The Foggiest Notion

Marc Breman

Book One of the Cryptic Chronicles

To my wife, Carol,
for giving this book its heart

To my mum, Wil,
for giving this book its humour

To my dad, Paul,
for giving this book its language

And to Sid,
for being the best cat in the world

A FEW INTRODUCTORY WORDS

Dear Reader,

As we have known each other now for at least five seconds, and I'm warming to you already, I feel a few words of reassurance are in order. If you are not as yet well versed in the gentle art of the cryptic crossword, do not panic. The possession of the cruciverbalist's particularly warped way of thinking (that's a crossworder, in case I've lost you already) is by no means a necessary requirement for the reader of this book – indeed, in the greater scheme of things, it may not even be desirable.

You will be taken gently by the hand at the solution of each clue, and may cheerfully ignore the explanation altogether, study it and memorise the technique it reveals, or nod impatiently at it as it confirms what you had already deduced several pages previously.

I have included the empty grid at the beginning, and did toy with the idea of providing all the clues as well, revealing the whole thing as it would have appeared in the newspaper, but decided that being able to solve at least some of the clues beforehand would diminish the hopeful enjoyment of the book. Instead, I have added an updated grid at the end of every chapter in which solutions have been found.

While writing this book, I found that a particular song invoked the mood I needed to be in. To amuse myself, I ended up hiding some of the lyrics in the text, and finally even the title itself. There is no prize for identifying the song, but if you think you know what it is, by all means get in touch and I'll let you know if you are right.

THE GRID

CHAPTER ONE

They appeared at the last stroke of midnight. That's the way it happens. Whether they took the time to get acquainted with their new existence, or hit the ground already running, is unknown. Setting off from one of the most inhospitable, and therefore uninhabited, parts of the earth, there were no witnesses. What is certain is that, like every other lethal force that had occasionally arrived unseen at the start of a new day, a basic instinct for self-preservation told them exactly which direction to take.

Considering the number of them, some eleven in all, their size, variable but ranging to a full forty-feet high, and their astonishing turn of speed, the noise of their progress should have alerted every earthquake-monitoring station around the world. As it was, two hours and many miles had passed before their presence was even noticed.

A six-year-old boy in northern China had woken from a nightmare, and rather than wake his parents at the other end of the room, he had been distracted by the brightness of the light coming through the window. He had opened the window and was leaning out, staring at the moon shining down from a cloudless sky on to the other houses in his village, trying to impose on it a face he was sure should be smiling and benign but kept realigning itself into an expressionless mask, when a sound made him turn his head to the barren landscape to the south.

In the fraction of time it took them to reach him, the sound split into two increasingly distinct components – a random beating of many low, muffled drums, and the quiet hiss of the wind through their thick white fur. They swept through and around the village on either side of the boy's house, and within seconds the noise, which had never risen much above a murmur, was all but inaudible. The village betrayed no sign of their brief visit, save the barking of a dog.

The boy watched the receding figures reach the hills to the north and disappear. Despite their speed, he had had time to see clearly in the night's glow that each of them wore, in a dark oval that covered barely half the front of their heads, the same expressionless face he had been staring at just moments before. The events of the rest of the day would determine whether this vision would live with him for the rest of his life, or be erased from his memory within twenty-two hours.

A solution would have to be found.

*

Colin Holly was, and always had been, a creature of habit. On this particular morning, without having made a single conscious decision, he found himself at the usual newsagent's, buying his usual newspaper, and suffering the usual awkwardness when trying to pay for it. The newsagent would always be reading a paper on the counter and would never look up. Holly would hold the money out and then be ignored, during which he could never bring himself to clear his throat, let alone place the money on the counter and walk out.

Eventually, eyes and presumably mind still fixed on the previous day's events, the newsagent would absently take the money and, if necessary, return the appropriate change, all without so much as a sideways glance at the till. Holly wondered whether, despite having repeated this ritual every morning for the best part of two decades, he would even recognise the newsagent if he walked past him in the street, never actually having seen his face full on.

The shop lay on the corner of a square in north-west London, technically a triangle, which would have felt considerably more like a rural village had it not been in the shadow of a huge seventies hospital building. Most of the shops along two sides of the triangle had been taken over by the usual chains, but a few independents still held out, a baker's, an Italian deli, a Polish restaurant. Holly had most of his modest needs catered for here, and seldom had cause to use any of the many buses that were always lined up along the third side, the hypotenuse of this triangle, and it had been a good many years since he had used the train station at the far corner.

For the moment, his routine was still dictating his actions. He folded the newspaper and clamped it under his arm so he could hide both his hands in the pockets of his sheepskin jacket, away from the bitter winter wind. He set off for home, his house already visible a couple of hundred yards away, indistinguishable in the featureless terrace but for the fact that it nestled exactly at the point where the road made a forty-five degree turn to the right, giving an otherwise dreary street an unexpectedly enigmatic ending. Cryptic, Holly would have said.

Halfway back, he made his customary involuntary glance at the first-floor bay window at number 29 and flinched, as he did every morning, at the vertical blinds that repelled him as much as they would have repelled the previous occupant.

Eric had been the only person in the area that Holly visited, and he had done so frequently until Eric's sudden death of a heart attack in the summer. At sixty-four, Eric had been a full two decades older than Holly, but they'd shared an almost identical lack of interests other than an aversion to rhetoric and a love of crosswords. Why waste time saying anything five times, they both agreed, when you could say it just the once and even then encrypt the meaning? They had spent many happy mornings together pondering the daily crossword in Holly's paper, with much silent appreciative nodding at the way an everyday word could generate such a convoluted, seemingly unrelated sentence, the clinically logical distilled from the apparently illogical.

Silent, that is, until the last couple of months of Eric's life, when he had suddenly become rather too talkative for Holly's liking, and the talk increasingly surreal. Crosswords seemed to have turned from an enjoyable pastime into a religion, and Eric had taken Holly to task on numerous occasions for not taking them seriously enough. Holly had put this down to the onset of dementia, and had found himself dropping by not quite so frequently, when one day the door had been opened by a young lady with bright pink hair, wearing a sullen expression and precious little else, who informed Holly that her uncle, well great-uncle, not that there was anything great about him, had pegged it without any warning and left the place in, well look at it.

Holly had almost finished expressing his condolences when the door was slammed in his face. The girl's use of words may not have been very artistic, but he couldn't help but admire her lack of rhetoric. He felt, on the whole, that Eric would have approved.

*

The endless corridors, empty but for the occasional trolley or wheelchair, shivered at the wind that moaned its ever-changing counterpoint through the broken windows and the cracks in the double doors, some fully open, some half-open, most closed, which punctuated the maze. The snow was swirling in too through the tattered curtains, settling in small drifts in the corners, blurring the distinction between outside and inside. This unification was completed by the fog that occupied the centre of every available space but not the edges, seemingly repelled by the walls, floor and ceiling.

The symphony of wind was occasionally joined by another voice, a wordless utterance that started at male speaking pitch and rose steadily until it became a shriek, coming to a sudden end, as though by a cleaver.

Barely noticeable against the fog, a darker shape moved slowly, smoothly and silently along. At a particularly loud and drawn-out shriek, it stopped by a window and seemed to look up. Its breathy voice was as hard to distinguish against the wind as its form against the fog.

'Patience.' The consonants formed an almost empty framework, the tenor vowels being barely audible. 'He will be here soon. He will have to come here. And then he'll be ours.'

Another, more doleful shriek came from outside and concluded the conversation between the two.

Two solutions that should have been found, but weren't.

*

With a mere dozen or so houses to go, an obstacle suddenly presented itself, an obstacle in the form of Holly's immediate neighbour, Gus. Holly hadn't noticed Gus on the other side of the street until he had emerged from behind the parked cars and started to cross.

Holly's first impulse was to hide behind a wall, a dustbin, a car, anything, even cross the road the other way. Typically, though, he just froze and hoped he hadn't been spotted. Not that there was the slightest antipathy between the two. It was just that Gus made Holly very uncomfortable, and Gus knew it, and revelled in it.

For all that he must have been well into his eighties, Gus was the closest approximation to the classic naughty schoolboy that Holly had read about when he was a boy. Gus now wallowed in his antiquity, as it allowed him to play his ideal role of wide-eyed, senile innocent, a role that Holly, from the safety of an empty shopping aisle, had seen him play many times in the small local supermarket, on one occasion reducing the poor owner to tears. Indeed, Gus had repeatedly been barred from the premises, but in perfect keeping with the lack of grip on reality that was the cornerstone of his assumed character, he wandered freely back in whenever he felt in need of some entertainment.

Apparently, he had just been barred again. He was being rather forcibly escorted home by his long-suffering niece who was scolding him bitterly, to his obvious delight, particularly as she was in her WPC uniform, giving him the impression of being frogmarched home by the law.

'I only asked him,' Holly overheard, 'if a packet of peanuts says "may contain nuts", what else it might contain.'

More remonstrations, by which time they had reached his gate. Holly had by now resumed walking, albeit at a snail's pace, and as they had now stopped he was faced with the decision of whether to stop as well, maybe attending to a wayward shoelace, or bite the bullet and try to sneak into his own gate, the one before, without them noticing. He decided on the latter.

'Now don't forget,' the young policewoman was saying, 'seven o'clock this evening. Tom will be there, and there's something I want to ask you about.'

Holly had reached his gate.

'Intriguing, my dear. I shall make every effort to reach the rendezvous at the appointed hour, but who knows what kind neighbour may invite me in for a cup of cocoa?'

Holly winced, threw a faint fleeting smile in the direction of the voice without taking his eyes off his own front door and hoped fervently that his key would behave itself. It took pity on him and acted with commendable efficiency. The door was open just long enough to admit a reproachful 'Uncle Gus!' before rattling shut.

Once inside, Holly took off his jacket to reveal an old maroon and white sleeveless jumper over a conspicuously unironed white shirt, brown trousers and shoes, both nondescript, both with their heyday long behind them. He hung up his jacket and went straight through to the kitchen at the back of the house, filled the electric kettle and switched it on – back to routine, although in the event routine only had five minutes left to live.

Waiting for the water to boil, coffee granules already in cup, he would have time to scan the front page headlines. Today was Friday December 8 2006, according to the paper's format, a full eleven years after the death of Princess Di, and yet there she was on the front cover, main story yet again, together with a rather smug story about the previous day's storms across Britain that apparently only this paper had seen coming.

Truth be told, he was no big fan of the *Daily Voice* ('It's your Voice!', as the television advertisement generously proclaimed), but it had been his wife's paper of choice. He had loyally continued buying it after her death and now couldn't bring himself to stop. Fortunately he had the cryptic crossword to justify this habit, the very puzzle he and Eric used to gloat over. To an aficionado like Holly, compilers of cryptic crosswords were surprisingly individual, and this particular compiler had a liking for the slightly surreal that Holly found appealing.

Today's puzzle was now the next order of business and would normally have taken up the next few hours of his time. Holly took his coffee and the paper upstairs to the room at the front of the house which, in the absence of any need for more sleeping arrangements, he called his office, actually more of a junk room with a table in the bay window. He sat at this table and opened the newspaper to the puzzles page, muttering 'Get in there', mimicking the silhouetted head next to the paper's name on the front page in the cockney accent he fondly imagined the character to have.

He had started reading the first clue, 1 Across as always, the first word of which he saw ruefully was 'Eric', when he became aware of three things.

The first was that it had suddenly got slightly but noticeably darker, although the pale winter sunshine had not diminished outside.

The second was a low rumble, very quiet at first but getting steadily louder to the point that the windows rattled and he could feel the table shake.

The third was that he was not alone in the room.

CHAPTER TWO

In the absence of any other noise in the house or in the street, the rumble initially appeared very quietly, growing in volume only slowly, and was still quiet enough for Holly to have been able to hear the rustle of paper from the other side of the room, which indeed he did. Looking over to the back wall, he noticed to his surprise (which, as was his nature, he didn't show) a man he was sure hadn't been there when he'd entered the room, sitting at a desk he had never seen before, a desk piled high with books that were not his.

The man was roughly fifty years of age, Holly thought, thin with sunken cheeks and pronounced cheekbones, a receding hairline that went back past the top of his head, giving the remaining short black hair the appearance of an atoll round a lagoon, and was wearing worn black trousers, scuffed black shoes and a white short-sleeved shirt, open at the neck. The rustling Holly had heard had come from the newspaper the man had just put down. Holly noticed that it was not only the same paper as his but was open at the same page.

The man was staring quizzically at the top of the window above Holly's head, and Holly distinctly heard him mutter the word 'liars', barely audibly. The rumble was getting louder.

Suddenly the man noticed Holly and jumped violently. After a couple of seconds he seemed to pull himself together. Keeping his eyes firmly on Holly he shouted, slowly and clearly, 'He loves the riser!' at the top of his voice, a voice so close to the one Holly had just used to mutter 'Get in there' that Holly suspected mimicry.

Holly was now starting to panic, although he still wouldn't allow his outward appearance to betray the fact. The noise was becoming disconcertingly loud, and he was wondering how he was going to evict this obvious madman from his house when, seemingly in response to the lunatic's shout, Holly could just make out hurried footsteps on the stairs.

The door burst open. The first person through was a man of average height and slightly oriental eyes, wearing a dingy white boiler suit and a faded red soft woollen hat, from under which emanated a scraggly pair of greying sideburns that reached the man's shoulders. He rattled, as though his pockets were full of loose change. He spotted Holly and stopped in the doorway, allowing the second person to pass him.

This was a teenage girl with dark brown hair in a ponytail, wearing jeans and a green jumper so threadbare a white T-shirt was clearly visible through it. She spotted the man at the desk and shouted 'Where...', by which time she had located Holly. Her eyes widened and she froze. The noise was now almost too loud for speech, but Holly was sure he saw the girl's mouth shape the word 'you'.

The noise and the shaking of the house snapped them all out of their mutual staring session. The rumble had been joined by an irregularly rhythmic metallic clanking. The girl looked frantically round the room.

'Uncle Sid, what is it?' she screamed at the man at the desk.

He nodded emphatically at the window and screamed back, 'Liars!'

They all turned to the window. Holly noticed a metal bar going across the middle pane of the bay, about a foot from the top and carrying on in both directions, with wooden slats going up from it at regular intervals. That would account for the slight darkening of the room, he thought with satisfaction. That's one mystery solved, albeit small comfort in the face of the other mysteries that seemed to be piling up by the second.

Just as the noise level seemed to have reached a plateau, it jumped another notch and the room went darker still. Cracks started appearing in the ceiling and plaster cascaded down. Three of the window panes cracked, one shattering altogether, making the noise, if not louder, then sharper.

To everyone's relief there followed a reduction in volume as sharp as the last increase, and then a steady decline, leaving the four occupants of the devastated room looking dazedly at one another. The man the girl had called Uncle Sid was the first to move.

'Satin words!' he barked, and rushed out of the room through the still open door. The other man followed him down the stairs, jingling as he went.

The girl beckoned hurriedly to Holly. 'Come on!' As much to get out of the room as to find out what on earth was going on, he unhesitatingly got up, and was just leaving the table when she added, 'The paper! Don't forget the paper! And the pen!' He picked up the two items as ordered and followed her.

Downstairs, they found the front door open and the two men standing in the street, looking back at the house. Joining them, the cause of the noise and destruction was all too apparent.

The street had acquired a railway line. It appeared in the middle of the street at the far end, started gently veering over towards the outside of the approaching curve and slowly rotated until the tracks were flat against the front of the houses. It then rose steadily until it reached the top of Holly's house at the bend, after which it gracefully descended again before righting itself in time for the square and a bend in the opposite direction. Here it duly mounted the facade of the old cinema building before turning right and crossing a road, twenty feet in the air, and then disappearing from view. The bewildered quartet were just in time to see the end of the train that had just passed them do precisely that.

Holly stiffly stood in suppressed amazement, surveying the damage. The ten or so houses either side of the bend were shrouded in a haze of masonry dust, which vainly tried to hide the jagged cracks in the walls, the broken windows and even the odd fallen chimney. Despite the horror he felt at seeing what had happened to his home, he was not surprised to find that he could so completely understand why the tracks had to mount the houses, making the train bank sharply and allowing it to take the bend more efficiently without slowing down. Like a roller coaster, he thought.

What did surprise him was that no-one else seemed to have rushed out of their houses to see what had happened. Indeed the only other people in the street were a couple walking hand in hand away from them towards the square. The girl had noticed that too.

'Is this normal?' she asked. Holly looked blankly at her. 'Were these tracks here yesterday?' she persisted. Holly shook his head slowly. 'Have to ask. It's impossible to be sure.' And to all three, 'Inside. Quick!'

She ran back through the door, followed by the others, her two companions making a big show of politely ushering Holly in ahead of them. In seconds they were all standing in the kitchen, where the girl immediately took charge with what Holly felt to be an air of routine.

'Right. Always look for a priority, and this is the most obvious priority we've had for a while. The house isn't going to survive another train journey, so start looking for anything that might relate to that.'

Holly realised in the ensuing silence that the other three were all looking expectantly at him, while all he could bring himself to do was look helplessly back at each of them in turn.

'In the grid!' she snapped, almost immediately softening in self-reproach. 'Oh that's right, you haven't done this before. Sorry. Look in the crossword.' She nodded at the folded newspaper Holly was still carrying. He didn't move, indeed seemed incapable of movement.

'You really are the silent, undemonstrative type, aren't you?' The girl was talking quietly now, and in response to his complete lack of reaction, 'I suppose that was always going to be a rhetorical question. OK look. I expect you're wondering where we've all escaped from, or when you're going to wake up. But however you want to deal with it, please humour me and play along, treat it as an intellectual challenge if you like, because believe it or not the preservation of this house, not to mention us in it, really does depend on solving the relevant clues in that crossword in the shortest possible time. So start looking for any mention of trains or rails.'

The challenge idea had the desired effect, as she knew it would. Holly had indeed been considering asylums and dreams together with a number of other possibilities, none of which appeared satisfactory, much less plausible. Indeed he had rejected the word plausible altogether, narrowing his search to the merely possible, but he wasn't having much luck even there. So the idea of a crossword puzzle and a return to rules he understood proved irresistible, even comforting. It offered familiar territory, and maybe a welcome opportunity to find some logic in this almost overwhelmingly illogical situation.

He lowered the paper and then, slowly, his gaze. Reassuring though the crossword might have been, it had also assumed an importance and a gravity that he found unsettling. Equally disconcerting were the men he now had on either side of him, looking over his shoulder, men, he noticed for the first time, who were both taller than he was.

Forcing himself to focus on the task in hand, he started scanning the Across clues for any transport-related words. He paused at, then rejected, the words 'on board' in 14 Across, coming to a full stop at 'train' in 26. He looked up at the girl, who was staring intently at him, and muttered the word pensively, whereupon the man to his right, the one with the whiskers, spoke for the first time, causing Holly to jump violently. It was a very different voice to his companion's – slow, deliberate, bordering on emphatic.

'Drill – educate – guide – rear – school – instruct – teach – prepare – coach –' The man was looking eagerly down at Holly as he spoke. The words were all slightly questioning, as though being offered for Holly's consideration, for which the man also helpfully left pauses.

'Uncle Jasper.' The girl's eyes never left Holly, but her gently reproachful words were obviously aimed at the man Holly was now staring at as though in a trance, and had the effect of both breaking that trance and of stopping the stream of synonyms that Holly had feared would continue for all eternity.

Looking back at 26 Across, he considered the clue 'Craftsman's train, as ordered (7)' for a moment and then said slowly, 'No, "ordered" is an anagram indicator,' – Uncle Sid on his left now eagerly thrust himself even more uncomfortably close – 'seven letters, so probably an anagram of "train as"…'

'Ant sari,' said Uncle Sid, breathlessly.

'…meaning a craftsman.'

'Maker,' offered Uncle Jasper.

'At rains,' purred Uncle Sid.

'Smith,' from Holly's right.

'In a star,' from his left, both sides getting more animated.

'Wright!'

'As in, rat!'

'Artisan!' they chorused in triumph. Holly's head by now was sandwiched between two expressions of unbridled joy, both looking to him for confirmation. Finding the combination of emotional display and proximity particularly alarming, and noticing that the solution was indeed the correct one, he nodded solemnly at each of them in turn. Delighted, the two victorious expressions turned to the girl for final approval, but were instantly disappointed.

'No,' she said bluntly, 'artisan isn't relevant to our train problem. Keep looking.'

The uncles both wilted visibly and retreated, much to Holly's relief. He resumed his search for likely candidates among the clues, and had just started on the Down clues when he found a word that was almost overqualified for the job.

'Tracks!' The two men jumped, even the girl flinched.

The men showed renewed interest, but Holly had the presence of mind to take a couple of steps back this time to give himself breathing space.

'Sounds promising,' the girl said, cautiously, 'what's the rest of the clue?'

' "Tracks seen in court",' Holly read out. 'Nine letters.' He looked up and, as he always did when trying to solve clues, instinctively focused on an imaginary point in the distance that transcended the walls of his surroundings. 'Court.'

The girl looked enquiringly at Uncle Jasper, who duly obliged. 'Tribunal – bar – bench –'

Holly shook his head. 'No, it's meant to sound like that type of court, but I don't think it is.'

'Chase – pursue – serenade – woo –'

On the last word, Uncle Jasper earnestly leant towards Holly, who said hurriedly, 'No, no, that doesn't seem right either.'

'What type of clue is it?' the girl wanted to know. 'Are we looking for a word hidden inside another word?'

Holly paused, looking at the clue. 'No,' he said at last, 'I don't think the answer is made up of several bits, as there don't seem to be enough bits in the clue. It looks to me like a good old-fashioned cryptic clue where the whole sentence means something, well, cryptic.' He paused again, then turned to his whiskered colleague. 'I think the court involved is a tennis court,' and continuing immediately in an effort to waylay the list of sporting venues that was threatening to appear, 'and the answer is…' He hesitated, not for dramatic effect as the others thought, but to check his reasoning so as to minimise the risk of looking foolish. 'Tramlines.'

Again all eyes went to the girl, this time meeting with an altogether more enthusiastic response. 'Excellent. Write it in.'

Holly did so, then looked up. 'Is that it, then? Are we

safe now?' There was a smug, slightly mocking tone to his voice. Truth be told, he felt a bit disappointed. He'd played along with this mad charade, and it hadn't presented much of a challenge after all, certainly not enough to warrant the seriousness of the girl's demeanour.

But then he noticed that the girl's demeanour had changed. Her eyes had widened and her mouth was opening wordlessly in fear. Only then did he hear the distant rumble, the same rumble as before, the rumble that said this was no charade, if only because the look on the girl's face told him that she believed absolutely that this may be the last sound any of them would ever hear.

CHAPTER THREE

'No! That's not how it works! It has to go all the way across the grid! What's the next clue?'

Knowing Holly wouldn't grasp what she meant fast enough, the girl snatched the paper from the table where Holly had left it and followed the one written solution with her finger to the word directly below it.

'Twenty-two!' Looking down for the relevant clue, she read out, ' "Wind key inside part of wall".' She slammed the paper back down on the table in an effort to detract everyone's attention from the increasing noise, then glared up at Holly. 'Five letters. "Wind key inside part of wall". Where do we start? Why would you wind a key in a wall?'

Finding another imaginary focal point far more comforting than returning the girl's stare, Holly played the sentence over in his mind a couple of times.

'Alright, well, "key" usually means any letter from A to G, musical keys. So it's either one of these letters inside a part of a wall, meaning "wind", or the letter inside a synonym for "wind", meaning part of a wall.' He looked over at the man in the boiler suit. 'I'm guessing the letter is inside another word for "wind".'

'Furl –' the list had barely started when the plates and glasses in the cupboards began to rattle, 'loop – spiral –' Uncle Jasper was now having to raise his voice, 'twine – wreathe –' glass could be heard breaking at the front of the house, 'coil – twist –' shouting by this time.

'That's not working!' Holly shouted. 'Try "wind" as in "bend"!'

Uncle Jasper continued without hesitation, 'Deviate – ramble – zigzag –'

One of the wall units came crashing to the ground, just missing Uncle Sid, spraying broken crockery and glass halfway across the room. The girl screamed but didn't move.

'Meander – curve –' now barely audible above the overwhelming noise of destruction.

At this point there was an almighty thud, which they all felt rather than heard, and a huge cloud of dust burst through the door. Holly instinctively shut his eyes tight, then put his hands over his ears in a vain effort to reduce the decibel level. He had never felt such disorientation, nor such despair. This is it, he thought. Part of a wall must have come down, surely to be followed by the rest of the house. Part of a wall.

Suddenly he realised which part of the wall it was. He opened his eyes as little as he could against the swirling dust but as much as he needed, and managed to locate the newspaper on the table. He was relieved to find the pen still in his hand, then instantly horrified to see that the paper was completely blank, having somehow lost all trace of grid and clues, before realising that it was covered in a thick layer of masonry dust. He brushed this aside in a single movement, located 22 Down and entered five letters. He had no idea what effect this would have, just a feeling that it was what was required.

The effect was instant. The noise stopped. Holly was initially unaware of any other changes as his eyes were still only admitting the smallest amount of light. Opening them gingerly a little more, he noticed first that the dust was gone, then that the floor was clear of the shattered remains of what it amused him to call his best china, and on opening them fully, that the cabinet was back on the wall. Next to it, also only now regaining their vision, the uncles found themselves huddled together in a terrified embrace. As they disentangled themselves with some embarrassment, Uncle Jasper reached into one of his pockets and pulled out a piece of string with what Holly recognised as an old camera film case attached to one end that he held against the door frame as a plumb line to convince himself it was back in the correct vertical alignment.

'Was that you? Did you do that?' The girl was staring at Holly with a broad grin of admiration. Not waiting for a reply, her eyes moved to the door. 'Hang on, got to check.' She ran out of the room. The two men followed her, as much, Holly thought, out of shame as curiosity.

Holly himself stayed in the kitchen, sitting down heavily on one of the two chairs by the table. In truth, he may have just regained his breath, but certainly not his composure. His ears were still ringing from the noise, and his mouth and nose still felt clogged with the dust he had been inhaling barely a minute before, even though he knew the dust had gone. Indeed, as he looked round the room, he could see no trace of the devastation that was so recently encircling him. Everything was exactly as it had been when he made his coffee before going upstairs. He was beginning to think that he hadn't gone upstairs after all but had fallen asleep at the kitchen table, his mind using the crossword puzzle he had been contemplating as a springboard and whisking him off on an escapade so fantastic he wasn't sure whether to congratulate himself or seek advice, and he was now waking up to resume a normal day, when his trio of tormentors burst back in.

'That was intense,' the girl was saying with a note of awe in her voice. 'Damage level eight at least there for a minute, wouldn't you say?' Her question was met with puzzled expressions from her two colleagues.

'Never mind.' She turned back to Holly. 'It *was* you, wasn't it? You *are* good! Come on then, what was it?' The girl was bouncing excitedly in front of Holly and giggling, an infectious, slightly obscene giggle that Holly found a little disturbing.

It was now his turn to look with concern at the doorway.

'Oh no, it's all back to normal,' the girl reassured him, 'no trains, no tracks, no cracks. They've been solved. But what was the word?' She snatched the newspaper from the table and looked at the second word that had been entered into the grid. 'Gable,' she read out, still smiling but clearly none the wiser. 'Didn't get that, did you, Skipper?' she threw at Uncle Jasper, who looked ever so slightly peeved. She turned to Holly, expectantly.

After the few seconds he needed to remember how he had arrived at the solution, Holly explained. 'It's "gale" with a B in it.' He turned to Uncle Jasper. 'It wasn't "wind" as in "turn", but "wind" as in "breeze", or in this case, "gale". So "wind" – gale – "key in" – including the letter B – "part of wall" – ,' he looked back at the girl, 'gable.' He paused, a muted version of the girl's admiring smile threatening to invade his own face. 'It's classic misdirection. Misdirection is the art of the crossword compiler. A good clue is like an illusionist's trick. It sends you the wrong way. You hit a dead end and the trick has worked. In this case, "wind" was chosen as a synonym for "gale", a noun, but used in the sentence in such a way as to imply the verb "wind", as in "turn".' He was staring off into space again by now. 'That's class.'

He eventually became aware of the silence that had ensued, and looked round as a movement caught his eye. It was Uncle Sid, a wry smile on his face, shaking his head.

'A recluse has our honey,' he said, wearily.

A barely stifled laugh came from Uncle Jasper, a mild rebuke from the girl. 'Uncle Sid, language!' Holly looked in bemusement from one to the other. Giving up on any idea of making sense of the conversation, he once again sought refuge in the rationality of the crossword puzzle.

'So, "tramlines" and "gable" go together to cause a train to run along the front of my house, is that how it works?'

'That's it, yes,' the girl said, eagerly. 'The clues come in pairs, and have to be solved in pairs. Solving just one isn't enough. It often happens that we know the situation they're causing, we've come up with one of the solutions but can't crack the second. That can be really demoralising.'

'Indeed.' Holly cast his mind back to the recent events in his kitchen. 'I can see how that might get one down...'

'No!'

In the split second of the girl's cry, Holly saw her reach out to him in desperation and noticed the look of panic on the uncles' faces. Then there was a brief moment when his vision became a blur and his ears felt pressurised, as though he was on a plane about to land, after which he found himself blinking in the sun, standing on the deck of an old sailing ship.

1		2 T		3		4		5		■	6	7		8
	■	R	■		■		■		■	9	■		■	
10		A					■	11						
	■	M	■		■		■		■		■		■	
12		L							■	13				
■	■	I	■		■		■		■		■	■	■	
14		N			■	15						16		
	■	E	■		■	■	■	■	■		■		■	
17		S				18		19	■	20				
	■	■	■		■		■		■		■		■	■
21		22 G			■	23								24
	■	A	■		■		■		■		■		■	
25		B					■	26						
	■	L	■		■		■		■		■		■	
27		E		■	28									

CHAPTER FOUR

Seasickness hadn't been a problem for Holly for some time. Admittedly, when his mother had first taken him on a ferry, just the short hop across to France, he had thrown up the whole way, but by the return journey he had already figured out that if he stayed outside on deck and could see the waves, all would be well. It had been a particularly icy January and he had caught pneumonia, but both he and his mother thought that a small price to pay for the lifetime of potential sea travel that was now open to him. The fact that in the following three decades he had been afloat just the once caused him no great regret.

The intense queasiness he now felt was therefore nothing to do with seasickness, and far more likely to be down to the fact that it had taken less than a second for him to reach the ship he was now on from the comfort of his own kitchen. The overriding lack of logic in the situation once again proved to be his undoing. He found himself on his knees, hands with palms down against the planks on either side of him, head back, eyes closed and with his mouth open in an effort to persuade his reluctant lungs to work.

As he rocked backwards and forwards, gasping rather feebly for air, he felt a pair of hands grasp his shoulders. Opening his eyes, he saw the girl sitting in front of him, looking back at him with an expression of great concern.

'It's OK, it's OK, it's OK, it's alright. It's OK.'

After a moment's hesitation, she leaned forward, put her arms around him and held him tightly. Far from restricting his limited breathing even further, he felt an instant relief – slight, to be sure, yet so overwhelming that, much against his nature, he threw his arms around her and clung on just as firmly. It did not escape him that, although the girl had been essentially an intruder in his home surroundings, she was now the only familiar object in this wholly new and inexplicable setting.

He had closed his eyes again, and as he slowly managed to take ever deeper breaths, he became increasingly aware of the movement of the ship. Finally confident his respiratory system would continue without his constant vigilance, he opened his eyes and let his arms fall by his sides. Taking her cue, the girl did the same. Without looking at her, Holly got to his feet, shakily but just steadily enough not to need the helping hands that were being offered to him, and took the half-dozen steps to the edge of the ship. The sight of the water was just as reassuring as it had been all those years before, and for a few moments he lost himself in it. Then, having regained most of his composure, albeit with the vital support of the parapet he was leaning on, he looked around him.

Holly was no expert in ship design through the ages, but was fairly confident in dating this one to the sixteenth century or thereabouts. It had a Drake-y feel about it, he thought. The condition of the ship seemed to belie this, as it looked as though it had been built the day before, not a nick or a scuff anywhere. Also, apart from the girl still kneeling a few paces away, it seemed completely deserted. He listened for any sign of activity, but could hear nothing but the sea, the creaking of the timbers and the plaintive cries of gulls.

This last sound, plus the knowledge that gulls never strayed far from shore, made him look over to the other side of the ship where he noticed, with some relief, that they were indeed not on the open sea but a mere half a mile from land, going parallel to the shoreline. He stumbled across to the opposite side without taking his eyes off the land in case it took umbrage at a lapse in attentiveness and disappeared.

The type of landscape gave Holly little clue as to where they might be – rocky, low-lying, the occasional patch of sand, leading back to a range of small hills that hid whatever lay behind, some muted vegetation – overall a rather dusty appearance that reminded Holly of Spain, although he wasn't sure Spain still had such a stretch of coastline without a single hotel to be seen.

Having gathered this much information, he now felt far more at ease with his surroundings. He turned back to the girl, who hadn't moved, still looking at him, now with a faint smile.

'Where are we?' he asked calmly.

The girl stood up. Holly was struck by the way she dusted the knees of her jeans, despite them already being considerably frayed. He watched her walk over and stand next to him, rest her elbows on the side of the ship and gaze at the land that was gliding silently past.

Just as she was about to answer, he said, 'What's your name?'

She looked clearly surprised by the question, then just as clearly delighted.

'Oh. Well. My name,' she turned her head to look at him, then down at the water, 'is Kia.' She turned back to him again, giving him a more searching look – a fruitless and frustrating search, as his expression didn't change. Having regained his composure, he wouldn't relinquish it again without a struggle.

'So, Kia,' he said, eventually, 'where are we and how did we get here?'

Kia sighed and surveyed the shoreline. 'As to where we are – specifically, I don't know. Generally, I know exactly where we are, and we're here because you brought us here.' Holly's expression became even more blank, if that was possible. 'It was your last remark, if you recall it. You really have to be careful what you say here. But then,' she gave him her best schoolmistress look, 'self-control doesn't seem to be a problem for you.' She saw him blink three times, particularly noticeable in the absence of any other movement. 'Exactly. Anyway, you said "I can see how that might get one down".' His eyebrows lowered in puzzlement. 'One Down. If the Solver names a clue, he goes to the location of that clue, or one at least associated with it.'

Holly's voice was croaky, as though he hadn't spoken all day. 'Solver?'

'Everything revolves around the day's crossword puzzle. It all happens because of what is in that grid. And don't say the word "grid", incidentally,' Kia said, hurriedly, 'because that's the word that takes you back to the house. And if I don't manage to grab hold of you like I did last time, I get stuck out here.'

His mouth opening and closing silently, Holly resembled a blinking goldfish. He made a supreme and very visible effort to regain coordination, resulting in a repeat of the word 'Solver?'

'The clues have to be solved. The words in the grid, in pairs as you recall, represent a situation, place, or person that didn't exist yesterday. Most are quite harmless, or at worst just odd. Some we're even sorry to lose. But then there are those like our train this morning.' Her voice lowered momentarily. 'I must say,' she said, absently, 'we haven't had a crisis like that for a long while. I have a strange feeling about today.' Then back to her previous tone, 'So obviously those have to be identified and dealt with first. That's why we have to prioritise. If we had just started at 1 Across, we'd have missed our train.'

She didn't want to interrupt the flow at this point by giggling, as the pun had been unintentional, but she couldn't help herself. Holly seemed not to have caught it, and was apparently getting back in touch with his inner goldfish. Kia stifled her laughter and pressed on.

'But things do get missed, and some clues don't get solved by the end of the day. Then whatever situation the clues refer to become a permanent feature.' She waited for a sign that any of this was registering, but gave up. 'And we seem to be the only ones who notice today's new oddities. You saw the people in the street after the train had nearly destroyed half a dozen houses. If you'd asked them, they would have sworn on oath that those railway tracks had been there the day before. And if you hadn't solved those two clues, tomorrow they would have been right.'

Holly was staring into space, still frowning, his mouth now fixed open, his eyes darting left and right. Slowly he turned to Kia and raised his eyebrows. Strange gurgling sounds came from his throat as he struggled to formulate words. Kia's expression betrayed her curiosity as to what his reaction to all this would be.

'Solver?' he rasped.

Kia sighed. 'Most days we can manage ourselves. Not just me, I'm pretty hopeless at them, to be honest. Not the worst. My mum's the worst. She reads a clue and tries to make sense of it as a sentence.'

Holly nodded faintly in agreement. 'The most fundamental mistake you can make,' he said, still a little hoarsely, 'is to take a cryptic clue at face value.' He was relieved to be back on safer ground, and Kia was relieved he'd rejoined the conversation.

'So I really just coordinate the team.'

'Team? You mean the uncles back there? They're an interesting couple.'

'Oh, they're wild, you have no idea.'

'And I suppose "Skipper" would have felt right at home here?'

'Uncle Jasper? Oh no, there's nothing nautical in that. We call him Skipper because he's a scavenger – he can't go past a skip without rummaging through it. You'd be amazed what he finds. And you'd be amazed how hard it is to get him to put most of it back. Just because something's functional, doesn't mean we have to find a function for it. He doesn't get that. What he does get, thankfully, is synonyms, so he's invaluable. As is Uncle Sid. Uncle Sid only talks in anagrams, which can be very confusing, but you get used to it.'

'Right, I see. So "liars" meant "rails"?'

'That's it.'

'And "Satin words" becomes,' he held up a hand to prevent being spoon-fed the answer, 'becomes "downstairs".'

'Right again.'

'And he got you running in with the words,' frowning, trying to remember the exact words, 'was it "He loves the riser"?'

'Yes, he uses that a lot. It's "The Solver is here".'

Holly nodded, then, frowning again, 'What was it he said at the end – something about honey?'

It was hard to tell in the bright sunshine, but he thought he saw Kia blush slightly.

'Oh, he didn't mean that,' she said dismissively. 'So anyway, there's a member of the team for every type of clue. I expect you'll meet the others later. And as I said, normally between us we can cope. But sometimes, when something big happens...'

'Like a train going up the side of the house?'

'...like a train going up the side of the house, yes,' she faltered, wincing at the memory of it, 'then we're sent a Solver.' She looked pointedly at Holly, who drew his head back, surprised.

'So I've come to your rescue?' he said with a hint of a smile.

'Steady,' she reprimanded. 'I said Solver, not saviour. A lot of the Solvers are a complete waste of time, frankly, because they're convinced it's all a dream. So they either swan around acting the superhero or wander off exploring and want nothing to do with us. But you're not like that, are you, because you know.'

His smile had gone, and for a moment they stared intently at one another.

'That's why you reacted the way you did when we arrived on this ship,' she continued. 'Because you know,' she lowered her voice, 'that this is real.'

CHAPTER FIVE

People disappear all the time, even in the normal course of events, some voluntarily, some involuntarily, most of them reappearing at some stage and in some shape or form. Disappear, in these cases, means that society has momentarily turned its back on an individual who is then absent when attention is returned. It does not mean vanish into thin air while in full view.

This latter definition was the one witnessed in Holly's kitchen by the two uncles whose lives, it must be said, wandered a considerable distance from the normal course of events. They had seen people disappear before, and had even disappeared themselves, albeit from someone else's view rather than their own. One of their colleagues, indeed, had not returned from one of these disappearances, so could be said to have disappeared in both senses of the word.

Despite their experience in the matter, Uncle Sid and Uncle Jasper had been staring uneasily for some time at the spaces previously occupied by Kia and Holly. Aware that the others needed only to utter a single word in order to return, the uncles knew that the reason for their continued absence was either that the word hadn't been needed or that it couldn't be used. Not knowing which was what made them uneasy.

And so they instinctively fell back on that experience, telling them as it did that the others were almost certain to return, that they'll be back, or 'Hey, black belt,' as Uncle Sid said, as much to reassure himself as Uncle Jasper, who nodded earnestly, muttering 'shortly – soon – presently' in agreement. After a further brief expectant stare they abandoned their vigil and busied themselves in their daily routine.

Uncle Jasper led the way into the living room. Being the most technically minded of the group, it was his job to program and operate the digital TV recorder. In order to prioritise and concentrate their efforts where they were most needed, all the morning's news programmes were recorded, starting with the seven o'clock headlines, allowing them not only to watch them whenever they liked but also to pause and rewind items of particular interest or concern. This frequently gave them advance warning of any imminent threat that may not have been immediately apparent.

He had been about to flick through the day's first recordings when Uncle Sid's shout had come from upstairs. Having to ignore the fact that the house had collapsed around them and been rebuilt since his last attempt, he now joined Uncle Sid on Holly's sofa – a frayed beige corduroy two-seater, the left seat worn smooth – and used two handsets to issue the appropriate series of commands, an operation watched with a certain amount of resentfulness by Uncle Sid who, despite repeated attempts, always succeeded in either recording the wrong channel or wiping something prematurely.

The top headline at seven had been the previous day's adverse weather conditions, many details of which were only now coming through. Christmas shoppers in Shrewsbury had returned to the car park to find that the Severn had burst its banks and left their cars wholly under water. A 350-foot tanker had hit the rocks off Seaford in East Sussex. This story had sent a questioning look between the two monitors but no more and they moved on.

A 130-mph tornado had hit Kensal Rise, a north London suburb not far away, and had damaged 150 houses. This elicited a more prolonged and more quizzical look, but again no real conviction that this was one of today's emergencies.

Indeed it was no easy task, sorting out a potential anomaly in reality from an event that was merely highly unusual. The Kensal Rise twister seemed to them an utterly fantastic phenomenon, but they would have seen it on the previous day's evening news, had they watched it, which would have ruled it out of today's proceedings. Unfortunately, the importance of the news before the day's grid had been finished meant that none of them could bring themselves to watch any afterwards.

The only eye-catching story in the local news was a group of pupils demonstrating outside their school, having decided that a particular subject was no longer worth studying. For reasons not yet fathomed by the reporter at the scene, the protesters were blocking the street – in truth a cul-de-sac, so no great inconvenience was caused – marching round in a circle carrying placards proclaiming 'maths stinks', 'down with subtraction' and 'go forth and multiply yourself'. Uncle Sid muttered 'ten studs' with some contempt, but hadn't managed to stifle a laugh first.

Moving over to a recording of another channel's news, the top headlines were much the same. A couple more stories followed, both of which were updates, one a long-running court case and the other a missing woman. Uncle Jasper raced through these at eight times normal speed, much to the annoyance of Uncle Sid, who was always convinced they'd miss something more relevant.

'Kippers! 'Owlers!' he'd shout. Skipper would pretend to be too deep in concentration to hear, consequently going no slower at all. This cycle would only be broken when a real contender appeared, as was the case now.

It had started as a minor story about a Liberal Democrat MP who had been reported missing during the night by his wife. He had been at a committee meeting at the Commons in the evening, and had been expected at his home in Hertfordshire at around one in the morning but had never showed. The story had only come to light because the wife was a minor celebrity herself, most recently as a presenter of a consumer affairs TV programme.

Uncle Jasper's thumb was already heading for the fast-forward button when a breaking news banner appeared at the bottom of the screen, followed by an announcement, read rather falteringly by the newsreader from a piece of paper he had been handed, that another MP's whereabouts were unknown – also a Liberal Democrat, also having attended the same committee meeting.

Then the floodgates opened. Wives and husbands of missing MPs were ringing in one after the other, either having only just noticed that their other halves hadn't come home or having finally run out of possible locations to phone. After ten minutes had passed, nearly every political party was represented by its representatives' absence – all indeed except, mysteriously, Labour and the Tories.

In the event, they hadn't all attended the same committee meeting as the first two reported missing, that had been as far as that coincidence had gone. There had been charity functions, social gatherings, simply commuting for those who lived further away from Westminster, and one or two had even gone to bed as normal and had simply not been there at daybreak.

By the time the news editors decided to let another story have a look-in, however briefly, seventy-eight missing political persons reports had been filed, home affairs reporters up and down the country breathlessly announced themselves to be completely baffled, and the deputy leader of the Labour Party had already got himself into trouble by claiming that the only reason the absentee list didn't include the names of any Tories was that the whole lot of them could have stayed out all night and their wives would have thought nothing of it.

On the other side of the screen, the two uncles had been getting increasingly restless, Uncle Jasper tapping his knee nervously with the TV remote, Uncle Sid muttering 'my dog alight' on more than one occasion. They both had the feeling that this day was shaping up to be one like no other before. These morning news sessions were supposed to throw up things that ranged from the mildly eccentric to the fairly wacky. In recent times they had encountered a magnetic strain of rhubarb, a rainbow that managed to convey cargo from one end to the other, and an inexplicable worldwide blanket ban on puppet shows, nothing that would have provoked more than a scratch of the head and an entry into Uncle Jasper's ever-present notebook. A fast-depleting House of Commons was in a different league.

The 'and finally' item, the feel-good story that news programmes were starting to bring back after a lengthy absence, concerned the third birthday of the apparently celebrated toddler who lived in a specially converted warehouse in Wapping, what with him being already nearly twenty-feet tall and weighing not much short of a ton. He had been delighted at his presents, which included a full-size bulldozer and a scaled-up pair of binoculars through which he was already happily scanning the Thames in both directions from the high windows. The only hiccup had come when he had blown out the oversized candles on his huge cake and inadvertently set fire to some curtains, for which he had very contritely said, 'sorry, Mummy'.

Uncle Sid's jaw had long since dropped, and it was only with a supreme effort that he regained sufficient control of it to utter incredulously, 'ham sweats!' Uncle Jasper could only wearily agree.

'Mess – shambles – mayhem – chaos.'

CHAPTER SIX

The ship ploughed smoothly on, its course unchanging. The sun maintained its comfortable warmth, unhindered by a single cloud. The sea remained calm and benevolent. Only the cries of the gulls had diminished, as they had given up their pursuit and were gradually returning to shore.

Holly sighed and turned his gaze to the land. His eyes followed the retreating birds. The leaders were already circling above a point where a river met the sea in a series of small cascades. Holly felt his mind wander gently from one feature of the scene to another, until one in particular snapped him out of it.

'That river,' he said, nodding in its direction. 'Does it look red to you, or is that just in my head?'

Kia looked over. 'Oh yes,' she said, casually, 'I haven't been there for a while.'

The water that came tumbling off the hills was indeed a full-blooded red that rapidly diluted after reaching the shore until it blended seamlessly with the sea's murky dark blue.

'So that was an unsolved clue?' Holly asked, unable to take his eyes off the spectacle. Kia nodded regretfully, obviously regarding it as a failure on her part.

'Crimson. I think that was the word we couldn't get.'

The disappointment was lost on Holly, who found the scene totally enchanting. The utter normality of it, save one detail, a tiny detail yet one that changed everything, a detail of transformation, and even then only a fleeting transformation that in a very short time, apparently twenty-four hours, would become the new normality. Holly continued to stare, unable to believe that he could ever, let alone within a day, find this view anything other than awesome.

'I must confess,' he said, slowly and cautiously, 'half of me would really like this to be real.' The cascades were already out of view, only a red smudge by the coast was still to be seen. He turned to Kia. 'Needless to say, the other half is screaming in abject terror.' He walked over to the middle of the ship, a little falteringly but not as much as he had expected, and put a hand flat against the mast, the foremost of the three. 'Logically,' he said, smiling at the irony of the word, 'either this is real,' his eyes followed the mast up into the bright sky, squinting, 'and I will have to deal with it,' he patted the mast reassuringly, 'or I'm imagining all this,' he turned back to his companion, 'in which case,' his restless gaze wandered briefly, finally settling on a part of the sky just above the hills, 'I'm imagining it for a reason.'

He kept his focus, both on the arbitrary spot above the horizon and on this train of thought, retracing his logical steps. Satisfied the train was still on the right track, he walked back to his companion, who was still keeping a respectful silence. 'Unfortunately, as to what that reason might be,' he sat down next to where Kia was standing, with his back against the timber, legs straight out in front of him,

'I haven't a clue.' He smiled apologetically up at her. 'Cryptic or otherwise.'

As he looked at her, a recent memory was triggered. 'You haven't asked me my name.' He could see she was struggling for a reply, so he continued, 'I expect names must be a problem, what with this constant conveyor belt of – Solvers. Dispensable, almost.' He saw the look of relief on her face. 'But that's not the case here, is it? You already know my name. Don't you? You recognised me the moment you saw me in that room before the train arrived.'

The smile on Kia's face was unconvincing. 'Oh, I've seen you around.' Under the corrosive force of his unwavering stare, the smile dissolved. 'OK, I've heard a lot about you. Eric mentioned you.'

Just when Holly had thought he was getting the hang of the place, another shock. 'Eric – was here?' he managed at last.

Kia nodded enthusiastically. 'Oh yes, a couple of times. Did very well the first time.' Her face clouded over slightly. 'Not quite so successful the second. But he kept saying how he wished you were here. Said you made a good team.'

For a moment, Holly was speechless. The idea that someone he knew had undergone the same experience seemed to reinforce the reality of it all, and also made sense of Eric's rather sudden change of attitude towards crosswords. Holly tried to imagine how Eric would have coped with this sensory overload. Rather better than me, he concluded ruefully. Quiet though Eric had been, his mind had been much the more open of the two, much less shockable, worldly-wise without being world-weary – a demeanour that must have come in handy when dealing with his Day-Glo-haired relative, Holly thought.

And yet, despite this resilient demeanour, Holly had seen for himself how the experience had affected Eric, with the development of a mild fanaticism that had rapidly made Holly less enthusiastic to visit. The clues were no longer tackled in the numerical order that had made the exercise so much more of a challenge, no flippant guesses were tolerated and the grid simply had to be finished, and if that took until midnight, so be it. Eric had clearly accepted this as real, and had taken his responsibility as a Solver to heart. Indeed, Holly thought, this responsibility may well ultimately have been what caused his heart to fail.

He looked up at Kia.

'I'm sorry to be the one to tell you,' he said, softly, 'but Eric died a few months ago.'

Kia's face showed genuine sorrow but no surprise.

'Yes. Yes, I know.' She smiled appreciatively. 'But thanks for telling me anyway.'

She sat down next to Holly, hugging her knees to her chin. 'He must have been a good friend,' she said, looking at Holly expectantly, like a little girl waiting for a bedtime story, he thought.

For all its appearance of a statement, this was clearly a question, and Holly considered it briefly. 'Well, he was certainly a friend,' he said, as though realising it for the first time, 'and that already says a lot. I'm not really one for socialising, and don't suppose I'm particularly genial company.'

Kia nodded, whether in agreement with his self-assessment or encouragement to continue, Holly wasn't sure. Giving himself the benefit of the doubt, he continued.

'To be honest, I was always happy to leave all that cordiality business to my wife. She was born to it. Unfortunately none of that ability ever rubbed off on me.

God knows she tried.' He was staring dreamily through the floorboards in front of him.

Kia's attentive expression was unaffected by the ensuing pause. 'Tell me about her,' she prompted, gently. Without taking his eyes off what he wasn't looking at, Holly resumed.

'She was amazing. She was outspoken, she was loud, she was conscientious, she was witty...' He shook his head. 'She was everything I'm not. No idea what she saw in me. One of life's eternal mysteries.' He smiled. 'But she'd made up her mind. And she was unstoppable.' Still smiling, he sighed. 'But of course, she wasn't unstoppable, as I found out when I got a phone call to say she'd been involved in a "traffic incident", a textbook, sanitised term wholly inadequate to describe what turned out to be a head-on collision with a lorry.' He leant his head back against the wood and closed his eyes. 'She'd been out shopping for Christmas,' he said, his voice trailing away, 'and for the baby. She was five months pregnant.'

Nothing could be heard now but the sea and the ship, no wind, no gulls. The sun was getting hotter, and Holly enjoyed it stinging his face. It seemed so long since he'd felt such strong sunshine that he wallowed in the discomfort of it burning through his jumper. He lost himself in the creaking of the timber, faint but broadcast directly into his head via the railing, a slow, complex, repeated rhythm like the rocking of a giant crib.

An indignant female voice broke the spell.

'The lorry driver was drunk.'

Holly opened his eyes and turned blinking to Kia, who was sitting upright on her knees with a belligerent look on her face.

'What? Hardly. He was a teetotal Norwegian, an unlikely combination, but genuine as even the tabloids had to concede eventually. The poor man went into therapy and never drove a lorry again. Became a fisherman in the Arctic, I seem to remember. Said it was safer. No women drivers.'

Kia was not to be diverted. 'So why was he on the wrong side of the road?'

'He wasn't.' Holly may have looked puzzled at the line of questioning, but was inwardly amused at the way this girl instinctively rushed to the wrong conclusion to vindicate a fellow female. 'He wasn't even close to the white line. There was a bend in the road that Anna seems not to have even registered. If the lorry hadn't got in the way, she would have shot off the other side into a field.' He smiled warmly at the belligerence in her face that was stubbornly hanging on. 'It's natural, on hearing a story like this, to pity the casualty rather than the survivor, but Anna was not the victim here. Injured party, certainly, but no victim. She simply didn't turn when the road did. She did this thing of screwing her eyes tightly shut when she was thinking about something, and the fact that she was behind the wheel wouldn't have come into consideration. That's what I think happened. Not that she would ever admit that.' He chuckled bleakly. 'It was black and white, there were witness statements, camera footage. But she'd still be arguing her case now. She was never wrong.'

He noticed that indignation had given way to bewilderment, and marvelled at the loyalty Kia was showing to someone she'd never met. He leant towards her.

'The first time we went out together,' he said, conspiratorially, 'she gave me a lift home, and she drove into the back of the car in front while showing me how she had been looking over her shoulder when she had driven into another car the previous week.'

Kia turned her head to meet his gaze and held it. Slowly the smile on his face spread across hers, where it was amplified. She nodded and looked down, still smiling. He retired to his previous position.

'That was Anna.'

The hollow tone of his voice made Kia look up with visible concern. She studied him for a while, hoping he would continue. When he didn't, she asked, 'What did you do?'

The total lack of response made Kia doubt that he had heard her, and she was about to repeat the question when he answered.

'After the accident? I did what any sensible, well-adjusted man would do under the circumstances, and tried to drink my way out of the situation. And of course I fondly imagined that nobody would notice. Even at work.'

'You were – a teacher?'

'Yes. Primary. Private school. You can't fool kids, they were on to it straight away. Started calling me AlcoHolly. Precocious little...' He smiled briefly. 'But it didn't get any better. Losing Anna was bad enough, but losing the baby as well seemed to make it ten times worse. The increase wasn't linear, it was exponential.'

He glanced apologetically at Kia.

'Yes,' he said, nodding wearily, 'a maths teacher.'

Encouraged by a lack of negative response on Kia's part, he continued.

'Maybe because of that, it got to the stage where I couldn't bear to be round children, somewhat of a drawback in my line of work. So I took compassionate leave, which turned into sick leave, which turned, eventually, into permanent leave.' He shook his head in regret. 'I never went back.'

After another pause, he folded his arms in a gesture of muted defiance. 'But I did manage to stop drinking. It may have taken me three years, but I did stop, very suddenly. And do you know what stopped me?' He turned to Kia, who shook her head. 'I was coming into the kitchen one morning – that kitchen,' he said, remembering that Kia knew the room in question, and then realising that he was actually nodding at the spot where he'd been fighting for breath when they first arrived on the ship. 'I heard Anna's voice, clear as day. "Get a grip, Holly Oak." Using her stern voice. You didn't argue with that voice. So I didn't have my morning brandy, went to the newsagent's sober, and on the way back had my first conversation with Eric. And I haven't had a drink since.'

He waited proudly for some word of congratulation from Kia.

'Holly Oak?' she blurted, breaking into a broad grin followed by that lewd giggle.

It wasn't the response he'd hoped for or expected, but he smiled, blushing, slightly at first, then a deep red as he realised he was blushing.

'She called me that a lot,' he mumbled, 'a reference to dependability, I believe, you know, her rock, that sort of thing.' He cleared his throat. 'She said I was a calming influence on her. Can't imagine what she would have been like otherwise, if that was her being calm.'

A thought suddenly struck him, and he looked quizzically at Kia, who had stopped giggling, but not smiling. 'I've never told anyone any of this,' he said pensively. 'I just don't talk about these things.'

Far from finding this thought disturbing, Kia appeared even more amused by it. She merely shrugged her shoulders happily.

His brooding was interrupted by a sound, a faint blurred ticking. They became aware of it at the same time and both stood up to see where it was coming from.

CHAPTER SEVEN

The birthday party in Wapping was still going well, curtains notwithstanding. A fire crew had been on standby anyway, had indeed lit the enormous candles on the birthday cake in the first place, long before the birthday boy had been allowed anywhere near it. They had then retreated, along with a battalion of reporters from around the world, well beyond the wall of horizontal and vertical girders that separated him from his parents and the considerable number of staff that looked after him – cooks, nurses, seamstresses, childcare specialists, structural engineers, builders and the like.

Most of the hollowed-out warehouse was essentially a heavily reinforced cage, except for about a quarter, which was given over to kitchens, storerooms and normal-sized accommodation. The caged area itself had a single large door, which took three average people to operate but which gave the cage's inhabitant no trouble at all. It opened on to a walled compound that allowed him daily exercise, which he usually needed a fair amount of persuasion to take. This area also now housed his newly acquired bulldozer, or tractor, as everyone very wisely let him call it.

Coming back in through the door took him to a mostly open space that served as a bedsit, combining as it did the roles of bedroom, dining room, play area and TV room. The only part that was walled off was the bathroom, which the youngster would run to with great pride, having just been successfully potty-trained, invariably resulting in the triumphant cry 'I did it!'.

The furniture and fittings, apart from being scaled up in proportion to the occupant's size, had surprisingly few modifications. The only things that had presented the team with any difficulty had been an oversized handset for the TV and DVD, and the rigging up of a remote-controlled arm with a huge spoon on the end for feeding the lad on the increasingly rare occasions when he was too tired, lazy, or disinterested to finish his meal by himself but was still receptive to outside help.

Despite the boy's accommodation being quite accurately referred to as a cage, he himself could hardly be called an inmate, having never shown a single sign of frustration at the limitations of his environment. It was generally acknowledged that he was one of the best-natured, most even-tempered children anyone had ever met. Even during the terrible twos, there had been very few tantrums and amazingly little damage, considering how much destruction he would be capable of, whether deliberately or not.

Ironically, the only time they had had real trouble restraining him was when they were attempting to transport him out of the city so he could have more space and freedom. He had been eighteen months old at the time, an unsteady toddler already taller than his parents, sending a tremor through the house in Pimlico they were still living in every time he crashed down on to his well-padded bespoke nappy.

He hadn't wanted to get into the removal van that had been specially kitted out for the journey to his prospective new home deep in the Suffolk countryside, and had been whimpering miserably as the van went through the centre of London and out along the Commercial Road. But it wasn't until they had turned off at the Blackwall Tunnel and were heading directly towards their destination along the A12, away from the river for the first time, that all hell had broken loose.

Suddenly inconsolable, the pitiful youngster was deaf to his mother's entreaties and would-be soothing words, and his father had suffered a broken rib on what turned out to be the last time he would use his stern voice on his son, as the toddler crawled over to the back door of the van, brushing aside any opposition. Here he proceeded to scream relentlessly, pounding the door and shaking the bars that reinforced it, turning the heads of passers-by as the anonymous van and its accompanying cacophony trundled past.

They had only reached the Bow Flyover when it was decided, out of desperation, to do a U-turn, the van being unlikely to survive this onslaught even as far as the M25 ring road. Heading back in the opposite direction, the frenzy had immediately abated, and they hadn't gone far when a tentative smile had appeared, with just the one repeated, wide-eyed, happy question, 'Home?', one of the first words he had learnt.

So they had stayed in London, with just the one move to their present address. He had literally outgrown the old house, and relocation was arranged while he could still get through the door. His parents had been dreading the move, his father instinctively rubbing his long-healed ribs whenever it was mentioned, but all went well. The child somehow seemed to know that the journey would not be a long one, and complied happily enough, even with some excitement. And he had shown such instant delight at his new surroundings that his mother had burst into tears and sobbed uncontrollably for two solid hours, mostly out of relief, but also because the warehouse reminded her so physically of the new reality – that her son was getting too strong and unpredictable to hold, to comfort, to cuddle, that since his birth his increasing size had brought with it an increasing need for distance that she was finding hard to bear.

He had, after all, been born a perfectly normal eight pounds two and a half ounces and there had been nothing in either side of the family to suggest that he would grow up in anything other than a perfectly ordinary way. The surprising increase in weight and size had been steady and had started on day one, causing alarm, initially, and then merely bewilderment as none of the numerous scientists' scare stories had come true and his development, size apart, was unexceptional. The growth in media interest had matched his for a while, but unlike his had duly slowed down and even gone into retreat, save for big occasions like this third birthday.

His parents, meanwhile, had also come more to terms with their new regime, and although they couldn't wait until he was old enough for them to be able to reason with him – not long now, he was a frighteningly bright child – and try again to get him into a larger, more suitable location, this one seemed to be adequate for the moment. He appeared settled enough, and that was their main concern.

His mother looked at him now through his cage's walls, watching him with immense pride as he tried earnestly to make something out of the acres of wrapping paper his presents had come in, yearning to be able to reach in and gently push back the hair, still too blond to be able to tell if it would turn his mother's red or his father's almost black, that was so endearingly untidy over his forehead.

'Happy birthday, Gogglyboos,' she said, quietly, not expecting him to hear her over the constant noise of the festivities. He looked up at her immediately and broke into a huge smile.

'Goggy happy,' he said.

CHAPTER EIGHT

Maintaining its course exactly parallel to the coastline, the ship was approaching a pointed promontory that would pass, Holly estimated, about ten yards from them. At the end of this flat piece of land was a clump of a dozen or so trees that Holly could not identify. The ticking seemed to be coming from these trees. Holly was peering into them as they drew nearer, trying to make out the hidden creatures he assumed must be the source of the sound, when he realised to his astonishment that it was coming from the leaves themselves. They were round, mostly about three inches long and looked, Holly thought, like miniature table tennis bats. Each one was oscillating backwards and forwards at its own tempo, the smaller ones faster, the larger ones slower, producing a sharp tick with every movement.

Enchanted by this music, Holly waited until the ship had passed the promontory and the sound was receding before turning to Kia open-mouthed.

'Yes,' she nodded, knowingly, 'I've come across them before. Metronome leaves. Lovely, aren't they?' They listened together in wonder until the complex rhythms dissolved into the random surges of the sea.

'We must be very far south,' she murmured. 'Most of those leaves should have fallen by now.' She turned to Holly. 'So, Mr Solver.' She waved an arm in the direction of the land. 'There's a whole grid out there, and we haven't got very far. Ready to get to work?'

After a moment's thought, Holly smiled ruefully. 'To be honest,' he said, leaving the comfort of the railing and walking slowly past Kia towards the front of the ship, 'if everything's like the crimson river and the metronome leaves, I'd be tempted to leave well alone and stay here for the day.' Just a few paces from the bow, he stopped and turned round to confront a serious expression.

'If everything was like them,' Kia said, softly, 'none of us would bother.' She sighed. 'As it is, if we don't get cracking,' she nodded and smiled sarcastically in acknowledgement that they had both registered the pun, 'none of us might be here tomorrow anyway.'

Still unconvinced, Holly held his arms out to his sides, hands open to indicate their surroundings, took a couple of steps back and was about to plead the case for the defence of complete inactivity when he heard a man's voice behind him.

'Thirty-two point seven metres,' it said, calmly.

Any practical sense of self-preservation would have made Holly duck, run, or at least spin round to assess any danger. But he froze, arms out at forty-five degrees, shoulders half shrugged. He was relieved to see that Kia wasn't staring open-mouthed at some nameless horror towering over him, but that she had no more than a puzzled look and her eyes were darting restlessly round the area behind him. He didn't move, nevertheless.

Apparently having spotted something, Kia walked

over and had drawn level with Holly when they heard the voice again.

'Fifteen point eight metres,' it said in an identical tone. Sufficiently reassured to have Kia next to him, Holly lowered his arms and his shoulders and turned slowly round.

Bending forwards in unison, they could just make out a black metal box hidden in the shadows where the two thick beams met that formed the tops of the parapets, a box with a face about the size of a letter box. In the middle was a small screen with a faint, flickering, fine red light that reminded Holly of the laser barcode readers found at supermarket checkouts, and on either side a circular grille pattern had been stamped out, indicating the presence of speakers.

Visibly relaxing, Holly looked expectantly at Kia, who just shook her head in bemusement. 'Doesn't look too threatening,' she said, hesitantly, 'no more than a possible damage level two, I would have said.' Widening her eyes, she turned to Holly. 'Why did I say that? What on earth does it mean?' Getting no meaningful response, she continued, 'That must be one of today's things.' She looked back at the flickering light, having to squint to see it. 'As must this.'

Still attracted to the idea of prolonging his mini cruise, Holly made one last appeal on behalf of non-intervention. 'How can you be sure that this only appeared today, that this ship and this weird little contraption haven't been harmlessly sailing the seas for decades?'

Kia stared grimly out to sea. 'I can only be sure of two things,' she said. 'One is that all this,' she gestured around them, 'must be current because you brought us here by naming a clue.' She glanced at him for confirmation, which he reluctantly gave with a resigned nod. 'The other is that the house we need to return to is that way.' She pointed in the direction in which the ship was travelling.

'How do you know that?' he asked, uneasily.

She smiled at him. 'I suppose I get as many marks for the working out as for the answer?' He returned her smile, but it had already disappeared. 'The answer is that all unsolved things are programmed with a purpose. They have a homing instinct.'

Holly felt even more uneasy. 'Homing in on what?'

'Depends. Sometimes the house, sometimes the team.' She was beginning to look as uncomfortable as Holly felt. 'Usually the Solver.'

Unable to catch her eye, Holly nervously took a few steps away, then turned round. 'Why would they go after the Solver?' he asked, not at all sure he wanted to know. He could see the effort it took for her to face him in her determination to give him an honest answer.

'Because they don't want to be solved,' she said, simply.

Holly's mind reeled with the implications of this fact. He walked back up to Kia.

'Do you mean to tell me they –'

'Forty-one point two metres.'

They both jumped and fell silent, staring at the source of this dubious information.

Suddenly Holly looked sharply at his companion. 'Forty-nine point seven metres,' he said, brusquely, holding up an admonishing finger to stifle the question she was about to ask. To her bewilderment, he carefully retraced his last few steps, five away and five back. On the last step he looked eagerly at the little box.

'Forty-nine point seven metres,' it said, dutifully.

Holly grinned in triumph and turned to Kia, whose

face still registered only bewilderment. 'I suppose you'll be wanting *my* working out,' he said smugly. He'd got one over on this place for the first time and he wasn't going to squander the moment.

After what felt to him like a prolonged orgy of self-indulgence, in fact a period of four seconds, he decided he'd exhausted his gloat quota. In any case, he was impatient to impart his wisdom to a hopefully eager pupil. It had been a very long time since he'd done that.

'The reading it gave me the second time was eight point five metres more than the first, and I'd only wandered over there and back.' He paused, waiting for the information to register. Old habits. 'So it stood to reason, assuming this place follows the same physical laws, and it seems to, that it was telling me how far I'd walked.' Another pause. 'So I tested the hypothesis, added another eight point five metres, and it tallied. The results matched.'

'QED,' she said, mimicking his smugness.

'Well, hardly. But a productive line of enquiry as far as it went. And I don't see that it need go any further.' He looked puzzled. 'Of course, as to why it would be telling me how far I'd walked...'

'We don't ask why,' Kia said, reassuringly, 'ever. It's just because. Because the grid says so. Philosophy is a waste of time here.'

'I'm not sure it isn't a waste of time anywhere,' he mumbled. 'The only interesting question philosophy ever threw up is – why bother with philosophy?'

Despite Holly's plausible explanation, Kia moved away from the talkative device she'd been eyeing suspiciously since they had located it, then confronted the teacher, hands on hips.

'Speaking of laws,' she said in headmistress mode, 'as a Solver, you have already broken rule number one.' She left the same instructive pause he had. 'Namely,' she continued, a little more gently, 'never, NEVER – and I can't stress this enough – EVER, be parted from your copy of the grid, under any circumstances. We have our own copies, yes, but for a solution to stick, it can only be entered in the Solver's, if we have one. And where is yours?'

Holly had to think for a moment. It took him a while even to remember that the previous events had taken place in his own house, so remote did they now seem. 'On the kitchen table?' he ventured at last.

She nodded in agreement. 'No,' she said, confusing him even more. She reached behind her under her jumper and retrieved a folded newspaper from where it had been tucked into the waistband of her jeans. As she did so, Holly could see that she had three spare ballpoint pens clipped to that waistband. She held the paper out to him, puzzle side up. He could make out the grid with the two words he'd filled in.

Gingerly he took it from her. Since he'd seen it last, this grid had assumed so much more importance, and he was acutely aware that in taking possession of it now he was accepting the responsibility of its solution. Kia unclipped one of the pens and gave it to him. It was all swirling colours, mostly yellows and reds.

'Hold on to those,' she said, earnestly.

Holly took a deep breath, surprised at the amount of courage he was having to summon even to look at the paper. 'I suppose we should check out where we are?' he asked with some reluctance. Kia nodded grimly. Making sure his eyes went straight to 1 Down, not wanting to blunder into any of the other clues, Holly read out, ' "Skill around primitive vessel". Five letters.' He looked up. 'No doubt about being in the right place, then.'

Kia started fishing optimistically, as usual. 'Are we looking for some sort of sailing ability – seamanship, marine craft...'

Holly thought for a moment and then smiled. 'No,' he said, looking at her with some admiration, 'you're taking the clue at face value again. And yet somehow,' he hurried on, spurred by her look of disappointment, 'you have got the answer.' She brightened up. 'Craft,' he announced, 'is the answer. "Around" is c, short for "circa", meaning "about" or "around", "raft" is our primitive vessel...'

'Fortunately not,' said Kia dryly, surveying their considerably more luxurious conveyance.

'...leaving "skill", which is "craft".' He peered at the grid. 'And following on from 1 is – 14 – because they come in pairs...' He nodded proudly at Kia to show he had understood this point. She exaggerated the gesture back at him, but not unkindly. '...And that reads – "Apostle includes building a counter".' He looked at her expectantly.

She had already decided she wasn't going to make any haphazard guesses this time, suppressing thoughts of tables and carpentry. Fortunately she could see from his expression that this would not be necessary.

'You've got it already?' she asked in disbelief.

He looked slightly embarrassed. 'Well yes, but it's a classic case of working backwards.' He met with a blank stare. 'I was already looking for the answer before I saw the clue.' The stare was no less blank. 'It had to be about our informative friend here,' he explained, gesturing to the black box. 'So the apostle in question had to be Peter, and the building a dome...' Her expression was now one of concentration. '...So the counter, far from being some sort of table...' She looked a little dismayed that he'd so accurately followed her method. '...must be a Pe-dome-ter.'

He paused, not this time to wait for an acknowledgement of receipt of wisdom, but to ponder the matter himself.

'So the combination of "craft" and "pedometer",' he mused, almost to himself, 'generates this magnificent ship with this handy little device, no doubt installed by the health and safety brigade to make sure the sailors weren't having to walk further than they were sailing.'

Full of admiration and wonder, he pulled the top off the pen and was about to write down the fruits of his considerable labour when a firm hand stayed his arm.

'No, no, no. Not *here*.' Kia looked outraged but was clearly enjoying regaining authority. 'Think about it. You write that in, all this is solved, the ship disappears, we get very wet.'

Holly had to concede to the logic in that. He put the top back on the pen, on the other end this time so he wouldn't have to take it off again, and looked around the ship one last time.

'There may be a lot worse than this out there,' he said, quietly. Kia nodded. 'Out here, we won't know if anything particular needs solving urgently.' Kia shook her head. 'So I suppose we should be getting back.'

'Just say the word.'

Holly nodded and stuck out his elbow, waiting for Kia to take his arm. She stared at him in disbelief, rolled her eyes and grabbed a handful of his shirt sleeve. Sheepishly he cleared his throat.

'So it's back to the...' he faltered, suddenly sceptical that mentioning one short word, that him, of all people, uttering that word would have the power to transform their surroundings so completely. But wasn't that how they had got there in the first place? And if nothing happened, they'd be forced to endure a whole day of clear sky and calm sea.

Kia was raising her eyebrows at him in expectation. Maybe it was time he stopped thinking himself in circles and just...

'...grid.'

CHAPTER NINE

BIG BABY POLITICIANS PROTEST HURRICANE.

Uncle Jasper looked dubiously at this rather abbreviated version of the four news stories he had considered worth noting down. Fortunately each one had been so bizarre he knew he wouldn't have any trouble remembering them in more detail. He had also written, next to each one, the time shown on the recorder when they had appeared. Kia would want to go through them on her return, he was thinking, and was handing the notebook to Uncle Sid for his approval at the precise moment she and Holly did reappear in the kitchen. Both uncles brightened visibly as they heard the telltale '*shap*' that always heralded someone's materialisation or dematerialisation.

They found the two travellers where they had last seen them, by the kitchen table. Kia was still holding on to Holly's sleeve, her other arm ready to catch him should he need it. He did indeed initially look a little shaky, but after a brief moment's apprehension suddenly smiled and nodded reassuringly, first at her and then at the others.

'That was so much better,' he said with obvious relief. A questioning look at Kia from the uncles was met with a brusque 'don't ask' shake of the head. Eager to change the subject, Kia looked around the room.

'House still standing, then?' she asked. 'You didn't take another train?' The uncles shook their head vigorously.

'No,' Holly agreed, dryly, 'we didn't fancy the train either. That's why we took the boat.'

'Took bone?' Uncle Sid asked Kia.

'Took boat,' said Holly, slowly and deliberately, as though addressing a backward child. A silence ensued as Uncle Sid slowly turned to face Holly.

'Took – bone,' he said, even more emphatically, waving the relevant article in Holly's face. Kia stepped hurriedly between them, put a hand on Uncle Sid's outstretched arm and lowered it.

'Ah yes, notebook, quite right.' Turning to Holly, she explained, 'They record the TV news every morning and then go through it to see if anything urgent stands out. If it does, it goes into the notebook. It's an invaluable routine,' she said warmly and, she hoped, soothingly, smiling at the balding man. 'So we'll do that in a minute. You go and set it up.'

Uncle Sid let himself be guided by Kia to the door, still scowling at Holly as he went, a scowl that only intensified on seeing Uncle Jasper's smirk, a smirk that broke into laughter when Uncle Sid threw the notebook at it.

'But first,' Kia turned back to a still bewildered Holly, 'we have to resolve our transport problem.' Holly apparently had to resolve the problem of understanding what she meant first. 'The ship,' she continued, 'and its talkative crew of one.' She watched his expression change from puzzled to crestfallen. 'We don't know what else its role might be. It doesn't seem to pose much of a threat, but I can't see that it's much of an advantage either. We can't take the chance.' By now she sounded almost apologetic. 'Trust me. It's got to go.'

Holly had to play counsel for the defence one last time.

'What if we just popped over there once in a while for a breather? Surely that would be an asset worth hanging on to?'

Shaking her head regretfully, Kia remained firm.

'We don't know where it's going, or if anyone else is on it by now. We might appear in the middle of a storm at sea, or it might have sunk, then we'd join it on the ocean floor. Believe me, things are going to get complicated enough round here. We need to get it out of the equation, and who better to do that than a maths teacher?'

That, and the playful punch on the arm, finally produced a thin smile. Holly lifted the paper he still dutifully held in his hand and studied it briefly. Then, with some effort, he put it down on the table and, using the red and yellow pen that suddenly felt way too gaudy for so weighty a task, wrote the word 'craft' at 1 Down. Here he hesitated, but Kia's stern gaze was too much for him, and with a grimace he added 'pedometer' at 14 Down. Then he sighed and straightened up.

Kia gently smiled her approval.

'Well done,' she said, patting his arm. 'That wasn't easy, I know. But it was necessary. There are just too many risks involved. Even if the ship hadn't posed a threat to us, it could have affected any number of other people in ways you can't possibly imagine, and certainly couldn't predict. You'll come to realise that you simply can't be too careful. Speaking of which, write in that one we got earlier while you're at it. It might give us a head start later. Artisan. You remember.'

Indeed he did remember, especially the way the uncles had arrived at it from two different directions. He located

26 Across and entered the seven letters.

'Great,' said Kia, walking to the door and gesturing to Holly to go through first. 'Let's go and see what the rest of the day holds in store for us.'

She waited until Holly had almost reached the door and then coughed in a loud and ostentatious way, nodding at the newspaper he had again left on the table. He frowned at himself, retrieved it and shuffled out of the room without looking at her.

They went into the living room and found Uncle Jasper sitting on the sofa directly opposite the television, brandishing a remote control, and Uncle Sid in the armchair, tapping his knee in impatience and pointedly ignoring Holly. As Uncle Jasper had taken the well-worn half of the sofa, Holly sat self-consciously in the other, having first gallantly offered it to Kia, who rolled her eyes again, clearly preferring to stand. Holly couldn't remember the last time he had sat on this part of the sofa, and was amazed at how alien it made the room look.

'So,' said Kia, hopefully, 'find anything unusual?'

'Bizarre,' was Uncle Jasper's response, spoken with an air of disbelief. 'Out – landish.'

He proceeded to show them the stories he'd deemed noteworthy, locating the times he'd recorded in his notebook.

Each story provoked a surprisingly different response. The hurricane was swiftly dismissed as Holly had seen it on the news the previous evening, although he wasn't sure if that counted any more.

'If it were one of today's – er – inventions,' he had asked, 'couldn't I just have imagined I'd seen it last night, just as the people outside weren't surprised to see a train rumbling down the middle of their street?'

'No,' Kia had reassured him, 'memories can't be invented for you, as you're not, well, from round here.'

Holly had been mightily relieved to hear this. He had suddenly realised the possibility of having to question the reality of everything he thought had been his life so far. Typically, he had also immediately seen the advantage of maybe being able to 'solve' some of his less pleasant memories. There were always pluses and minuses.

His scientific mind had far more trouble taking in the birthday celebrations for the enormous child. Indeed the three men were united in their amazement, and were just thinking things couldn't get any stranger when they heard Kia cooing, 'Ooh, he's so cute!' They silently turned their amazement on her, but she was adamant. 'Well he is! Look at the way he apologised for setting fire to those hideous curtains. He's just adorable!' The men turned to each other, shaking their heads and raising their eyebrows. Holly was aware of feeling accepted as part of the team for the first time. Even Uncle Sid seemed to have forgotten their recent misunderstanding, and it was he who then drew them all together by pointing at the television and saying earnestly 'Switch hat!' by way of introducing the next item.

This was *The Case of the Disappearing Politicians.* Holly had always had what he considered a healthy disrespect for politicians. If you can't believe what they say, he had long ago reasoned, then there really isn't any point in listening to them at all. He had voted a couple of times just after he'd got married, because his wife had said that if he didn't, whoever he voted for, then he wouldn't be in a position to complain at their decisions. But then he had figured he wasn't much of a complainer anyway, so that really wasn't a great loss, and he had lapsed.

All of which made it more surprising to him to see how incensed he was that someone was spiriting them away. He may have had no time for them and would have crossed the street to avoid one – more likely pretend to be tying his shoelaces as he almost had on spotting his neighbour Gus that morning – but they were symbols, however annoying, of democracy and that in itself seemed to Holly to be worth at least a modicum of indignation. Plus of course he found it a particularly intriguing puzzle that screamed out for a solution.

But if he found that story baffling, the next one was utterly beyond his comprehension. The idea that anyone could fail to find mathematics as fascinating as he did was a source of constant wonder to him. But that there could be a dislike so strong that it brought students out in the streets waving banners made him doubt that he and they had even been born on the same planet.

He was so utterly spellbound by this incomprehensible vision that he failed to notice the others nudge each other, nodding at him, barely stifling their laughter, and it was a while before he realised that the ringing he had supposed had been part of the news story was in fact his own doorbell.

<table>
<tr><td>1 C</td><td></td><td>2 T</td><td></td><td>3</td><td></td><td>4</td><td></td><td>5</td><td></td><td>■</td><td>6</td><td>7</td><td></td><td>8</td></tr>
<tr><td>R</td><td>■</td><td>R</td><td>■</td><td></td><td>■</td><td></td><td>■</td><td></td><td>■</td><td>9</td><td>■</td><td></td><td>■</td><td></td></tr>
<tr><td>10 A</td><td></td><td>A</td><td></td><td></td><td></td><td></td><td>■</td><td>11</td><td></td><td></td><td></td><td></td><td></td><td></td></tr>
<tr><td>F</td><td>■</td><td>M</td><td>■</td><td></td><td>■</td><td></td><td>■</td><td></td><td>■</td><td></td><td>■</td><td></td><td>■</td><td></td></tr>
<tr><td>12 T</td><td></td><td>L</td><td></td><td></td><td></td><td></td><td></td><td></td><td>■</td><td>13</td><td></td><td></td><td></td><td></td></tr>
<tr><td>■</td><td>■</td><td>I</td><td>■</td><td></td><td>■</td><td></td><td>■</td><td></td><td>■</td><td></td><td>■</td><td>■</td><td>■</td><td></td></tr>
<tr><td>14 P</td><td></td><td>N</td><td></td><td></td><td>■</td><td>15</td><td></td><td></td><td></td><td></td><td></td><td>16</td><td></td><td></td></tr>
<tr><td>E</td><td>■</td><td>E</td><td>■</td><td></td><td>■</td><td>■</td><td>■</td><td>■</td><td>■</td><td></td><td>■</td><td></td><td>■</td><td></td></tr>
<tr><td>17 D</td><td></td><td>S</td><td></td><td></td><td></td><td>18</td><td></td><td>19</td><td>■</td><td>20</td><td></td><td></td><td></td><td></td></tr>
<tr><td>O</td><td>■</td><td>■</td><td>■</td><td></td><td>■</td><td></td><td>■</td><td></td><td>■</td><td></td><td>■</td><td></td><td>■</td><td>■</td></tr>
<tr><td>21 M</td><td></td><td>22 G</td><td></td><td></td><td>■</td><td>23</td><td></td><td></td><td></td><td></td><td></td><td></td><td></td><td>24</td></tr>
<tr><td>E</td><td>■</td><td>A</td><td>■</td><td></td><td>■</td><td></td><td>■</td><td></td><td>■</td><td></td><td>■</td><td></td><td>■</td><td></td></tr>
<tr><td>25 T</td><td></td><td>B</td><td></td><td></td><td></td><td></td><td>■</td><td>26 A</td><td>R</td><td>T</td><td>I</td><td>S</td><td>A</td><td>N</td></tr>
<tr><td>E</td><td>■</td><td>L</td><td>■</td><td></td><td>■</td><td></td><td>■</td><td></td><td>■</td><td></td><td>■</td><td></td><td>■</td><td></td></tr>
<tr><td>27 R</td><td></td><td>E</td><td></td><td>■</td><td>28</td><td></td><td></td><td></td><td></td><td></td><td></td><td></td><td></td><td></td></tr>
</table>

CHAPTER TEN

'Would I be correct in assuming this to be the residence of a Mr Holly?'

Holly opened his mouth to answer.

'A Mr Colin Holly?'

Holly tried again, with no more luck.

'Formerly in the employ of Westlink Manor Primary School?'

This time Holly waited, expecting another interruption which, needless to say, didn't come. But it did give him time to have a look at the man now standing on his doorstep.

The coat and the hair were the features that struck Holly first – thin, mousy, sand-coloured hair swept over to one side, just not thin enough for Holly to see if it was a comb-over, and a beige raincoat that almost reached the man's feet and had clearly seen better days. These were offset with a number of similar-coloured accessories – shoes, brown, socks, beige, eyes, red-rimmed but otherwise brown, in his left hand a small, thin notebook with a brown cover, in his right hand a pen that was strikingly black against its monochrome surroundings. Colour aside, Holly had the impression that everything about the man was covered in a thick layer of dust.

As the man looked as though he could comfortably hold his expectant expression for the rest of the day, Holly thought he'd have another go at answering.

'That is correct,' he said, rather stiffly.

'Correct is what we aim to be. Or at least factual. There is a big difference, you know. Don't get me started.'

Holly had no intention of getting the man started. Getting him leaving would have suited him just fine, but there seemed little chance of that. The man had assumed his expectant stare again, and Holly had no idea what it was he was expecting.

'Well, what can I do for you, Mr...?' he finally dragged out of himself.

'Noose. Roger Noose. Roving reporter for the Voice.'

Holly felt a certain dismay that this man represented Holly's own newspaper, but not greatly surprised. He had after all given up reading the articles a long time ago, focusing entirely on the back page headlines and the crossword puzzle.

The thought of the puzzle reminded him of more pressing matters, and he saw no reason to waste any more time with this character.

'I'm sorry,' he started to say, 'I really don't...'

'It's about the kids demonstrating outside Westlink. May I come in?' The question was clearly rhetorical. He had barely finished the sentence when he brushed past Holly and entered the house.

Left standing alone in his own doorway, Holly found the situation too amusing to suppress a wry grin. He was also relishing having a moment to himself, a respite from this madness he knew would be all too brief. So he just stood there for a few seconds, staring at the spot outside where he had tried in vain to evade his neighbour Gus just that morning, marvelling at how much had already happened since then. Gus would love all this, he thought, seriously considering the possibility of knocking on his door and inviting him along, for moral support if nothing else, or maybe even to take Holly's place.

But he immediately rejected the idea. Gus was hardly the moral support type and, for all Holly knew, might not be any good at crosswords. It struck Holly not only that he felt so responsible to the team for solving today's clues, but also how possessive he felt towards that responsibility. After all, since he had last seen Gus he had totally rebuilt his own house and sunk a sailing ship. He wasn't going to let anybody else step in now and have all the fun. And he had to admit, much to his own surprise, that he was having fun.

This realisation sank Gus's chance of involvement in the day's proceedings. Holly took a deep breath and closed the door.

The house was unsettlingly quiet. Holly feared for a moment that he would find it empty, that all his house guests had vanished, figments of his imagination after all. Why was the reporter not interrogating the others? Perhaps he was giving them one of his lingering expectant looks.

In the event, the reason why the journalist wasn't conducting interviews was that he had apparently spent all that time, as if to prove his true hack credentials, snooping around Holly's kitchen. On hearing Holly's footsteps he made it back in the hallway just in time to be first through the living room door.

'Oh hello,' he said, cheerfully, on finding the room occupied. Holly followed him in and made the necessary introductions, intrigued what all these characters would make of each other.

'Everyone, this,' he said, turning to the new arrival, 'is Mr Noose.'

'Noose,' the dusty man agreed, 'Roger Noose. Here on behalf of the *Daily Voice*.'

'So that makes you a Noose reporter,' Kia exclaimed in delight.

'No, no, I'm a news reporter. Noose is my name.'

Kia continued staring at the man, her beaming smile undiminished, eventually transferring her gaze to Holly, who found a sudden need to frown heavily at the carpet.

'Roger Noose,' the man continued, by way of explanation. The uncles, who had both got up to greet the newcomer, were eyeing him with unbridled glee.

Increasingly aware of the ensuing silence, Holly resumed the introductions.

'This is Kia, Uncle Sid and Uncle Jasper,' he said, gesturing to each in turn.

'Ah, the extended family,' the reporter purred, 'how refreshing.' Spotting the notebook in Uncle Jasper's hand, he waved his own in the air. 'And what do we have here – another devotee of the journalistic arts?'

Before Uncle Jasper could reply, Uncle Sid snorted. 'Into old boy Kelly,' he muttered.

The reporter turned to him with a puzzled look.

'Not sure I understand the reference,' he said. 'Is it in connection with a former pupil of the school?'

'What school?' Kia asked.

'Westlink Manor. Lower Manor Lane. Ten minute walk away. Maths students demonstrating outside. Surely you've heard about it?'

‘Yes, we’ve just seen it,’ Kia said, evenly, ‘on the Noose.’

The grins reappeared on the uncles’ faces, and Holly was glad the reporter wasn’t looking at him.

‘Well that’s why I’m here,’ Mr Noose continued, obliviously. ‘To get the inside story. After all Mr Holly here did teach at that establishment for a number of years.’

All eyes turned to the subject of this new revelation.

‘That was your school?’ Kia demanded in disbelief.

‘Our holy cos?’ echoed Uncle Sid, much to Mr Noose’s bewilderment.

‘Why didn’t you say?’ Kia wanted to know.

Holly shuffled awkwardly. He had always hated being the centre of attention, particularly this sort of attention.

‘Well,’ he began, tentatively, ‘it’s all very nostalgic, you know, but I really don’t see the relevance.’ Nobody seemed convinced so he continued. ‘I can’t imagine that, after all these years, anything I might have to say on the subject could be remotely,’ he paused to throw Kia the most fleeting of glances, ‘Nooseworthy.’

The uncles could contain themselves no longer, and exploded with laughter. The merriment was compounded when Mr Noose did finally react with indignation but, to the uncles’ wonder and delight, for the wrong reason.

‘No, no, no,’ he began, promisingly, ‘you shouldn’t laugh at the poor man’s insecurities.’ Turning to the incredulous poor man himself, he continued, ‘You would be amazed, Mr Holly, how the distance in time, with the right words, becomes null and void. Null and void. Any comments you might make, on the record of course, would sound as relevant today as, well, however long ago it was that they really were relevant. After all, mathematics, the study of constants, could be said to be a constant itself.’ He beamed at Holly, clearly very pleased with himself. 'You see? Context. Context is everything. Verbiage as scaffolding. A metaphor here, a simile there, and everyone will be hanging on your every word. You just need the right journalistic architect. And I,' he rose as tall as his dusty frame would allow, 'am a craftsman.'

Kia was the first to react. 'Did you hear that?' she asked Holly. 'He's a craftsman.'

Her knowing look spread to Uncle Jasper's face. 'A smith,' he said, eagerly. 'A wright.'

Uncle Sid took up the reins. Smiling malevolently at the reporter, he hissed, 'As in, rat.'

All three turned to Holly. Unfortunately, he still hadn't made the connection, and his face was registering little more than mild panic. Only after Kia pointed vigorously at the paper he had forgotten he was still holding did the penny drop.

'Oh,' he breathed slowly, turning to Mr Noose for the first time with any degree of respect. 'You're the artisan.'

The artisan, still a little dubious about having possibly been called a rat, reacted predictably to what he thought was flattery.

'Well,' he nodded, 'years of hard work, built on the bedrock of natural linguistical ability, and that's what you get. Artisan, craftsman.' He turned jovially to Uncle Jasper. 'No point just rattling off a series of synonyms, is there?'

Uncle Jasper's smile disappeared and his eyes narrowed. Uncle Sid happily shook his head in agreement. There was a healthy rivalry between the two, synonyms versus anagrams, although they were generally evenly represented.

'No,' the thick-skinned reporter continued, 'artisan is a perfectly good word. The *mot juste*, if you'll pardon my French. You're a puzzling man.'

Holly, to whom this last remark was addressed, wasn't initially too sure what to make of this non sequitur until he realised he had indeed been looking at the crossword.

'Yes. Yes I am. Do you dabble, Mr Noose?'

'Go on, try me,' the reporter simpered.

Locating the word that preceded 'artisan' in the grid, Holly said, 'OK then, see what you make of this. "Old bait used daily". Seven letters.'

Mr Noose took a few tentative bites on the end of his pen. 'Something to do with maggots, I expect.'

'No,' said Kia, shaking her head in resignation, 'that's what I thought, so it can't be right.'

Holly gave her a sympathetic smile. 'Daily?' he enquired, looking at each of the others in turn. 'Any ideas?'

'Every twenty-four hours?' the reporter offered, hopefully. 'Seven times a week?'

Holly shook his head, his eyes glinting. 'Misdirection,' he murmured.

Uncle Jasper shook his head, but not without some admiration. Uncle Sid just looked briefly heavenwards.

'It's actually a noun,' Holly went on, in fuller voice. 'A daily, as in a newspaper.'

Mr Noose furrowed his brow, deep in thought for a few seconds, and then shook his head firmly. 'No no,' he said with conviction, 'that's nine letters. It doesn't fit.'

'A type of newspaper,' Holly continued patiently. 'The word "used" is an anagram indicator.' He looked over at Uncle Sid, who in turn gave an even more irritated Uncle Jasper a triumphant look. 'And it's an anagram of "old bait". Which is...?'

'Tabloid!' said Uncle Sid, beaming.

'Which is indeed a type of newspaper,' the journalist

conceded with reluctance, 'although nowadays we prefer the term "non-broadsheet". One must move with the times, if you'll pardon the pun.'

'Well, then I'm afraid,' said Holly, starting to enter the word into the grid, 'that this word makes you old Noose.'

'Oh, I hardly think so. Forty-one in this game isn't...'

And with that, there was suddenly one less person in the room.

1 C		2 T		3		4		5		■	6	7		8
R	■	R	■		■		■		■	9	■		■	
10 A		A					■	11						
F	■	M	■		■		■		■		■		■	
12 T		L							■	13				
■	■	I	■		■		■		■		■	■	■	
14 P		N			■	15						16		
E	■	E	■		■	■	■	■	■		■		■	
17 D		S				18		19	■	20				
O	■	■	■		■		■		■		■		■	■
21 M		22 G			■	23								24
E	■	A	■		■		■		■		■		■	
25 T	A	B	L	O	I	D	■	26 A	R	T	I	S	A	N
E	■	L	■		■		■		■		■		■	
27 R		E		■	28									

CHAPTER ELEVEN

The laughter this time was more widespread and more prolonged. Kia was having to support herself against the armchair Uncle Sid had been sitting in. Uncle Sid himself had to wipe tears from his eyes, eventually managing to say an admiring 'neon ice!' to Holly, slapping him forcefully on the shoulder. It was only at this point that Kia realised that Holly hadn't joined in the merriment.

'You're shaking,' she said in some surprise, gesturing to her teammates to calm down.

Holly had been staring at the point formerly occupied by the reporter, and was now fixed on the crossword grid in his hand. He was indeed trembling all over, quite subtly, but the newspaper seemed to amplify his movements, and that's what had given him away.

'How do you feel?' asked Kia, cautiously. Once again, she couldn't tell from his initial lack of response whether or not he had heard her. Only after she and the uncles had exchanged puzzled glances did Holly break the silence.

'I knew what was going to happen.' His quiet voice expressed surprise and dismay. 'I knew, if I put that word in, that he'd... But then actually seeing him... Or rather, then not seeing him... The power...'

He looked up at Kia, clearly struggling to find the right words.

'With the ship,' he settled on, finally, 'I just wrote the words in, and I assumed the ship disappeared, but I didn't actually see it. And it was just a ship – a nice one, to be sure, but still just an inanimate object. But he – he was...'

'You did what you had to do,' Kia said, sternly. 'You did the right thing.'

'Well, yes, I'm sure one less tired hack in the world...'

'But there isn't one less, that's the point.' Kia went up to Holly and gently held the newspaper in his hand steady. This time it seemed to conduct a lack of movement the other way, and Holly's shaking started to subside. 'This time yesterday Mr Noose didn't even exist. So there are now just as many tabloid artisans in the world as there were then.' She paused until she was sure Holly had grasped the importance of what she was saying, and then added, 'Unfortunately.'

Reassured by his faint smile that he was on the road to recovery, she let go of his newspaper.

'So,' she went on more forcefully, 'don't get the idea that seeing off a man with no past, no natural future, no more than the merest whim as the reason for his existence, should make you some sort of – killer.'

With a last admonishing look, she went and sat heavily in the armchair, side-saddle, both legs crossed over one of its arms. Uncle Jasper couldn't resist making full use of her last word as she went.

'Assassin!' he whispered playfully at Holly. 'Murderer!'

Holly squinted at Uncle Jasper, smiling yet quizzical. He was beginning to understand Kia's affection for these two mischievous eccentrics. They had such well-defined roles within the team, and yet there seemed to be so much more to them than their mere functions.

The thought of these functions gave Holly an idea. Holding up a 'don't go away' finger to the bemused Uncle Jasper, he started to read frantically through the list of clues, muttering to himself as he went. This incomprehensible monologue ended in an abrupt 'Aha!', at which he lifted his head and challenged Uncle Jasper with, 'Calculations!'

Uncle Jasper looked surprised until he realised what was expected of him. 'Assessments?' he offered, eagerly. 'Computations? Estimations? Forecasts? Reckonings?'

Holly glanced down at the paper, then turned, upheld finger and all, to Uncle Sid. 'I'm their cat!' he exclaimed, wondering what the probability would be that he would ever use that particular sentence again.

Unfazed and without hesitation, Uncle Sid said, 'Arithmetic!'

The finger and the expectant look turned back to Uncle Jasper, who shrugged and happily conceded, 'Arithmetic.'

Holly nodded triumphantly at both of his colleagues in turn. Kia watched intently as he entered the word in the grid.

'What's this one, then?' she asked.

Holly waited until he had finished writing, and then looked up.

' "Calculations worked out I'm their cat",' he recited. 'Calculations means arithmetic, which is also an anagram of "I'm their cat".'

'Yes,' Kia said, wearily, 'even I'd figured that out. I meant, why this clue?'

'Well,' he explained, 'it may not be a priority for you, but this school demonstration is starting to bug me. The idea that anyone could protest about the study of mathematics is just too fantastic for words.'

'Really?' Kia cast her mind back to the expanse of bobbing placards. 'Maths stinks,' she recalled. 'Sounds more than reasonable to me.'

Uncle Sid nodded solemnly in agreement. Uncle Jasper shook his head and raised his eyebrows at Holly in disbelief. Grateful for at least some support, Holly continued.

'No, it has to be resolved. Especially as it was my school. Makes it personal. And maybe also out of guilt at Mr Noose's demise. That was supposedly why he was here, after all.'

Kia gave an indifferent shrug. 'Go on then,' she sighed. 'Finish it off. At least it's one more thing we won't have to worry about, and it might give us some useful letters.'

'OK.' Holly peered eagerly at the grid to see which word preceded 'arithmetic'. 'Let's see. Twenty-sev...'

He was drowned out as all three shouted incoherent warnings at him. He was visibly annoyed at himself for his momentary lapse of concentration. He had to follow the rules, or at least be aware of them.

'Oh I'm sorry,' said Kia with a look of exaggerated concern. 'Perhaps you wanted to drop in at the old school? Look up some old friends?'

Ignoring her, Holly returned to the newspaper.

' "Queen returns, getting eastern king to hum". Four letters. R blank E blank. Shouldn't be hard.'

A silence ensued as four brows furrowed. Kia was the first to break it.

'How about "reel"', she suggested. 'You can hum that, can't you? I know it's a dance, but it's the music as well, isn't it?'

'Yes, it is,' Holly said with some hesitation, unwilling to have to tell her yet again that she was on the wrong track, 'but if you put all the bits together, "queen" is usually ER, our queen, Elizabeth Regina, "returns" means it's backwards, so RE, "eastern" is just an E and "king" is just a K, so you get "reek". For which "hum"," he said, looking over at Uncle Jasper for confirmation, 'can be a synonym.'

Uncle Jasper nodded solemnly.

'Although,' Holly went on, 'you would naturally expect it to mean "sing".'

'There's nothing natural about it,' Kia muttered in dejection. 'You have to have a warped mind for this stuff.'

She picked up the copy of the paper Uncle Sid had been looking at and gazed morosely at the page their puzzle was on, together with half a dozen others, all variations on the same theme.

'Look at them,' she moaned. 'Alphabet puzzles, circular puzzles, word searches, themed crosswords. They're all – twisted. Granted, these cryptic ones are the worst of the lot, but all word puzzles...'

She stopped, her eyes fixed on a particular clue. The uncles exchanged nervous glances. Holly, who had been looking at the word he had just written into the grid, still grappling with the concept of anyone protesting about being taught the noble art of manipulating numbers, sensed the tension and looked up. Kia seemed to be the centre of attention.

'What is it?' he asked, but got no reply. 'Kia?' He walked over and touched her arm, making her jump. 'What is it?'

'This clue,' she said, regretfully. 'Eleven Across. We have to solve it.'

'OK. Any particular reason?'

Kia looked back at the paper. 'I said "all word puzzles" just as I was looking at the words "all word puzzles" in the clue.'

The expression on the uncles' faces went from nervous to grim. Holly could see that this meant something to them, but it didn't to him.

'Well, surely,' he reasoned, 'seeing the words would make you say them?'

'No,' again sounding remorseful. 'I knew I was going to say them before I said them and then I saw them and then I said them anyway.' She looked up at the uncles, almost apologetically. Uncle Jasper seemed transfixed, but Uncle Sid managed a reassuring smile, as faint as it was unconvincing.

Holly was so baffled by this, that out of the innumerable questions that occurred to him, the only thing that came out of his mouth was, 'What?' Succinctly put, he thought to himself, what a boon it was to have such an incisive, inquiring mind.

Kia turned to him with the same pained look.

'Don't ask me why,' she said, which cheered Holly somewhat, as at least he hadn't done that, 'but it's always significant. And it's never good news.'

However intriguing Holly found this, he had to admit that it was hardly the strangest thing he'd had to take on trust since the morning, so he let it pass.

'Right. Well. Let's have a look at it, then.' He found the relevant clue and read out, ' "Judge all word puzzles".' He looked round hopefully, but was confronted with the usual hopeful faces, only now with a little more trepidation, he thought, so he sighed inwardly and applied himself more diligently.

'Well, it's seven letters in total, and the words before "puzzles" contain seven letters, so "puzzles" could just be an anagram indicator, albeit rather a dubious one.' He looked inquiringly at Uncle Sid.

Kia handed the paper to Uncle Sid, who peered intently at the clue. Suddenly, to his amazement, Holly watched all the blood drain from the poor man's face, and Uncle Sid began shaking his head vigorously.

'What?' asked Kia, anxiously. 'It's not an anagram?'

Uncle Sid turned to her and carried on shaking his head, but Holly could see that he wasn't refuting her question, but trying to refute something else.

'It is an anagram, isn't it?' he prompted, gently. 'What is it?'

He located the clue to work it out for himself, but before he could do so, Uncle Sid, who hadn't taken his eyes off Kia since she had spoken, made a single utterance in a pinched voice, as though having to force it through a throat that had all but closed.

'Law Lord,' he squeaked.

Holly heard an intake of breath in each ear. He was startled enough to see Kia's expression of fear, but was even more unsettled to see that Uncle Jasper's face was now the same colour as his boiler suit.

'That's just a type of judge, as the clue says,' he offered, but without any real conviction. 'Or is this someone specific, like the local magistrate?'

Kia made a visible effort to compose herself.

'Oh, he's a little more than that.' Her voice was barely above a whisper, as though she suspected that someone was listening at the door. 'Law Lord,' she clearly had difficulty even saying it, 'is one of the names used to describe the Compiler.'

Holly felt a chill ripple through him.

'Law Lord, as in, he makes the rules?'

Kia nodded, very slowly.

The events of the day so far had been hard enough to assimilate, Holly thought, without having to factor in the possibility that one individual might be responsible for it all. A crossword had to have a compiler, he could see the logic of that, but how it applied to this particular case completely escaped him. He was almost relieved to be denied the opportunity to contemplate the matter further.

'Finish the line.' Kia's voice, back to its usual strength, was grim and resolute.

Having calmed down somewhat, Uncle Sid now turned to Holly and the plaintive head-shaking resumed. Grappling with these conflicting instructions, Holly went with grim and resolute. Consulting the paper, he located the clue to the word that preceded 'law lord'. Taking a deep breath, he said, ' "Opposed to making a profit on the way". Seven letters, A blank A, four blanks.'

Looking round, he saw that Kia was staring fixedly at the wall opposite, unable to make eye contact with anyone, and the other two seemed to have gone into some kind of shock. He figured he wasn't going to get any help with this one.

' "The way",' he began, falteringly, 'usually means a road, so it could be R, RD, or maybe ST for street, "*on* the way", so at the end.' He checked the others, but found no change. 'If the A in the clue is the first A of the word,' still no response, 'then we're looking for a four-letter word, second letter A, meaning profit.'

Uncle Jasper did no more than wince at this, which Holly took to mean that there was an obvious candidate but no inclination, or maybe capability, to give it.

‘“Gain”,’ Holly directed at Uncle Jasper, ‘is another word for “profit”.’ Uncle Jasper could only nod wearily. ‘And “opposed to” could be synonymous with “against”, A – gain – st.’ Another reluctant nod. Holly mulled over the resultant combination. ‘Against law lord.’ He felt disappointed at the lack of revelation the solution had brought. ‘What is?’

Kia’s voice, when it eventually came, sounded distant. ‘Lines like these always refer to the Solver.’

‘What does that mean?’

‘It means,’ Kia said emptily without taking her eyes off the wall, ‘that in some way or other, you are on a collision course with the highest authority there is.’

1 C		2 T		3		4		5		■	6	7		8
R	■	R	■		■		■		■	9	■		■	
10 A	G	A	I	N	S	T	■	11 L	A	W	L	O	R	D
F	■	M	■		■		■		■		■		■	
12 T		L							■	13				
■	■	I	■		■		■		■		■	■	■	
14 P		N			■	15						16		
E	■	E	■		■	■	■	■	■		■		■	
17 D		S			■	18		19	■	20				
O	■	■	■		■		■		■		■		■	■
21 M		22 G			■	23								24
E	■	A	■		■		■		■		■		■	
25 T	A	B	L	O	I	D	■	26 A	R	T	I	S	A	N
E	■	L	■		■		■		■		■		■	
27 R	E	E	K	■	28 A	R	I	T	H	M	E	T	I	C

CHAPTER TWELVE

'Kia seems a bit quiet.'

'Don't be absurd. Kia's never quiet.'

'Hah! No! I don't mean she wouldn't be her usual deafening self. Just that we haven't seen her for a while.'

'Well now that you've said that, we will of course be seeing her today.'

'Ah, tempting fate, you think? Throwing destiny a tasty morsel on a line and reeling her in? Or maybe just spinning her a line?'

'No doubt a line you've spun before.'

'Hah! No doubt. I don't think there are any new lines. My round?'

'No, that would only be a new line if *I* used it.'

'No, I didn't mean... Oh I see! Hah! Yet another point to the baron. *Le capitaine – nul points*. Same again?'

The baron nodded absently and resumed watching the world go by.

The setting for the conversation was a circular, stainless steel table on the pavement outside a pub. This pub, the Luminous Steed, named in honour of a fabled faithful companion of a local highwayman, a fable of decidedly dubious origin, was located on a corner of the busy shopping area that included Holly's newsagent. The table was the middle one in a row of five, the others being unoccupied – understandably, given the time of year, although, being sheltered from the wind and getting the full benefit of the winter sun, the two companions found the situation infinitely preferable to the pub's grim, atmosphere-free interior.

The men were in their mid twenties. The captain, the one with the explosive laugh, had now got up and was carrying two empty beer glasses towards the pub's entrance on the corner. He was wearing an old pair of trainers, combat trousers and a light brown padded jacket that tried hard but ultimately failed to contain the bright multicoloured shirt beneath it. His shoulder-length hair was long at the front with a side parting and apparently needed pushing away from his face with a cuff before he barged open the door.

By contrast, the baron was all in black – black baseball boots, black jeans, black T-shirt and black leather jacket. His hair, which was shorter than his companion's and gelled back, would also have been black, or at least a close approximation, had he not already been going grey for some time. Fortunately this process had been quite even, resulting in a salt and pepper arrangement that he had been told, but not convinced, made him look distinguished.

It being lunchtime, the street was like an ants' nest. It seemed to the baron that everyone had just realised that they were out of something essential. He and the captain loved this time of day, particularly when they were up in time to meet up and see it, and felt they could spend their whole lives just sitting with a pint and watching the activity of others, which is why they did.

They had done so from innumerable different locations, all fully licensed, but the Steed kept dragging them back. Reasons they had come up with for this preference included the comfort of the seats, the wide view over the square to one side, the bus stop directly across the road, which offered more leisurely scrutiny of its occupants, and of course their mutual favourite beer, Bentley's Best. There also used to be the allure of the regular lock-ins in the downstairs bar, but this had all but ceased since the recent change in management, and anyway the new landlady wasn't someone even the captain would have wanted to get locked in with.

All this aside, they would still have ended up at the Steed more often than not, because it was the location where they were most likely to run into Kia and the team. The pair greatly enjoyed rising to the daily challenge, having even been helpful in finding solutions in the past, and while they were never actually sought out, the odd chance encounter had certainly proved beneficial to all concerned. The baron picked up a copy of the paper every day just in case, the only thing he could ever have been said to do religiously.

It was as the baron was scouring the crowds in search of one of these familiar faces that he spotted a decidedly military gentleman walking directly towards the pub – so directly, indeed, that while everyone in his vicinity was charging left and right, he seemed almost to be walking on the spot, but for the fact that he was getting bigger – and so military in his bearing that his uniform was superfluous. The purpose with which he moved in contrast to the pinball behaviour around him even made the captain stop in his tracks momentarily as he returned to the table with the recharged glasses. He barely had time to exchange intrigued glances with the baron and resume his seat before the army man had crossed the street and come to attention in front of them.

The officer's demeanour and energy were those of a young, lean, imposing figure of a man, particularly impressive as the man himself was actually short, plump and balding. There seemed to be more of his dark hair on his upper lip than on top of his head, a fact that became apparent as he took off his cap and cradled it to his chest.

'Would I be correct in assuming,' his voice was deep and husky, as though from a lifetime of shouting at people, 'that you are – affiliated?'

The captain turned to his companion.

'He could tell that just by watching me walk from the door to the table,' he said, clearly impressed. Turning back to the man in uniform, he asked, 'Are you a medical man?'

The officer looked a little peeved.

'Well, yes I am, as a matter of fact, but I fail to see the relevance. The point is – reconnaissance tells me that you two are – local but not native – if you get my drift.'

The two men either didn't or weren't letting on that they did.

'Er, well, this is our local,' the captain offered, hopefully.

'And we do pretty much live in it,' conceded the baron.

'No. No.' The army man gave them each a suspicious look. 'You're wandering off course.'

'Of course. We are wondering,' the captain agreed, 'exactly what it is you're getting at.'

The officer seemed unsure how to proceed. As he contemplated his options, his eyes darted restlessly about while the rest of him remained completely motionless. He finally settled on directness being the best policy for this situation, albeit the least natural to him. He leaned forward, his voice a forceful whisper.

'All right. I'm looking for the Team. I believe you might know where they are.'

'You mean the local team, Hardly United?' suggested the captain. 'They'll be training. They're away to Den City tomorrow.'

The man scrutinised each of the seated companions – twice – and then straightened up, military bearing firmly back in place.

'I do apologise,' he said, more with contempt than contrition. 'I appear to have been misinformed.'

And with that, he turned to leave.

'Perhaps,' ventured the baron, forcefully enough to ensure the officer didn't move, 'if you were to give us a – clue, to whatever it is that needs – solving, we could help you with your – puzzle.' He turned to his drinking companion. 'A little heavy-handed?'

The captain, whose mouth was attending to his beer, shook his head.

'No,' he said eventually, putting down his glass, 'never send a trowel to do a shovel's work.'

The man in uniform may not have moved off, but neither had he moved back, in fact he hadn't moved at all. Even his eyeballs were stationary. The baron tried again.

'It might be advantageous if you were to describe your primary target in more detail,' he said, trying to sound as military as possible, looking over for the captain's approval, and getting it. He was then gratified to see that he had scored a direct hit with his own primary target, as the officer finally returned his still rather disdainful attention on them. After a deep sigh, clearly expressing his reluctance to dealing with civilians, he resumed his mission.

'Intelligence informs me,' he began, 'that the Team's liaison officer is a little girl, about so high.' He held his hand horizontal, not much higher than the table.

Before he had a chance to ask what the devil these two undisciplined layabouts obviously found so confounded amusing, a female voice came from behind him.

'I'm afraid your intelligence is a good two foot short of a length.'

He span round just in time to see a teenage girl with a ponytail brush roughly past him and slump heavily into a chair next to the two men.

'But then, who needs intelligence on a day like this?' she lamented. 'Perseverance, that's the thing.' She looked up at the baron, who had got to his feet on the girl's arrival, as he always did. 'I'll have a half of perseverance, if you're buying.'

CHAPTER THIRTEEN

'Tough day, Kia?' the baron asked, sympathetically.

She nodded. 'Definitely one for the record books, wouldn't you say, boys?'

Holly and the uncles were just catching up with her, clearly having been unable to match her pace, and for the moment could do little more than nod.

The excursion had been Holly's idea. He had been so alarmed at seeing the other three each staring catatonically in a different direction that out of desperation he had suggested taking them out to lunch. Anything to get them out of the house, he thought, not to mention out of themselves. The Steed was the nearest place, and although it had changed hands, décor, even themes since he had set foot in it last, the food advertised on the boards outside had nearly drawn him inside on many occasions.

So he had herded his group of zombies out of the door and propelled them in the appropriate heading. Sure enough, it wasn't long before they had reverted to type, with much hilarity at the expense of the unfortunate Mister Noose, or Rose Nose Tim as Uncle Sid called him.

Only Uncle Jasper seemed a little subdued, due no doubt to the slight limp he had developed but which, on inquiry, he had dismissed and shrugged off. Holly initially thought Uncle Jasper may have picked up an injury when the house was collapsing round them, but rejected the idea, remembering that after a solution everything was supposed to revert to its former state.

The man in the boiler suit had soldiered stoically on, but not fast enough for Kia, who saw no reason to reduce her normal pace and so had built up a sizeable lead, which increased after Skipper's excited discovery of a new skip that insisted on getting his full attention. Uncle Sid had inevitably decided to show avuncular solidarity, merely getting his order in early with a shout of, 'I meant pins! Regal!'

Just before crossing the road to reach the pub, they passed the newsagent's in which Holly had bought his paper that morning. Without stopping, he glanced in through the open door, curious as to whether the newsagent was as engrossed as he had been earlier, but there were too many people in the shop to allow Holly a clear view.

By the time they had reached the other side of the road, Uncle Jasper having reluctantly abandoned his treasure trove, Kia was already sitting at a table with two men, while a third, wearing what Holly would have described as a serious military uniform, was standing rigidly next to them. Holly was surprised to realise that he was curious about these people, that he actually wanted to meet them, hardly a feeling in keeping with his usual antisocial self.

As they approached the table, they heard, and responded to, Kia's question. Holly was amused to see that one of the seated men had leapt to his feet in Kia's presence, remembering Kia's reaction to his own gallant efforts. The difference between chivalry and chauvinism, he reflected, was only a matter of perspective.

The uncles clearly knew the two men as there were nods and friendly smiles all round. Only the army man seemed detached, yet ever vigilant.

The only man still seated, more accurately sprawled over his chair, was the next to speak. Holly found the man's shirt, although almost totally concealed by his jacket, also almost impossible not to stare at.

'The baron here tells me,' the man was saying, gesturing to his companion, 'that he was nearly run over by a train this morning, here in the middle of the road, when he went over there to get his paper, and that it had vanished by the time he came out.'

Before Kia could even open her mouth, Holly's curiosity got the better of him.

'I'm sorry, you saw it, and you remember seeing it?' he asked the man dressed in black. He looked at Kia. 'How is that possible? I thought after a solution that was it, people swearing blind it never happened, and all that.'

'People, yes,' Kia laughed, 'but these aren't people. They're creations. And rather exotic ones at that.'

'Captain Persona,' the seated man announced with exaggerated pride. 'At your service. And this is my colleague and collaborator, the woefully inappropriately named Baron Nonentity.'

'No, no,' mumbled the baron, 'I'm sure it's not...'

'They arrived one day,' Kia continued.

'Actually two days,' corrected the captain.

'That's right,' agreed the baron. 'We travelled separately.'

'The point is,' Kia struggled on, 'they appeared out of nowhere, just like our train, only marginally less destructive. And we must have been having an off day – or two – because their clues seemed to have slipped under the radar.'

'Of course,' said the captain, cheerfully. 'I'm insoluble.'

'In water, maybe,' snorted the baron. 'You dissolved easily enough in the Bentley's last night.'

'Heavy night, Captain?' scolded Kia. 'Out riding the wild Steed again, were we?'

'I did get rather luminous, didn't I?' asked the captain sheepishly.

'Almost fluorescent,' agreed the baron. 'And yet we live on to drink another day. What would everybody like?'

He proceeded to take orders from everybody, both for drinks and for food from those who were having it, plus a supply of banknotes from Holly who insisted on paying for everything. Armed with all this, he disappeared into the pub. The only person to refuse either food or drink was the officer, who mumbled something about always being on duty, the only thing he had said since the team he had been looking for had turned up.

Business over, the captain turned to Holly, who had sat down with the uncles at the adjacent table, next to the captain.

'So this is today's knight in shining – knitwear?'

Kia nodded, despite Holly's protestations.

'Yes indeed. Holly here has really done us proud. So far today he has derailed a train, sunk a ship, rebuilt a house, stopped a demonstration and dispatched a particularly annoying member of the press.'

The captain whistled in admiration.

'And he hasn't even had lunch yet. Hah! He's a one-man assault squad. You don't have anything against pubs, do you?'

'Other than the fact that I can't make as much use of them as I would like?'

'Why's that? The money? Remortgage the house! It's got to be worth it. Not the money. The wife? Keeps you on a tight leash? No? The liver! I've put myself on the waiting list for a new one. Don't need it yet, but it pays to think ahead.'

Kia gripped the captain's arm in an effort to stem the flow.

'Holly's in recovery,' she hissed at him. 'Or remission, or whatever it's called. How long since you had a drink? Thirteen years?'

Holly nodded. The captain slumped back even further into his chair, no mean feat.

'My God, that's already a life sentence! You'd get less than that for murder. And I bet you could murder a pint! Sorry! Hah! There I go again. Best foot forward and the other firmly in my mouth!'

At this point the officer decided he had heard enough. He cleared his throat.

'Look here,' he rasped. 'I take it you're the outfit I've been after. There's something jolly important you need to know regarding today's operations.'

All eyes turned to him.

'Who's this, then?' asked Kia with more than a hint of amusement.

But the answer didn't come from any of her companions, nor from the subject of her inquiry, but from a new voice, a cold, suave and businesslike voice.

'He's a disconnect facing anonymisation, and he's just run out of wriggle room.'

CHAPTER FOURTEEN

Wasting drinks did not feature in Baron Nonentity's world. He could be ham-fisted, he could be clumsy. Particularly on the way home from the pub, he would be at least as likely to trip over a kerb he had negotiated a thousand times before as the next man. He had narrowly escaped death on many occasions through wandering in front of unnoticed cars and buses, even a train that very morning, although here he would have pleaded extenuating circumstances, the train not having existed the previous day. But put a tray of drinks in his hands and he would be as sure-footed and vigilant as a mountain lion stalking its prey, always assuming its prey was at least five per cent proof.

Carrying a tray barely big enough to contain its cargo of four and a half pints plus an orange juice, he was prepared for the woman at the bar to start gesticulating wildly during her animated conversation the second he came within striking distance. He could sense that the double-hinged doors to the kitchen would fly open as he approached them. And he correctly surmised from the shadow through the frosted glass that a trio of adolescent revellers would burst through the outer doors at the precise moment that he would have been halfway across the threshold himself, had he not waited patiently to one side until the danger had passed.

So it certainly wasn't going to put him off his stride to discover, once outside, that the company of two he had formed on meeting the captain at the table that morning had now swollen to twelve – five more, even, than when he had gone inside.

A quick glance was all he needed – fortunately, as that was all he would allow himself until his tray had safely touched down and taxied to a halt – to observe that the newcomers had considerably raised the standard of dress. They were all sharply suited, the central figure, clearly in authority, in a dark blue three-piece, the other four in mid grey without waistcoats.

The baron deposited the tray on the table he was now sharing with Kia as well as the captain, handed the drinks for Holly and the uncles to the captain to pass on in turn to the next table, and resumed his seat, all the while listening to a tirade from the officer – a tirade directed at the suits, at Mr Blue in particular, who met it with a fixed, humourless smile, an expression mimicked by his grey minions on the pavement behind him – a tirade that displayed indignation, certainly, but also fear. The dauntless leader of men, seasoned campaigner and apparent recipient of numerous decorations, was scared.

'– how dare you,' the phrase that had greeted the baron as he had stepped outside, 'how dare you confront me here, in public, in front of all these – people, with your ludicrous accusations? This is a private arrangement. Private! Strictly need to know. And your demands are unreasonable, sir, unconscionable. You – you alter the rules of engagement whenever it suits you. The terms change from day to day. You signally fail to nail down your objectives. And your methods are more than questionable, they're – they're indefensible. I will not pay! I WILL not pay, do you hear?'

His adversary's smile didn't waver.

'Dear me,' he oozed, 'quite the blamestorming session. But I'm not sure you have the full optics on the situation.'

The colour of his suit was not the only thing that set him apart from his colleagues. He was clearly older, as indicated by the greying at the temples of his otherwise dark, short hair, currently supporting a pair of black sunglasses, and the numerous wrinkles on his face, mostly around the eyes, which gave the impression that he was smiling, even when he wasn't. He was also the only one to sport a deep tan.

'I don't mean to break your crayons,' he continued, 'but I had no idea you'd be here. It was pure chance we decided not to have lunch al desco today, and pure chance that has provided us with this happy opportunity for some face time.' His smile managed to shed a few more degrees of warmth. 'But I have heard a rumour, by word of mouse,' he went on, leaning slightly forward and speaking a little quieter, although still loud enough for everyone to hear, 'that accuses you of stalemating. Naturally, I kicked the idea into touch. Plenty of people out there who like to imagineer these things. No, he's just realised his situation has reached critical mass, I told myself, and he's buying himself some much-needed foot-on-the-ball time. And yet here you are, zero-tasking.' He straightened up and turned his head to address his companions without breaking eye contact with the officer. 'Looks like we're going to have to adopt a more cradle-to-grave approach with this client.'

The targets of this remark seemed enthusiastic at the idea, but its subject bristled.

'Client? I'm no client of yours. Prey would be more...'

'Perhaps,' the blue suit interrupted, leaning forward once again, 'we could improve his 360-degree thinking. We could provide him with more of a helicopter view. Without a golden parachute. That would certainly put his bouncebackability to the test.'

'This gentleman is with us.' Kia had clearly had enough, both of what she saw as bullying and of being ignored. 'And any business you may have with him is also our business.'

Foolhardy, Holly thought to himself, very foolhardy. But he wished he'd said it himself.

The humourless smile switched allegiance all too easily.

'A third party? By all means, let's triangulate. We enjoy a bit of healthy coopetition, don't we, boys? Are you and he – affiliated?'

Only the captain and the baron exchanged glances at the use of the word the officer had used earlier, but dismissed it as coincidence. The reaction was lost on Kia.

'I don't even know his name,' she confessed. 'But then, I don't know yours either.'

'Well, then, slapping our credentials on the front burner would seem to be a must-do.' He turned ever so slightly in her direction, hands still in pockets. He clearly never made more of an effort than was absolutely necessary.

'I am the Director,' he started the introductions, naturally, with himself, 'the CEO, or maybe PM, of this outfit, and this is my Cabinet, my Filing Cabinet. That gentleman over there is the Gofer.'

With the vaguest motion of his head he managed to indicate the man furthest to his right, a thin, spotty young man with flat brown hair combed forward in a fringe. His tie was the only thing he wore of any individuality, as was the case with every member of the Cabinet. His was red.

'The Gofer gets things done,' the Director continued. 'It's his job to operationalise. If you're not sure whether you're looking through the right lens, he's the man to peel the onion. And here,' he minimally singled out the man to his immediate right, 'we have our head of creative input, our spark of originality, the Copier. He looks after our marketecture.'

The Copier looked barely out of his teens, had dark spiky hair and sported a tie depicting a seemingly endless line of piano keys.

'Behind me,' the words specially chosen by the Director so that he didn't have to move whatsoever, 'keeping a weather eye out for clients, current or prospective, is the Scanner.'

The weather eye was not in evidence, hidden as it was behind a pair of mirrored sunglasses, but the lookout function was obvious enough, judging by the frequent sweeping turns of the Scanner's head from side to side, self-conscious motions clearly designed to generate a high interest rate in his shoulder-length blond hair. Mimicking both this movement and this colour, the Scanner's tie faded repeatedly between yellow and white.

'And finally,' again, no gesture needed, 'but at least as buzzworthy, I give you our chainsaw consultant, the Stapler.'

The man to the Director's left was the largest and arguably the most imposing – arguably, that is, for anyone foolish enough to want to argue with him. His head was shaved, as much for effect as to hide a fast-receding hairline, his tie was a ridiculously elongated Union Jack, and his version of their ever-present smile was distinctly lopsided which made it, deliberately or not, a sneer.

'The Stapler, as his name implies, keeps everything together, and – ties up loose ends.'

Appropriately, just as the Director had tied up the final loose end of his introductions, the pub door opened and two women appeared, each carrying three plates which, after making the necessary enquiries, they placed in front of the relevant recipient, not too arduous a task, as only two different dishes had been ordered, both varieties of ploughman's. This being a gastropub, the ploughman's consisted of a chunk of ciabatta with a choice of either Sardinian Cheddar or Fourme d'Ambert, the resident blue cheese, with a garnish of caramelised onion and rocket. Kia, Holly and Uncle Sid had gone for the Cheddar.

The Director eyed the proceedings with malevolent amusement, while still standing uncomfortably close to the army man.

'Not hungry?' he asked, noting that the officer was the only one not eating. 'Strange. I've got you down for a reality sandwich.'

The officer was struggling, but ultimately stuck, for a suitable response. Kia felt for the poor man and decided to step in as soon as a mouthful of dry ciabatta would allow.

'So, Mr Director,' she managed at last. 'That's your team accounted for, so it's my team's turn. Starting from the far left...'

'Forgive me,' the Director steamrollered, 'but your identity really isn't the long pole in my tent. What does float my boat is your credit rating.'

The captain waved a fully loaded fork in the air to delay matters while he too finished his mouthful.

‘I’m sorry,’ he spluttered, not having waited quite long enough, ‘but I’ve lost the thread. Are we camping or sailing? I’ve never been one for activity holidays. The two words just don’t go together, to my way of thinking.’

‘Mutually exclusive,’ the baron managed to squeeze past the blue cheese, nodding.

‘Irreconcilable,’ offered Uncle Jasper, eagerly.

‘Ten fit after Dolly,’ agreed Uncle Sid with solemnity.

Kia was trying very hard not to laugh, and nearly succeeding. Holly felt increasingly nervous.

The Director’s smile hadn’t wavered, quite the opposite of Uncle Sid’s ‘totally different’, and his eyes hadn’t left Kia. Other than the fact that he hadn’t spoken for a few seconds, there was no indication he had even heard this frivolous interruption.

‘So if this gentleman’s business is your business,’ he took up where he had left off, ‘then you’d better make sure you’re belts and suspenders before you decide to join him behind the eight ball.’

‘I played pool in suspenders once,’ announced the captain, this time mercifully between mouthfuls. ‘Rugby club rules. Or so they told me. Hah hah!’

A pause ensued, as the Director waited for the sniggering to subside and the focus of proceedings to return to him. When he was satisfied he had everyone’s full attention, he took a step back, much to the officer’s evident relief.

‘OK, people,’ the Director said quietly, ‘this is where the rubber hits the road.’

Before the captain could even open his mouth to tell the story of how he had once run a half-marathon in wellington boots, the three members of the Cabinet who had been standing alongside the Director each took a couple of steps forward to take up positions between the tables, effectively blocking every exit for the people sitting at them. The Gofer was at one end, staring down at Uncle Sid, the Copier stood squarely in front of Holly and the captain, and Kia all but disappeared from view behind the towering figure of the Stapler. Only the Scanner remained unaffected, blithely continuing his lighthouse impression.

If Kia was scared, she wasn't going to show it. What she did show was irritation.

'I'm sorry,' she said, having to look round the Stapler to be able to see the Director, 'but what exactly do you think you're doing?'

'Exactly?' queried the Director. 'I shall be exacting this gentleman's debt. From you.' He looked round to make sure the message was getting through. 'Your hard hats here,' he went on, indicating Kia's colleagues, 'seem to be heavily incentivised to pick up this portfolio. So in case this is beyond their bandwidth, perhaps you could cascade down to them that they have just picked up his option. Transfer of liability. Effective immediately.'

'You can't do that!' the officer protested, looking hopelessly back and forth between Kia and the Director. 'You can't just impose my obligations on to somebody else! Certainly not on to innocent civilians! And you don't have the resources...'

'I'm afraid you underexaggerate our capabilities,' the Director purred. 'Our organisation is all about organisation. We are many, and we are everywhere. And just last night, we successfully de-integrated ninety-three politicians.'

CHAPTER FIFTEEN

Not for the first time today, Holly felt a responsibility to his team, that it was somehow down to him to do something to get them out of this situation. Unfortunately, this time, he had no idea what that something should be. He thought of saying the word 'grid' to return to the house, but going back on his own wouldn't be of any use, and even if he got every member of the team to link hands he didn't think it would work, as he hadn't spoken the number of a clue to get here. Fortunately, he was soon to be shown the way.

His view had shortened considerably, being almost entirely taken up by the Copier, whose jagged peaks of hair made him seem to Holly even more mountainous. Holly could only marvel at the way someone who looked so ludicrously youthful could now appear so ominous. Directly in front of Holly, commanding his attention, was the keyboard tie. He wondered if he would ever look at a piano in the same way again.

He looked round to see how the others were reacting to this news that had suddenly elevated, or lowered, the Cabinet from entertaining novelty act to mortal threat. The first thing he noticed was that everyone had stopped eating.

To his left Uncle Sid was glowering up at his particular mountain, the Gofer, an immoveable object with a fringe, bushy eyebrows and that ever-confident smile. Uncle Sid was gripping his cutlery very tightly and looked like he was muttering to himself. Holly fancied he could see the red of the Gofer's tie reflected in Uncle Sid's eyes.

The eyes were the only parts of Uncle Jasper that were moving at all. He had relinquished his knife and let his arms fall by his sides. His head was completely still, his eyes moved steadily from one member of the Cabinet to another, and his face betrayed no emotion of any sort. Holly decided that should he ever need a poker partner he should look no further than Uncle Jasper.

Captain Persona, on the other hand, as Holly turned to his right, was a study in bewilderment, his head moving restlessly to look at every person present, his mouth opening and closing in its struggle to formulate a question that was proving elusive.

Beyond him, the baron had acquired a pensive look which was initially directed nowhere in particular and then switched to a point down on the table in front of him. Whether or not this was his lunch, Holly couldn't tell.

And finally, Kia provided a neat symmetry by mimicking Uncle Sid's scowl. She was refusing to be outstared by the lopsided sneer towering over her, and looked for all the world like she might attack the Stapler at any moment. Holly doubted whether the Stapler would even notice.

'Ninety-three.' The Director was looking smug, but then they hadn't seen him looking anything else. 'No trace. No trails. No heads-up. No time to sunset them, that's too long-game. Just vector them out, dot a few t's, cross a few i's and Bob's your broker.' The smile became a touch broader. 'Forgive the anecgloat.' The moment of genuine good humour departed as quickly as it had arrived, and the smile reverted to its default setting. 'So let me bottom line it for you. You have exactly,' he looked at his watch, the first time he had taken even one hand out of his pockets, 'no time at all to turn a dead cat's bounce into an upcurve.' The hand scurried back to its refuge. 'Or it's flatline time.'

The Cabinet instinctively took this as a cue to shift their weight momentarily, a gesture designed to remind the seated company of their considerable presence. The Director cocked his head to one side and continued looking at Kia. He was clearly lying in wait for the response.

But the response was not what he was expecting. And it didn't come from Kia.

'Stop me if I'm driving beyond my headlights,' the baron began, his eyes still firmly fixed somewhere on his table, 'but if we could just parking lot the takeover bid and circle back to the matter in hand, viz. the asking price,' he looked up, squarely at the Director, 'then maybe we can touch base and talk turkey.'

All eyes and a pair of mirrored sunglasses turned on him. Among the home team, jaws were dropping like flies. Holly had been convinced the baron had been reading this speech out verbatim from something on the table until he had looked up. The members of the Cabinet were squinting suspiciously at this would-be comrade. Even the Scanner had been torn away from the tennis match he was watching, and for a few brief moments his twitching locks were given a well-earned rest.

The Director looked genuinely pleased.

'Ah,' he sighed, appreciatively. 'A fellow jargonaut.'

‘Well, let’s see if we’re singing from the same hymn sheet,’ the baron continued, ignoring his gaping colleagues. ‘If you want us to mission critical this contract, then we’re going to have to parachute in some amendments, make sure everything’s fit for purpose. Are we in agreeance?’

The Director’s hands finally both appeared as he folded his arms. He was having to think. He took his time thinking.

‘You’ve got the sausage,’ he murmured eventually, ‘but where’s the sizzle?’

The baron was compelled to respond quickly, fearing some culinary comment from the captain, but he needn’t have worried. The captain’s jaw was still way too slack.

‘I don’t want to be a complete meanderthal,’ the baron hurried on, ‘so I’ll gist it for you. We don’t want this to be too back-of-the-envelope, so we’ll get our alpha geek to ballpark some figures and then run them up the flagpole, see who salutes.’

‘And your First Lord of the Treasury is – who? Surely not your sartorially challenged rent-a-quote here?’ He indicated the captain with the merest glance. ‘I had him firmly bucketised as an ignoranus.’

The only person seated to register amusement at this was Uncle Sid, but he made up for it by registering a great deal.

‘No,’ said the baron, hoping he had the self-control to postpone his own amusement until later. ‘No, but if you just lateral your attention one more notch, I’m sure you’ll find the back of the net.’

Everyone’s focus was transferred again, this time to Holly.

There had been times in his life when Holly’s customary complete lack of visible response to a given situation had left him frustrated and angry with himself. This was not one of those occasions. Indeed, he felt his natural reserve had actually come to his rescue, as his visible response would have been surprise and panic.

'This is – the Calculator,' announced the baron, 'our resident figure skater, and he will now power-up, shift into high gear and run down some stats, the end game of which will be an offer you will not be able to refuse.' He leant across the captain towards Holly and tapped on Holly's newspaper which was lying on the next table. 'And he will input it here.' He caught Holly's eye and held it. 'I humbly suggest,' he almost whispered, 'that the figure begins with a fourteen.'

Holly remained staring at the baron, and only finally lowered his eyes to look at the paper when the baron's tapping on it became more insistent. After a few moments of scrutiny, he nodded slowly and picked up his pen.

Taking the baron's hint, he looked at 14 Across, the first of a pair of words that spanned the width of the grid. 'Sheet left on board (5)' he read. Moving immediately to its companion, 15 Across, he saw 'Former spouse wrong to charge for blackmail (9)'.

The Director also looked at the paper, but with contemptuous glee.

'Treeware,' he sneered. 'How quaint.'

'Quaint but impactful,' the baron reassured him. 'The Calculator is called in whenever we need to solution a problem we may have, and his clean-up rate is top-of-the-tree.' He noted with some relief that Holly was already writing something. 'There – that's the opening equation factored up, now just a few more variables to dial in.'

'Better make it a two-comma,' the Director snorted, turning to Kia and giving his smile a lascivious twist. 'Got to make sure the juice is worth the squeeze.' Kia rose to the bait and bristled obligingly.

‘The Brain, we call him,’ the baron went on hastily, hoping it wasn’t too obvious that he was trying to buy Holly time. ‘And there,’ indicating Uncle Jasper, ‘we have – the Muscle.’ Uncle Jasper raised an quizzical eyebrow. ‘And there the – Sinew.’ Uncle Sid squinted back in bewilderment. The baron turned to Kia, who flinched. ‘And this is the Heart – of the outfit,’ he said, smiling briefly. That just left the captain. ‘And this is...’ the captain looked challengingly at him during a lengthy pause, waiting to see what organ of the body he was going to be presented as, ‘...the Mouth,’ the baron decided on, much to everyone’s relief. ‘As you can see,’ he turned to the Director, ‘although they are seated next to each other, the Mouth and the Brain are not connected in any way whatsoever.’ The captain could only nod in rueful agreement.

‘Well,’ considered the Director, still addressing Kia, ‘that just makes you a tasty selection of offal, unfortunately hardwired to the wrong end of the food chain.’ His tone became harsher. ‘You seem woefully undertooled, and that’s interdepartmental. So unless you can upskill dramatically, I suggest you tell your team to stop wallpapering fog and go back to their knitting.’

Holly cleared his throat and, leaning sideways, held his newspaper out so the baron could see what Holly had just finished writing. For 14 Across he had written the word ‘panel’, and had almost completed the line with ‘extorti_n’, leaving a blank to allow for a second opinion.

The baron duly gave it with a nod and a grin. ‘Knowledge is power,’ he murmured. Looking up at the Director, he said, ‘So you think we’re boiling the ocean?’

‘I think,’ the Director told him a little wearily, now with only the vaguest hint of a smile, ‘and I hate to be the one to have to shoot the puppy, that you have a big learn ahead, and that the best way to kill something is to go,' his eyes swivelled over to Kia, 'for the heart.'

Reacting to another subliminal cue, the Stapler immediately shot out a huge hand and grabbed Kia by the neck, lifting her a few inches off her seat. Unable to breathe, let alone speak, she set about beating his arm with her fists, with as much effect as if it had been a crane holding her aloft.

The uncles both shot out of their seats at this attack, but were effortlessly shoved back by the Gofer.

The baron held up his hand in a vain attempt to placate the two men.

'In that case,' he said calmly to Holly, 'we'd better add another zero.'

Holly nodded solemnly and duly complied, filling in the missing letter. Now happily without any qualms or a shred of guilt, he looked up just in time to see the Director, by now totally bereft of smile, give him one final chilling snarl and then disappear into thin air, along with his Cabinet, faithfully synchronised to the last.

1 C		2 T		3		4		5		■	6	7		8
R	■	R	■		■		■		■	9	■		■	
10 A	G	A	I	N	S	T	■	11 L	A	W	L	O	R	D
F	■	M	■		■		■		■		■		■	
12 T		L							■	13				
■	■	I	■		■		■		■		■	■	■	
14 P	A	N	E	L	■	15 E	X	T	O	R	T	16 I	O	N
E	■	E	■		■	■	■	■	■		■		■	
17 D		S				18		19	■	20				
O	■	■	■		■		■		■		■		■	■
21 M		22 G			■	23								24
E	■	A	■		■		■		■		■		■	
25 T	A	B	L	O	I	D	■	26 A	R	T	I	S	A	N
E	■	L	■		■		■		■		■		■	
27 R	E	E	K	■	28 A	R	I	T	H	M	E	T	I	C

CHAPTER SIXTEEN

Kia fell back in her chair with her head back, gasping for air, just as Holly had done on the ship. The officer collapsed into a chair at the end next to hers, staring at the members of the team with almost as much fear as he had shown his previous tormentors. Holly stood up to see if Kia was all right, but was beaten to it by the uncles, which in the event saved him the embarrassment of being impatiently waved away, as they were. Reassured that Kia was making a full recovery, he turned to the baron, who he noticed with amusement was also standing, no doubt for the same reason. He held out his hand, which was gladly accepted.

'Nice work,' he said. 'Good to see someone keeping their head in all that. And well spotted, getting the right clues.'

'No, that was more luck than judgment,' said the baron, shaking his head. 'You did all the hard work. "Pane". I wouldn't have got that.'

It was Holly's turn to shake his head.

'Head start,' he said, holding his paper out so the baron could see it. 'I already had the P and the N.' He checked the table in front of the baron, and found what he was looking for. He had guessed that it was a copy of the same puzzle that the baron had been staring at earlier, but this one was still blank. 'You a fan?'

'Definitely. A local rag is even daft enough to let me write one for them occasionally. Strictly gentleman amateur status.'

Holly not only was impressed but even looked it.

'Well that's taking it to a whole new level. I couldn't do that.'

The baron resumed his head-shaking.

'Actually, no it isn't,' he said, 'and yes you could. Think about it. If you're solving a puzzle, there's only one solution, and you have to find it, but if you're writing it yourself, it's a blank canvas. Granted, your first few words will then limit your options for the rest, but there's still a choice, as there is with the cluing. I have great fun with that, but it doesn't help me trying to solve anyone else's. We still have a go most days though, don't we, just in case we can be of any help?'

Still seated between the two, indeed back to his customary slump, adrenalin having made him sit up briefly under the weight of the Filing Cabinet, the captain, to whom this question had been addressed, shook his head cheerfully.

'Don't look at me,' he beamed. 'I can't tell me epigrams from me anagrams. I'm as rubbish at crosswords as Kia. No offence,' he added in Kia's direction.

Without looking at them, Kia gave another dismissive wave, which at least told the others that she had recovered sufficiently to take an interest in their conversation.

'So where did you dig up all that nonsense you were spouting?' the captain wanted to know. 'Sounded worryingly convincing. You're not one of the funny handshake brigade are you, on the quiet?'

'Heavens, no. No, I came across a list of the stuff on the Internet just last week. It's all good clean fun.'

'I don't even understand,' the captain continued, clearly charmed by his own ignorance, 'how you knew to entrust this task to Holly here. You weren't even there, were you, when we heard about his house-building and ship-sinking exploits?'

'No,' the baron admitted, 'but he's obviously today's Solver, and that train that nearly caught me this morning was gone by the time I came out of the newsagent's, so I presumed that was his handiwork.'

Holly happily conceded the point, but with modesty.

'Speaking of handy work,' Kia's voice was hoarse, but everyone was relieved to hear she had one at all, 'what was the magic phrase that bankrupted our delightful troupe of entrepreneurs?'

Everyone edged in towards Holly, eager to hear the explanation – everyone, that is, except the military gentleman who was evidently not listening to anything but his own troubled thoughts.

'It was "panel extortion" that conjured them up,' Holly announced, eliciting nods of approval from the uncles. 'The first clue, "Sheet left on board", is "pane", as in sheet of glass, plus an L for left, making "panel" which can be a board, in this case a board of directors,' again the pause, giving everyone time to visualise, 'and then "Former spouse wrong to charge for blackmail",' he read out, 'nine letters. A former spouse is always an ex. "Charge" is often used for an -ion word ending, one of the most common endings there is, an ion being a charged elementary particle. "Wrong" was the hard bit, that took a while because it's more misdirection.'

The happy tone of his voice at this point provoked another roll of the eyes from Uncle Sid.

'On a giant,' he moaned.

Holly smiled apologetically at him.

'Oh, yes, again,' he answered. 'You see, "wrong" is used in the clue as an adjective, the ex was wrong, but that's falling into the trap. It's just a disjointed word, and is actually a noun, *a* wrong, in this case a legal wrong or injury, a cause for damages, called a tort. Ex – tort – ion, extortion.' He turned to Uncle Jasper. 'Which is, of course, synonymous with...'

'Coercion,' suggested Uncle Jasper.

'...blackmail,' finished Holly.

'Blackmail,' Uncle Jasper nodded, sheepishly.

'Blackmail,' came the officer's hollow voice. 'That's what it was all right.'

They looked over at him, most of them with some surprise, having completely forgotten of his existence. He was still sitting next to Kia, staring absently at the pavement, but had regained some of his military bearing.

'That claim of theirs, that they had made all those politicians disappear,' Kia asked him, gently, 'do you think there was any truth in that?'

He sighed, making a visible effort to pull himself together.

'I wouldn't put it past them. It's the sort of thing they did.' He looked up and gave Holly a haunted look. 'But then, it seems to be the sort of thing you do as well.'

Holly was so stunned by the comparison that it was all he could do to stare back. An awkward silence developed, and soon there were so many confused looks bouncing around that Kia felt she had to step in. She put her hand on the officer's arm, breaking his concentration, much to Holly's relief.

'It might look the same,' she tried to explain, 'but there's a world of difference.'

Holly was forcibly struck by just how appropriate that phrase was.

'Those thugs – don't belong here,' she went on, frustrated that she couldn't put it any better. 'Whereas the politicians – do. For better or worse,' she added, trying in vain to lighten the situation.

'Well, they're not back,' said Holly, pointing across the road at the boards outside the newsagent's which were still loudly proclaiming 'B-LIST MPS GO AWOL'. 'If that issue had been resolved, wouldn't those headlines have reverted to something else?'

'Yes,' said the baron, tentatively, 'but that doesn't necessarily mean that our suited friends weren't responsible. It might be connected to another solution.'

Conceding readily to this logic, as he always did to any logic, Holly returned his attention to his paper, eyeing it with suspicion.

'So,' the captain waded in, always eager to fill a conversational void, 'what did they have on you? Siphoning off the military budget? Awarding yourself non-existent medals? Taking the tank home at weekends?'

This finally snapped the officer back to his normal indignant self.

'Nothing of the sort. If you must know, it was a matter of honour.'

'It's usually honour,' the captain prattled on. 'Or some kind of offer. Or possibly both. Honour and offer. That's always good for a spot of blackmail.'

Kia managed to silence him with what she hoped was a frown, as much for upsetting the officer as giving the uncles a fit of the giggles. As it happened, both the remark and the ensuing hilarity had passed completely over the army man's head.

'I don't suppose honour plays a large part in your life,' scolded the officer, not pausing long enough to allow the eager captain to expand on his questionable theme with a heartfelt refutation, 'but in my line of work it's everything. In fact, it's what brought me here today, for my sins.'

Even the captain was now more interested in the reason for the visit than in any sins the gentleman may have committed.

'You specifically came to see us?' Kia prompted, anxious that his obvious regret at having done so shouldn't get the better of him.

'I have no recollection of hearing about you,' replied the officer, looking puzzled, 'and I have no idea what made me come here to find you, but I knew you had to be informed about a traitor.'

He made so little of these last few words that the effect was all the more chilling as realisation seeped through. Nobody spoke until the officer continued.

'This morning I received intelligence from a colleague at the hospital that one of her patients would be instrumental in your downfall today.'

More stunned silence, only broken when Kia found the obvious questions had become overwhelming.

'Well, who?' she demanded. 'And how?'

'As to how,' the army man said, frowning, 'apparently he's developed some sort of weapon, called a 4-18. Very hush-hush. No idea what it does.'

Kia looked round helplessly, but everyone had clearly found this more perplexing that informative.

'Alright, then,' she conceded, reverting to her original question, 'who?'

The officer shook his head.

'I don't have a name,' he admitted.

'Not even a rank or serial number?' quipped the captain to the annoyance of everyone except the army man, who seemed not to have heard it.

'But he's distinctive enough, because she said he's always c...'

Sound travels considerably more slowly than light, so for a split second the team could still hear the officer even though they could no longer see him. Once the echo of his last consonant had drifted off, however, they were left staring at an empty and silent space.

Kia was the first to suspect what might have happened. She spun round to Holly.

'What?' she demanded.

Holly looked up from his paper, pen in hand, vacant in expression.

'What?' he returned.

'What was that?' Kia expanded, gesturing at the void they had been left with.

'What was what?' responded Holly, desperately trying to see what she was pointing at, until suddenly the empty seat told him that what she was pointing at was no longer there to be seen.

'Oh no,' he mumbled, 'was that him?'

'Was what him?' Kia asked, suspiciously.

' "Common lad with desire to be a doctor",' Holly read out, a little crestfallen. 'It didn't occur to me that might be him.'

Kia gave him an exasperated look.

'What were you doing?' she demanded again, angrily.

'My job,' Holly replied in kind. 'I believe that's what I'm here for. That's what you've been telling me all day.'

Seeing, not without some pleasure, how taken aback Kia was at his uncharacteristic loss of composure, Holly lowered his voice.

'I've been going through the clues, trying to find a way of restoring these politicians to their rightful surroundings,' he explained. 'No luck so far, but on the way I came across this one and I got the answer straight away. Look. "Common lad with desire to be a doctor", seven, seven.' He looked round, defiantly. 'Nothing military in that,' he pleaded. 'And nothing difficult either. "Common" is general, and "lad with desire" is "son" with "urge" in the middle. General s-urge-on.' Another defiant look, but with noticeably less confidence. 'Which is a doctor.' He waited for someone to offer reassurance or commiseration, but no-one did. 'How was I supposed to know he was a general?'

'OK, OK,' Kia relented, more out of sympathy than genuine forgiveness, softening her tone but not her expression. 'Good work,' she said through her teeth. 'But your timing stinks. It seems we still have something big ahead of us, and the General had some vital information that might have made all the difference.'

Holly threw his paper and pen down on the table.

'Well alright, it may have had some bearing,' he conceded with obvious reluctance, 'but they're just clues. We'll get them anyway.'

Kia was now on full glare.

'Do you have any idea what's at stake here?' she shouted. 'Do you think this disappearing thing is only for them? Do you think we're immune? Do you think you're invincible?'

'It's not as though...' he began defensively.

Kia leapt out of her chair and leaned over towards Holly with her hands on the table between them.

'Do you want to know what really happened to your friend Eric?' she hissed. 'He didn't die a nice cosy death at home in bed. He died here. He was murdered. Here.'

1 C		2 T		3 G		4		5		■	6	7		8
R	■	R	■	E	■		■		■	9	■		■	
10 A	G	A	I	N	S	T	■	11 L	A	W	L	O	R	D
F	■	M	■	E	■		■		■		■		■	
12 T		L		R					■	13				
■	■	I	■	A	■		■		■		■	■	■	
14 P	A	N	E	L	■	15 E	X	T	O	R	T	16 I	O	N
E	■	E	■	S	■	■	■	■	■		■		■	
17 D		S		U		18		19	■	20				
O	■	■	■	R	■		■		■		■		■	■
21 M		22 G		G	■	23								24
E	■	A	■	E	■		■		■		■		■	
25 T	A	B	L	O	I	D	■	26 A	R	T	I	S	A	N
E	■	L	■	N	■		■		■		■		■	
27 R	E	E	K	■	28 A	R	I	T	H	M	E	T	I	C

CHAPTER SEVENTEEN

The snow had eased considerably, providing less ammunition for the wind, which doubled its strength in compensation.

The room the man was in was, appropriately, a waiting room. It was quite large, with several chairs lining the walls, one or two still upright, a grey metal filing cabinet with its bottom drawer extended and a coffee table. A lone fluorescent light struggled to function at one end. There were no windows, just a set of double doors at either end. The set next to the embattled strip light was half-open and led towards the interior of the building, consequently letting in little more than a dull glow. The other doors were shut and separated the room from a corridor with mostly absent windows along its entire length, so it was through the crack between these doors that the maddening noise was coming. The wind, having only one means of access, produced a single wildly fluctuating note, a demented clarinet solo.

Occasionally, a few snowflakes would make it through this narrow gap, catching both the light from the opposite end of the room and the man's jumpy attention, before joining the others in the form of a glittery fan on the floor.

The temperature was so low that the snow didn't melt, but the man didn't feel it. He was too ill to notice. He was also too preoccupied, trying to figure out how to hear someone's approach against an erratic backdrop of distant rising shrieks, and in a place where the sound of footsteps was forbidden.

The man was sitting in the chair next to the coffee table, on which a few sheets of paper had been thrown. It was a grey metal chair with a padded plastic seat, and one side of the back of the chair had come away from the arm, so that it wouldn't have been able to take the weight of an average person leaning back on it, but the man was so frail and thin that he made no impression on it at all.

He coughed – reluctantly, as he was so intently listening out for the other's arrival, which only made him want to cough more. In the event, the arrival was obvious enough. The doors only parted a couple of inches, turning the clarinet, suddenly and briefly, into a bass clarinet, but somehow that was sufficient to allow the shadowy figure to enter the room.

The man in the chair wasn't even sure whether the dark shape made contact with the ground, as he could see that the fanned out ice crystals by the door were still intact. It gave him the impression that some of the ever-present fog had congealed, although it did seem a little more dense than the last time he had seen it. And that unmistakable thin voice might also have gained a little substance.

'Have you brought the final figures?' it wheezed.

'They're here,' said the man, in a voice that would in normal company have seemed hoarse, but compared to the other voice sounded as clear as a bell. He gestured at the pages on the coffee table.

The apparition came forward, as slow, smooth and silent as ever, and picked up the sheets of paper – quite how, the seated man couldn't for the life of him make out. After a few moments apparently studying the data, it spoke again.

'Good. Just in time. It will be ready this evening. Can the same be said for you?'

The man nodded weakly.

'Yes,' he said, 'I'm to tell them that one of them...'

'A simple yes would suffice,' came the dismissive reply. 'There isn't time.'

'No, there isn't.' The man closed his eyes and leant his head back. 'I must be getting back.'

'You'll have to wait. I notice you walked here. Make sure you bring the trolley next time.'

With that, the figure left the room, filtering through the gap in the door, causing the same brief change of register in the wind.

The man in the chair was left to ponder how long he needed to wait before he could safely make his own exit. He reckoned eight or nine of those distant shrieks should be about right.

*

'He's usually referred to as the Culprit,' Kia was telling Holly in response to his ever more insistent questions. She was beginning to regret having let this particularly melodramatic cat out of its bag. 'He was certainly the culprit in this case.'

They had just started walking back to the house. The uncles had gone in front, Uncle Jasper once again wincing every time he put his weight on his left foot. Then came Kia and Holly, with the captain and the baron bringing up the rear.

'And what does he look like, this Culprit?' Holly wanted to know.

'Difficult to say,' was the terse response.

'Why?' Holly persisted. 'Is he in disguise? Does he wear a mask?'

Kia snorted. 'He'd need more than a mask.'

Holly was feeling increasingly disturbed that he was getting so little information on a subject that suddenly seemed very important.

'What is he, then?' he demanded. 'A gorilla?'

'No,' Kia said, dismissively. 'He's...' She was clearly having trouble finding the right words. 'He's more of a shadow,' she finally settled on, 'than a man. He's more...'

'Ethereal,' ventured Uncle Jasper between winces.

'That's it,' agreed Kia. 'More...'

'Spectral.'

'Yes, yes, that's enough,' she said firmly. 'I'm sure he's getting the idea.'

'He makes me foods,' Uncle Sid almost whispered to Holly with obvious discomfort.

'He's a caterer?' The captain was looking questioningly at everyone in turn. 'He poisons people?'

'No, no, no,' said Kia in exasperation. 'He's saying he's made of smoke. That's probably the best description.'

'But – how did a wisp of smoke kill Eric?' Holly asked incredulously.

'Smoke inhalation?' ventured the baron.

'Instantaneous lung cancer?' suggested the captain.

'We don't know,' lamented Kia. 'We got there just too late. And there's nothing wispy about this character, believe me. We've only actually seen him a couple of times. I wouldn't be at all sorry if I never saw him again.' She increased her pace a little as if trying to get away from that image.

'Well, what are the chances of seeing him?' Holly was pretty sure that being forewarned, in this case, was nothing like being forearmed, but wanted to know anyway. 'Where does he live?'

'Wherever it's cold, dark and isolated,' was the not remotely reassuring reply. 'Which could be anywhere. He may or may not be waiting at the end of any one of these clues.' She stopped and turned on Holly. 'And we won't have the foggiest notion until it's too late. Because the only person who may have been able to give us more precise information seems to have fallen victim to a bad case of Eager Solver Syndrome.'

She resumed her journey, leaving Holly standing, a picture of remorse. The baron was the first to catch up with her.

'Come on, Kia, give the guy a break. He hasn't done this before.'

Kia held up a hand to stop him.

'Don't,' she said.

'But it's his first time,' agreed the captain. 'He's bound to be useless occasionally.'

This was such a backhanded compliment it actually cheered Holly up and he sheepishly started trudging after them. Kia, however, started waving the hand that was still aloft, while the other was pressed against her chest.

'He did tidy up the officer's mess,' the captain added in an effort to be more positive. 'So to speak.'

'And anyway,' the baron went on, 'overeager is better than over-...' He looked over at the captain for help.

'The top?' offered the captain, doubtfully.

'No, no. You know, the opposite of eager.'

'Reluctant?' hissed Uncle Jasper between gritted teeth, limping more than ever. 'Disinclined? Averse?'

'Averse,' nodded the captain. 'I like that.'

'Yes, but over-averse?' questioned the baron. 'That's a bit lame, isn't it?'

The captain shrugged. 'Try it. In context'

'OK. Surely it's better to be overeager than over-av...'

The experiment was abandoned, as they all became aware that Kia had stopped and was holding on to a lamp post for support with one hand while the other was still up at her neck. Her face had gone red and she was clearly having the greatest difficulty breathing.

'What's the...' the baron began, but Kia waved him into silence. All five of her companions were now standing round her, concerned but helpless.

Slowly, Kia's breathing became slower and deeper, and the colour in her face started to subside.

Still gasping slightly, she said, 'What was that? Some sort of seizure.'

'Stress?' proposed Uncle Jasper, visibly relieved to have stopped walking. 'Strain? Overwork?'

Kia's breathing started to deteriorate again, and her eyes darted about restlessly. 'What the hell...?' she muttered.

'Got to be stress,' the baron agreed. 'Hardly surprising, having to do this, day in, day out. You can't be expected to do this without some sort of break?'

'I'm sure Kia wouldn't be over-averse to the idea,' said the captain triumphantly, instantly shaking his head and pulling a face. 'Didn't work, did it?'

'No,' agreed the baron, 'it didn't. But Kia does, and the work is incessant. It's small wonder...'

'Everybody shut up!'

Struggling as she was for air, Kia still managed to shout loud enough to turn the heads of a group of teenagers on the other side of the road, who laughed and shouted encouragement at what they saw as a repressed comrade, 'sticking it to the olds'.

Their voices slowly receded, and Kia's breathing came off the critical list and started to approach normality. Her companions were all keeping totally silent out of a mixture of respect and, they would freely have admitted, fear. Kia eventually drew a line under the episode with a deep sigh.

'Excuses,' she said to everyone, immediately having to contradict their very vocal but erroneous assumption that she was apologising. 'No! No, that's what you were making, first for our poor undervalued Solver,' she threw Holly a reassuring smile, 'and then for me.' She looked at each in turn for some reaction, but they were all waiting to see where this was going. 'That's the only thing I can put it down to. The excuses started, for some reason I couldn't take it, they stopped, it calmed down. It started again, and it was worse than ever.' She puffed her cheeks. 'I don't mind telling you, that was approaching damage level nine.'

At this, she lost her temper, making them all jump.

'That again! What does that even mean?' A look of determination came over her face. 'The hell with this!' she declared.

She snatched the paper out of Holly's hand and stared intently at it for a few seconds. Then she brusquely gave it back to him, having suddenly acquired a mischievous grin.

'I say, I say, I say,' she surprised him by saying in her best vaudeville voice. 'How do you turn a zebra into a crossing?'

Holly was convinced the poor girl had lost all grip on reality, even on what passed here for reality. If she had, he realised, then so had all the others, as he noticed they were all sporting the same demented grin and were crowding round him rather alarmingly. He even felt a couple of nudges in his back. There seemed no alternative but to comply.

'I don't know,' he replied hesitantly. Bowing to their increasing encouragement, he continued, 'How do you turn a zebra into a crossi...'

There followed that by now all too familiar '*shap*', the brief pressure in the ears, and Holly found himself in a charming cottage garden, surrounded by all his companions, or to be more precise, their heads.

CHAPTER EIGHTEEN

Despite the time of year, the sun was still warm enough for the elderly couple to sit outside with not too many more layers of clothing than they would have worn anyway at the height of summer. The garden was her favourite spot, and she was very glad of his company.

She had only discovered the place fairly recently and had moved in as soon as she could, quite rightly finding the location utterly enchanting. The landscape rolled pleasingly to a distant horizon, and the unique character of the area meant she had a panoramic view in every direction.

The three exterior sides of the garden were walled, old brick walls six-feet high with a sporadic cover of ivy all round. The walls themselves couldn't be seen, but this was again due to that unique character of the region rather than the ivy. Indeed, the ivy was the only reason you knew the walls were there at all, not just because it must have had something to cling to, but also because instead of being its usual green, it was actually the various shades of the old bricks and even, occasionally, the mortar. The walls, likewise, had taken on the features of the countryside beyond them, rendering them, to all intents and purposes, invisible.

This phenomenon was also noticeable where the couple were sitting. The garden table between them was of wrought iron and had been painted a cream colour, but that's not how they saw it. From where they were sitting, it took on the appearance of the grass beneath it, its actual surface, indeed its very presence, only revealed when superimposed on to the four objects that rested on top of the table, namely a teapot, two teacups and a raffia fan. These had in turn self-effacingly relinquished their own given designs to sport instead the cream wrought iron swirls of the table.

It was similarly impossible to tell at first glance what the couple were wearing. Seated as they were almost facing one another on chairs that matched the table, the only pattern that each could make out was the same cream swirls from the parts of the chair that the other was obscuring, the other parts of the chair of course being the same colour as the grass and therefore barely discernible. Had they both been sitting directly on the grass with their hands in their pockets, all they would have been able to see of each other would have been their heads.

The old lady reached for the pot, her sleeves instantly acquiring the same swirl pattern.

'Just eaten?' she asked, happily.

'The old school,' he replied, equally contentedly.

The tea having been offered and accepted, the couple settled back to lose themselves once more in the view. It was at this point that the team invaded their idyllic scene.

The second they arrived, looked round and realised where they were, they all acquired expressions of utter delight. All, that is, except Holly, who reverted to type and froze, not even registering the horror he undoubtedly felt.

His immediate desire was to shut his eyes tight, but he couldn't even bring himself to do that.

Kia's reaction couldn't have been more different.

'We're here!' she squealed and clapped her hands in excitement. Holly knew she had done this, not just because of the sound, but also because he could see, with what was now approaching nausea, her seemingly disembodied hands make contact with one another. Fortunately, she noticed the look on his face and stepped in to reassure him before he had a chance to realise that his own hands were also the only part of himself he'd be able to see.

'It's alright,' she beamed at him, grabbing his arm and making him flinch. 'We're all here. It's just an optical illusion.'

'Hah! He probably didn't think we were all there to start with,' laughed the captain.

'In certain cases I dare say he'd be right,' murmured Kia. She gestured around her. 'This wonderful place,' she announced to Holly, 'is the Chameleon Realm. Everything here tries to look like what's behind it.'

As Kia was standing between two of her companions with her arms out, Holly saw in astonishment that her left sleeve had suddenly taken on the white of Uncle Sid's shirt, which was otherwise nowhere to be seen, and her right sleeve had turned the light brown of the captain's jacket, save for the thin psychedelic blast from his shirt in the middle. As the team were standing in a row with Kia at the centre, her arms were the only things he could make out against the brick wall and the ivy behind. Apart from their heads floating on top.

'I bet all you can see is a brick wall covered in ivy with our heads floating on top,' Kia said gleefully, disconcerting Holly even more. 'And I bet the ivy's green.'

Holly's expression betrayed the fact that he found this so self-evident that it didn't merit a response.

'But it's not a wall, it's us,' she went on, 'or rather,' sensing that she was making things less rather than more clear, 'if we weren't here, you wouldn't be able to see the wall.'

She pushed the captain away and moved in the opposite direction herself to create a gap between them.

'Look,' she demonstrated. 'No wall.'

Holly was forced to concede that where her head had previously been bobbing in front of a wall covered in green ivy, there was now indeed no wall, just the ivy, and that had changed colour to a patchy terracotta.

As the identity parade in front of him had now dispersed and its members become more individually discernible, Holly could see that each one was clearly delineated by the same brick and green ivy pattern, and that this pattern remained static, different parts of it appearing and disappearing as his teammates moved in front of it.

'The wall is there,' Kia explained, 'but assumes the look of what's behind it, like a chameleon. In this case what's behind it is the countryside, so that's what it looks like.'

On peering more intently, Holly fancied he could just make out the outline of the wall against the sky, plus a few lines of mortar within it like ripples, as though it were made of glass.

'And the ivy is of course green,' Kia continued, 'but turns itself the colour of brick to blend in with the wall – despite the fact,' she hurried on in order to divert the objection she could see Holly was formulating, 'that the wall is no longer visible.' She smiled. 'As a wall. Lady!'

Before Holly could take offence at this, Kia rushed excitedly past him. He got a fleeting but very reassuring glimpse of the whole of Uncle Sid and then Uncle Jasper as Kia ran in front of them.

Turning out of curiosity, Holly spotted the elderly couple for the first time, or rather two elderly heads each suspended above an uncomfortably skeletal off-white design, either side of a collection of similarly patterned objects that were hovering in mid-air.

'So this is where you've been hiding,' chided Kia playfully. 'No wonder we haven't seen you in a while.'

Kia went straight up to the woman and gave her a hug. Normally this would have obscured the woman from Holly's view, but in this case it had the reverse effect, revealing the woman as she would have appeared anywhere else.

Holly had already been able to see the mid-length tufty hair of numerous shades of red, one of which was mirrored in the lipstick which smiled out of an otherwise pale, wide-eyed face. Revealed now were the mauve sweatshirt, the dark pink baggy cotton trousers and the scuffed pale green trainers that completed her outfit. As the woman leaned forward to receive and return the embrace, Holly could see the cream swirls of the back of the chair that had so worryingly seemed to be part of the woman's anatomy. Less revelatory were the words with which the woman warmly greeted Kia, which sounded like 'khaki anorak'. Holly assumed, erroneously as it turned out, that he had misheard.

'And I suppose,' Kia went on, taking the few steps across to the man, briefly revealing to Holly as she did so a round table of an identical colour and design to the woman's chair, a table that supported the previously hovering articles, which turned out to be a teapot, two teacups and a raffia fan, 'that it's no great surprise to find you here as well. Assuming the rumours to be true.'

Seeing the man who had by now become almost wholly visible made Holly start and glance quickly over his shoulder to check that Uncle Sid was still behind him, so exact was the likeness. The face was a little more sunken and cadaverous, the atoll of hair had acquired a snowy appearance, and the white shirt and black trousers, so far also identical, were complemented by the addition of an equally shabby black single-breasted jacket, which was open. Uncle Sid was indeed still behind him, grinning foolishly at the older man, as were the rest of the team, Holly noticed. He also noticed that the face of the subject of their attention had gone several shades towards the colour of his companion's hair, though not so much out of camouflage, Holly surmised, as out of embarrassment.

'So they are true!' Kia said, squealing again, and again accompanied by a short burst of applause. 'You're going to be looking out for a ring for her, then? Better be some stone, eh, Lady?'

'Bagatelle?' said the old woman, beaming, followed by 'Scrub yourself!' in mock indignation. She leaned towards Kia conspiratorially. 'The French media – mon Dieu!' she whispered loudly, and rolled her eyes. Suddenly spotting Holly, she pointed at him, shouted 'Rubbery lips!' and dissolved into a fit of laughter which slowly transformed into a fit of coughing.

Everyone was now laughing except the elderly man, who had regained most of his normal pallor and was just smiling fondly at his seated companion, and Holly, who was mystified but no longer as surprised to be mystified as he would have been that morning. He had reached the stage where he would have been more surprised if he hadn't found some new character mystifying. No more goldfish impressions from me, he resolved. So he waited patiently for the surrounding hilarity to subside, knowing that an explanation would be forthcoming, as indeed it was, though not one that made any immediate sense.

'Stones,' Kia said to him, starting off another wave of laughter all round as it became apparent that this had made things no clearer to Holly whatsoever.

'Come over here,' she beckoned to him, anxious that his patience had been tested far enough, 'and meet the rest of the team.'

She didn't know it, because of course he didn't show it, but to Holly this was already explanation enough. Just knowing that these two were part of the team, and knowing that each member of the team dealt with a specific type of clue, told him that the woman's seemingly random remarks were not the ramblings of a deranged mind but contained information that was very precise, almost mathematical. This thought gave him a warm glow and renewed confidence, to the extent that in the few steps required to reach Kia, he had identified the variable.

'This is...' was as far as Kia got in her introductions.

'Inserts,' Holly said with more eagerness than he was used to. 'Hidden words.'

Lady was clearly impressed.

'Ooh,' she intoned quietly, nodding at him.

'And those,' he continued in muted triumph, 'were gemstones.'

'Bribing officials!' Lady cried happily, clapping her hands as Kia had done.

Kia, the captain and the baron echoed her, shouting 'Bingo!' as she had done in her way, and everyone joined in to give Holly a round of applause.

‘Rubbery lips,’ Holly carried on regardless, now on a roll, ‘contains the word beryl,’ – nods of agreement – ‘the phrase “scrub yourself” has the word ruby in it,’ – more general consent – ‘bagatelle. Now, that’s a wonderful choice because it already means a trinket, albeit a worthless one, but actually contains the word agate,’ – he could sense Uncle Sid’s exasperation at his enthusiasm without turning round – ‘and the most desirable of all, “the French media, mon Dieu” denotes...’

‘I’m afraid I am on drugs,’ Lady chipped in gleefully.

‘...diamond. Precisely.’

CHAPTER NINETEEN

The introductions were briefly put on hold as Kia, Holly and the geriatric lovebirds watched the others revelling in their surroundings.

'Kids,' muttered Kia, watching them merrily exchange clothes by standing in front of one another. Particularly striking were the negative images created by giving the baron Uncle Jasper's white boiler suit and then kitting Uncle Jasper out in the baron's all black, the latter a distinct improvement, to Holly's mind. The sight of Uncle Sid trying to restrain the captain's irrepressible shirt was easily the most jarring.

Before Kia could bring in the last member of the team, Holly remembered an issue that needed resolving more urgently.

'What on earth was that vaudeville comedy routine all about?' he asked Kia.

'Oh, that,' she replied, a little sheepishly. 'Well, that damage level nonsense I was coming out with was getting on my nerves. It's bad enough listening to someone else going weird, but when you can hear it coming out of your own mouth and you can't stop it, that's never happened to me before. It's unbearable. It has to be solved.' She took a deep breath. 'So I thought if we could go directly to the location of the relevant clue that might speed things up a bit. I had a quick look at the clues and got a feeling that the word "injury" seemed appropriate. I had to find a way to get you to say "2 Across", as in "how do you turn a zebra in 2 across-ing".' She gave him an apologetic smile. 'Actually it's quite an old trick. One of Lady's, originally.'

The old lady took Kia's hand and squeezed it affectionately. Holly, though, had been looking at the clues and was clearly still not satisfied.

'That's all well and good,' he conceded, 'but the clue with "injury" in it isn't 2 Ac...' He broke off, not sure what would happen if he repeated the name of the location they were already at, if anything. 'It isn't 2,' he settled on, just to be safe, 'it's 6.'

Kia shrugged.

'That's the way it works,' she said simply. 'If there isn't a 2, we go straight to whatever comes after 1. In this case, 6.' She grimaced. ' "Six Across" is difficult to hide in a sentence, even for our expert here.' She gently rocked the woman's hands that were still holding hers. 'Anyway, we now know what sort of clue it is, because it brought us here, to you. This,' she said to Holly, 'is the Wise Lady. Lady, to her friends.'

'Salad years,' Lady agreed, flaunting her foible.

'Lady it is then,' said Holly, smiling. 'Delighted.' He turned to Kia. 'And do I detect a – family resemblance?'

Kia recoiled in mock horror.

'I certainly hope not! Probably a streak of madness common to both families?'

Holly reddened slightly.

'No, no,' he protested, flustered, 'it's just that you mentioned your mother earlier, and I just wondered...'

'In demand?' Lady spluttered. 'Remaining outside?' At which she collapsed into more laughter, again followed by a mild coughing seizure. Kia patted her gingerly on the back.

'No,' she said wistfully. 'Lady's not my ma. You'd know my mother soon enough. But getting back to the matter at hand.' She directed Lady's attention to Holly. 'Lady, this gentleman is...'

'Compartmentalised,' interrupted the old woman, having just got her breath back. Kia frowned at her.

'Don't call him mental, that's not nice,' she said hurriedly. Lady threw her a mischievous glance. 'Although God knows he'd need to be, to put up with all this. His name's Holly, and he's – well, he's definitely out of the ordinary, which is just as well, because this is turning out to be a far from ordinary day. Ah, I see you still use that fan.'

Holly sensed that the change of subject was intended to divert whatever pronouncement Lady had been about to make.

Kia's once again disembodied hand picked up the apparently wrought iron fan and held it up between her and Holly, which had the effect of revealing each one to the other.

'Ah, there you are,' she smiled, 'and,' her smile became a little strained, 'there's that jumper. Lady uses this fan,' she went on, before Holly could query that last remark, 'to find things.' She waved the fan about to reveal Lady, then the table and its contents. 'Things she might otherwise lose. Like her house.'

Following her gesture, Holly looked beyond the elderly couple and the table for the first time, noticing that this side of the garden was even more strange than the other three.

The blotchy orange ivy came to an abrupt halt at either side, leaving what at first glance appeared to be an uninterrupted rural scene, with a path in the middle leading away through a small front garden to a narrow country road that sloped off in both directions before meandering and then disappearing from view.

But then Holly noticed that there were interruptions. Hanging about four feet in the air were two dark squares, one on either side, each another four-feet high, Holly guessed. For a moment he took them to be paintings. Although details were hard to make out in the darkness of the images, they seemed to be room interiors, the one on the right quite plain, with a dining table at the centre with six chairs round it, in front of a closed door, the other a lot busier, a country kitchen with another table in the middle and a tall, wide dresser against the wall, bursting with knick-knacks, vases, dried flowers and all manner of crockery. The angle of the pictures, Holly observed, put the artist, and consequently the viewer, at the window.

Holly swayed left and right in an effort to see what was holding these pictures aloft, and noticed to his astonishment as he did so that the interiors moved with him, revealing more of the rooms. He also fancied he could see a few almost imperceptible lines across the pictures, again like ripples in glass, mostly horizontal with a few diagonals thrown in.

'They're shutters,' Kia explained, having keenly followed his line of vision. 'They reveal the inside of a house you can't see.'

Awestruck, Holly could only stare. The view had seemed simple enough, the floating panels aside, but the knowledge that this revelation brought gave it a depth and a grandeur that rendered him speechless. He started noticing the odd distortion in the image of what he had assumed was distant countryside – actually just a projection of that countryside on to a surface that was mere yards away from him – lines that shimmered and refracted the light slightly, betraying the outlines of the camouflaged house. He could just see the contours of the roof, and even thought he might have spotted them sooner against a clear blue sky rather than the assorted bands of wispy cloud that currently hung practically motionless high in the air.

As usual, his sense of wonder didn't stop him analysing what he was looking at, and it wasn't long before curiosity got the better of him.

'Why,' he asked tentatively, feeling almost ashamed to be questioning such a vision, 'do the shutters act differently from the rest of the house?'

Far from finding this a disappointing reaction or even just irritatingly pedantic, Kia glanced over at the Wise Lady.

'See what I mean?' she whispered. 'Nobody's ever asked that before.'

She screwed her eyes tightly shut, sorting out the explanation in her mind in advance before launching it.

'The house,' she began at last, 'acts as a single unit, rooms and all, which is why you can't see the door, and wouldn't be able to see the windows. The shutters seem to have been added later, so they behave independently to the rest of the house. So if they were open, you wouldn't be able to see inside the rooms, they would just look like the brickwork they were covering. So they have to be shut...'

She faltered, making the mistake of listening to what she was saying and thereby losing the conviction of her explanation.

'...for you to be able to see – through them.'

Here she ground to a halt, looking desperately over at Lady for reassurance. Lady duly beamed back at her and nodded contentedly.

'This pot only,' she declared.

'Yes, well done,' murmured Holly, as impressed with her answer as he was with the vision itself. Bobbing his head sideways again, it did indeed seem to be the only theory that consistently explained everything he could see.

'Second graduate on the right,' came another voice, ostensibly that of Uncle Sid, but with the slightest quiver of age. It was quiet, and was currently full of pride.

'Great!' called Kia, bounding over to the old man. 'I hadn't forgotten you,' she teased, giving him a hug as well. As she did so, she appeared to Holly to be wearing the old man's jacket back to front.

'Holly, this,' she said, straightening up, 'is Great Uncle Sid, known simply, to avoid confusion and to pander to his huge ego, as...'

'Old king, each time!'

'...Great. Yes.'

Holly could see that she was about to tell him the role Great Uncle Sid played in the team, but he had already figured it out, given that the old man had merely said his own name. 'Old king', Holly knew, was used to denote the letters GR, as in George Rex, old King George. 'Each' was often abbreviated to just EA, and 'time' was one of the many words that meant the letter T.

'Codes,' he said, cutting Kia off in mid inhale. 'Abbreviations. Acronyms.' He looked down at the unassuming, wiry character with undisguised admiration. 'Truly a man of letters.' He held out his hand. 'How do you do?'

‘Fellow students – nil,’ came the reply, along with a surprisingly firm hand. Holly congratulated himself on translating that into the appropriate greeting, ‘fellow’ being HE, ‘students’ being learners or LL, and ‘nil’ providing a zero, or O. Casting his mind back, he quickly worked out that Great’s previous comment had been to call Kia smart, ‘second graduate on the right’ breaking down to S for ‘second’, MA or Master of Arts, being one of many possibilities for ‘graduate’, and RT for ‘right’.

Standing in this garden, still shaking the old man’s hand, in the most surreal surroundings he had ever experienced, Holly realised that he hadn’t been this happy for a very long time, that he hadn’t felt so at ease in anyone’s company as he now did in that of this bunch of eccentrics. He not only felt accepted, and accepted as an equal, but as an equal among specialists, almost an elite. And this feeling was too strong even to be diminished by the sight of the quartet performing at the other end of the garden. Their quick-change routine had become quite advanced – having exhausted every possibility of horizontal and vertical splits, they had progressed to individually attired arms and legs. Their favourite to date was to give Uncle Jasper the captain’s explosive shirt, his own white-sleeved arms and the two distinct shades of black of the baron’s and Uncle Sid’s trousers for his legs.

Looking around him at the childish antics and the fond smiles, his thoughts grew dark. An uneasy foreboding made him aware how vulnerable they all were, how everything relied on them and yet all they had to rely on was each other. He noticed again, still with some surprise, how responsible he felt for them, almost paternal.

He also suddenly felt very tired. He relinquished Great Uncle Sid’s hand and sat on the grass in front of him. Just like on the ship, he felt he could sit in this garden forever, never tiring of the bizarre conversation or the fun to be had exploiting the laws of the Chameleon Realm. But he knew there were matters that needed resolving, hidden threats that needed to be identified and dealt with, that there was work to be done. And he knew that Kia was going to have to burst this happy bubble in order to address the issue.

Which was what she now did.

CHAPTER TWENTY

'OK, before we do anything else, could we please cure my affliction?'

All eyes and ears turned to Kia. Even the costume designing came to an abrupt halt.

'Well, both of them, actually. My two afflictions.'

The team were exchanging quizzical glances, especially Uncles Jasper and Sid who were clearly worried she may be talking about them.

'That weird breathing seizure back in the road?' she spelt out. 'Ring any bells? And that damage level nonsense?'

They all nodded knowingly, embarrassed yet relieved, even the elderly couple, who had no idea what she was talking about but were still relieved to see the others relieved.

'Now this damage level thing is actually itself only a damage level one at most,' she said, starting a fresh round of puzzled looks, 'but is definitely the most annoying.' She went over to the Wise Lady. 'And naming what I hoped was the relevant clue brought us to you. So let's see what you make of this.'

She brought her copy of the paper out from where she had hidden Holly's on the ship, tucked into her waistband at the back, under her jumper. Seated on the grass, Holly could only just make it out, as it had now assumed the green knitted texture of that jumper, blending in fairly well against the green ivy that defined the rest of it. He could see it clearly enough, though, when he held out his own copy that he found, with some relief, he still held in his hand.

'Six Across,' Kia began, grinning at Holly, 'not 2 Across, but close enough. It's only four letters. "Charming about injury".'

'Charming,' the Wise Lady pounced on immediately. 'Spanish armada. Both arms.'

Kia's face as it turned to Holly had gone its customary clue-solving blank, but cheered up as it saw Holly nodding in agreement. Feeling her expectant gaze, he explained.

'I'd assumed "about" was going to be a C for "circa" again, or RE for "regarding", or even an anagram indictor. It comes up a lot,' he said almost apologetically to Kia, 'it's very versatile. But there are no four-letter words for it to be an anagram of,' he waved aside the captain's generous offer to supply some, 'and the fact that this clue has brought us to the inserts specialist is in itself a clue.' He looked over at Lady who gave him an encouraging wink. ' "About" in this case means "surrounding", and tells us that the first word contains a synonym for the last word.'

Kia raised the paper and frowned at it, very hard.

'A synonym for "injury",' cajoled Holly. More frowning. 'In "charming",' he added helpfully.

'Harm!' Kia shouted, as though it was the first clue she had ever worked out for herself, which for all Holly knew it might very well have been. She looked over at Lady in delighted revelation. 'Which is also in "Spanish armada"! And "both arms"!'

Lady patted Kia's arm proudly.

'Cobra vomit,' she purred.

'Thanks,' said Kia, doubtfully. Buoyed by her success, she was keen to crack on. 'Now, the word before "harm" makes up the pair,' she said, consulting the clues, 'and the clue is – "Eric"...'

She faltered briefly, just managing not to look up at Holly.

' "Eric goes"', she pressed ahead, with some effort, ' "at disruption in class". Ten letters.'

There was an uncomfortable silence. Holly could see from their faces that they had all met Eric and were not at all happy to be reminded of him, or of what happened to him. This obviously being their overriding thought at the moment, Holly knew he would have to get the ball rolling regarding the clue himself. He cleared his throat.

'Um, well, "disruption" is a common anagram indicator...'

Great Uncle Sid lifted two fingers to his mouth and let out a piercing whistle, at which the younger version of himself dutifully came running up.

'...and it follows the words "Eric goes at"', Holly continued, marvelling at this display of what he took to be filial duty, 'which also add up to ten letters...'

'Categorise,' was Uncle Sid's instant response.

'...producing a synonym,' Holly concluded, 'for "class"'.

'Categorise!' Uncle Jasper confirmed from some way off, hands dejectedly in pockets. Holly wondered how Uncle Jasper knew which pockets to use, there were so many of them, but suspected that each had its own well-established role.

'Good work,' said Holly, nodding to each in turn. Uncle Sid looked eagerly at his ancestor for approval and received a brief solemn nod, with which he appeared quite content, seemingly taking it as both approval and dismissal, respectfully withdrawing from the older man's exalted presence.

'So that gives us – "categorise harm",' said Kia, tentatively, mulling over the words before gesturing to Holly to write them into the grid. That done, she waved the captain over. 'We have to test this, Captain,' she said. 'Do something threatening.'

The captain thought for a moment.

'How about a hearty rendition of the "Volga Boatmen Song"?' he suggested, eagerly.

'That'll do it,' Kia agreed, holding up a hand to make sure this remained merely a threat.

She waited. The others watched her eyes darting about in concentration that was only broken once when she had to hold her hand up again, this time more emphatically, as the captain mistakenly assumed she was waiting for him to burst into song.

Eventually, she relaxed.

'That's got it,' she said in quiet satisfaction. 'Not the slightest urge to assess the danger we were all just in,' then a little quieter, 'which I'm sure would have been off the scale.'

Holly, who was still seated between Kia and Great Uncle Sid, and was probably the only person to have heard Kia's last remark, was on the verge of laughing out loud when something strange caught his eye.

From his low vantage point on the grass, Kia's head was floating way above the top of the wall, which only reached halfway up her jumper. Just above the wall, between Kia and the house, Holly had spotted an indefinable movement, more like a distortion in the light, moving away from the house. It wasn't until it had passed behind Kia that it revealed itself to be a cat.

Alerted by the look on Holly's face, Kia turned in the direction of his gaze, holding up her paper so that she too could make it out.

'Zoso!' she cried happily. 'So that's where you've got to!'

'Yours?' Holly asked.

'Sort of,' Kia replied. 'Mum's really. But mostly mine now. She's a cat, you know, so she comes and goes as she pleases. Although how she got here...' She gave Lady a stern look. 'Nothing to do with you, I suppose?'

Lady shrugged, carelessly.

'Zoso?' Holly queried, not sure whether he'd heard the name correctly, and also not sure he hadn't heard it somewhere before.

'That's what Mum named her,' Kia explained. 'Can't remember why. A name she'd heard in California, was it?'

Holly watched Zoso – still imprinted on Kia's jumper – pause briefly, then give them a haughty look before disappearing behind the wall, only to reappear when no longer behind Kia, made visible by the now invisible wall, slowly making her way down the hill.

'Not an easy name,' Kia said, looking quizzically at Lady, 'to hide in a sentence of normal words. How on earth do you call her?'

Lady's eyes twinkled mischievously.

'Scatterbrain!' she barked. 'Formica table! Cardiac attack!'

Kia nodded in appreciation.

'Just "cat", I get it,' she said. 'Very good. And speaking of cardiac attack,' she addressed the others, 'let's quickly deal with my other little problem. I'm not going through that again.' She waved her copy of the newspaper around. 'So start looking for potential keywords – "breathless", "excuses" – "smarmy" maybe.' She fixed her eye on the captain. 'Maybe "over-averse" is in there somewhere.'

The captain looked briefly enthusiastic before realising that this may not have been a serious suggestion, after which he joined the baron to search through the clues in their copy of the paper.

Uncle Jasper had retrieved another copy from one of the innumerable compartments in his boiler suit, already folded to the same page as the others, and was holding it between himself and Uncle Sid. This brought the number of copies being simultaneously scanned to four. The only people not actively involved in this quest, Holly noticed, were his two most recent acquaintances. He considered offering to share with Great Uncle Sid, but as neither of the elderly couple had made any effort to participate, he concluded that their roles were more as consultants, helping out only when asked.

The captain had the first recommendation.

'Well, I was involved in these so-called excuses,' he admitted, 'and 7 Down mentions "bad jokes", which certainly sounds like me.'

Holly regretfully shook his head.

'Following Kia's "smarmy" route,' he said, 'I'm drawn to "overindulgence", two clues further.'

'A little harsh,' protested the baron, a point even Kia had to concede. 'As the main culp... – the main protagonist,' he corrected himself, 'I prefer "magnanimity" in 12 Across.'

There was a pause as everyone considered the baron's proposal under Lady and Great's patient, benevolent gaze, the only things audible being the rustling of leaves and the occasional distant birdsong. Holly was the first to respond.

'Looks promising,' he agreed. 'And its companion clue contains the word "terror", which may fit.'

Kia raised her eyebrows.

'Companion clue,' she teased. 'You really are getting the hang of it. OK, let's do it. What have we got? "Set clear tone in magnanimity", nine letters. "Set" and "clear".' She looked up, hopefully. 'Something to do with honey?'

'The quickest possibility,' said Holly, desperate not to laugh, 'is that "set" means Uncle Sid, and "clear tone" happen to amount to the required nine letters...'

'Not cereal,' said Uncle Sid, vehemently, then more tentatively, 'once alert? Lone react?' Then turning to Uncle Jasper, a far more confident, 'Tolerance!'

'Magnanimity,' nodded Uncle Jasper, glad to have been included, if only for confirmation. 'Tolerance.'

Having for a moment been worried that the anagram route may have been a dead end, Holly eagerly wrote the word into the grid, taking a moment to stare at it in satisfaction. The left-hand side of the grid was looking decidedly healthy, he thought. Smug attack over, he hastened to the second of the pair of clues.

'And the next one,' he announced, 'is a five-letter word, and reads "Deity in charge creates terror".'

He frowned at the clue, as though it was an impertinent child. For the first time today, nothing sprang to mind. Fortunately, Great Uncle Sid's quavering but authoritative voice sprang to his ear.

'In charge,' it said, simply.

Although this sounded as though the old man was merely repeating a section of the clue, Holly realised that

Great Uncle Sid's role in the team provided an additional clue in itself.

'IC,' he muttered, thinking out loud.

'What do you see?' asked Kia. 'Anything worth sharing with us?'

Holly shook his head.

'No, I mean the letters I and C,' he explained. 'The phrase "in charge" is often abbreviated as IC.'

'I see,' echoed Kia. 'And the terror, where does that come in?'

'It's not where it comes in,' lamented the captain, 'it's where it comes out that can be a problem.'

The baron tutted at him.

'Going commando again, are we, Captain?' he asked in mock sympathy, causing disgusted protests from everyone except the old couple, who didn't seem to be acquainted with the expression, and Uncle Jasper, who chuckled loudly. The captain just shrugged his shoulders happily, hardly the denial the protesters were hoping for.

1 C	A	2 T	E	3 G	O	4 R	I	5 S	E	■	6 H	7 A	R	8 M
R	■	R	■	E	■		■		■	9	■		■	
10 A	G	A	I	N	S	T	■	11 L	A	W	L	O	R	D
F	■	M	■	E	■		■		■		■		■	
12 T	O	L	E	R	A	N	C	E	■	13				
■	■	I	■	A	■		■		■		■	■	■	
14 P	A	N	E	L	■	15 E	X	T	O	R	T	16 I	O	N
E	■	E	■	S	■	■	■	■	■		■		■	
17 D		S		U	■	18		19	■	20				
O	■	■	■	R	■		■		■		■		■	■
21 M		22 G		G	■	23								24
E	■	A	■	E	■		■		■		■		■	
25 T	A	B	L	O	I	D	■	26 A	R	T	I	S	A	N
E	■	L	■	N	■		■		■		■		■	
27 R	E	E	K	■	28 A	R	I	T	H	M	E	T	I	C

CHAPTER TWENTY-ONE

'Yes, thanks for that,' said Kia, wearily. 'I don't think any of us needed such a graphic demonstration of what terror feels like. I meant what part does it play in this clue?'

'I think it's the definition,' said Holly, thankful to be changing the subject. 'A five-letter terror that ends IC...'

'Toxic?' suggested Kia.

'Attic,' said the captain with conviction, shuddering at some distant memory. 'I was locked in an attic once...'

'...a five-letter terror that ends IC,' interrupted Holly, 'and starts with a three-letter deity.'

There followed a pause, everyone thinking so hard Holly almost fancied he could hear the scratching of heads. The captain was, as usual, the first to break the silence, though more out of an aversion to it than any hope of contributing something of genuine use.

'God-ic?' he ventured.

'Set-ic?' muttered the baron, shaking his head and getting a sarcastic 'ooh' from Uncle Sid for his trouble.

'Asp-ic!' The captain again, immediately disappointed at the lack of enthusiasm that greeted this latest brainwave.

'Snake worshippers...?'

A shrill, warbling whistle made everyone jump and turn angrily to Uncle Jasper, especially Uncle Sid, whose particularly black expression betrayed the fact that this was a common occurrence which had nevertheless caught him out yet again. Uncle Jasper, in the meantime, calmly lowered the silver referee's whistle from his lips. The whistle was attached to a bunch of keys, at least fifty, of all manner of shapes and sizes, each identified by differently coloured stickers and pieces of string. That would account for the jangling, Holly thought. Uncle Jasper then returned the whole lot to its appropriate pocket, one of the larger ones at the hip.

Satisfied that he had everyone's undivided attention, he said, quietly and deliberately, 'Panic.' And then to reinforce the incongruity of his tone with his words, 'Terror.'

'Of course,' the captain nodded his admiration. 'Pan. The ancient Greek god of fry-ups. Hah! How could we forget him?'

'So – tolerance panic.' Kia mulled this over. 'Panic induced by other people's tolerance.' She vaguely nodded her approval. 'Sounds fair enough.' Checking that Holly had entered the new word into his copy of the grid, which he hadn't but quickly did, she grinned at the baron. 'Well come on then, let's try it out. You're the nice one. See if you can come to someone's defence – Lady's, maybe, for kidnapping my cat.'

Lady raised her eyebrows in indignation.

'Or Uncle Jasper's,' Kia continued, 'for still using that sodding whistle.'

Uncle Jasper chuckled like he'd just pulled off the best practical joke ever. But the baron solemnly shook his head.

‘No,’ he said. ‘No more Mr Nice Guy for me. Nice doesn’t get you anywhere.’

Kia’s reproachful look, however affectionate, produced the desired response, but from Holly, not the baron.

‘You can’t blame him,’ Holly heard himself say, much to his own surprise, addressing the ground as he always did when being remotely confrontational. ‘He was only making the perfectly reasonable point that...’

He broke off, suddenly realising, only a split second before everyone else realised, that he had just done exactly what Kia had asked the baron to do. He looked up to catch her triumphant eye, and then over at the baron, who smiled reluctantly.

‘Thanks,’ he said, ‘but I think you’ve just proved my point.’

But Kia was quick to contradict him.

‘Nonsense, Baron,’ she said, kindly but firmly. ‘On the contrary. Nice has come up trumps again. Holly seems to be a wonderfully tolerant man, who nevertheless feels the need to come to the defence of someone he thinks is being treated unfairly –’ her eyes darted over to Holly, who quickly looked away, ‘– possibly against his better judgment. And it’s precisely the fact that it is against his better judgment that makes him – well, as soppy as you.’

Both men were having the greatest difficulty knowing where to look. They briefly tried looking at each other, but quickly resumed their search.

‘And being petulant,’ she continued, remorselessly, ‘doesn’t stop you being nice, if nice is what you are. It’s just throwing your toys out of the pram. But still in a nice way.’

Great Uncle Sid was by now feeling so uncomfortable on his teammates’ behalf that he couldn’t help clearing his throat. Apart from immense gratitude, Holly also felt a certain amount of awe at the way the authority of this simple guttural sound brought Kia back to the point.

'The point is,' she went on, suitably chastened, 'that, however unwittingly, Holly here, by being,' she could see him starting to squirm already, 'the N-word,' rolling her eyes, 'has provided the perfect opportunity to see whether the last solutions have in fact solved anything.'

'Well,' said the captain, with his head to one side, 'you certainly don't seem to be having any trouble breathing.'

'Exactly,' she agreed, continuing to prove the point. 'And that's nice. Nice will always win the day.'

'Hah! It didn't do Uncle Gordo any good.'

Specifically, this meant nothing to Holly whatsoever, but he could tell from everyone's reaction that the captain, in his customary shoot first, think later manner, had broken some sort of taboo. He could also glean a little more information from the way each person reacted differently.

Great Uncle Sid, although still seated, had drawn himself to his full height and was glaring at the captain in imperious indignation, clearly considering him to have transgressed some unwritten law. Lady wore an expression of pained sympathy that she was distributing evenly between Kia and the younger uncles.

Uncle Sid also looked angry, but less imperious and more intensely resentful. In contrast, Uncle Jasper appeared more shocked than anything else, and was staring at the grass, shaking his head sadly. The baron was neither angry nor shocked – having spent far too much time in the captain's company for that, Holly imagined – but was looking anxiously from one person to the other.

Kia herself was the only one to betray no emotion at all, staring blankly and unwaveringly at the captain, who was in turn showing not a shred of remorse at having stirred up this hornets' nest, and was in fact smiling inanely at his companions, shrugging his shoulders.

From all this, Holly gathered that the ones most affected by this matter were Kia and the two uncles, which tied in with the person mentioned also having been an uncle, and also that the captain was more than happy to raise an issue he thought demanded airing.

'I'm sorry,' Holly said, determined not to let this silence go on too long and all too aware that he was not the person they wanted to hear those words from, 'but who are we talking about?'

It was a while before anyone answered. Having got this particular ball rolling, even the captain seemed reluctant to have it passed back to him. In the end it was Uncle Sid who regained possession.

'No cruel God,' he hissed slowly and quietly from between clenched teeth. The bitterness was still present, but was no longer directed at the captain, more at the world in general. Holly hadn't noticed either of the uncles actually move, and yet he was sure they were standing a little closer together than moments before.

Kia's trance finally dissolved, and she shifted her gaze. The captain, who had been dangling uncomfortably on the look on the end of her line, was visibly relieved, for all his bravado.

'Uncle Gordo,' she murmured to no-one in particular. 'Yes, he certainly was a nice man.'

'Reportedly.'

Holly was surprised by this seemingly dissenting remark, more surprised to find that it had come from Uncle

Jasper, and more surprised again to find that it had been addressed to him.

'Say,' Uncle Jasper continued, in the same deliberate delivery he had used while the house was crashing down around them. 'By the sound of it. We hear.'

The penny finally dropped, and Holly realised that Uncle Jasper, far from casting aspersions on Uncle Gordo's niceness, was actually describing the absentee's role in the team.

'Homophones,' Holly announced, having recognised the most common phrases used to indicate the use of words that sound the same as others but are spelt differently. 'He dealt with homophones.'

Uncle Jasper nodded absently, clearly never having doubted that Holly would understand.

'And where exactly did being nice get him?' demanded the captain, seizing the opportunity to resume his line of questioning.

'It got him a lot of respect!' shouted Kia in exasperation. 'And it got him sorely missed now he's gone.'

The captain was resolute.

'No,' he said in a kinder tone, 'I mean, where exactly, physically, did it get him?'

Kia sighed and looked at Holly, feeling his curiosity hanging over her.

'Well that's just it,' she told him. 'We have no idea.'

She looked round at her colleagues for encouragement, and got it. Lady even reached out and squeezed Kia's arm, or at least her hands did. Holly was amazed at how long it had been since he had been aware that they were still in the Chameleon Realm, how quickly its initially unnatural laws of nature had become second nature.

'He was a real gentle giant,' Kia started off. 'Such a nice man.' She ignored the captain shrugging his shoulders. 'Anyway, about this time last year, maybe a little earlier – only a couple of months after this place first appeared –,' nods all round, 'the Solver of the day made a last-ditch attempt to solve a particularly nagging clue. He meant to go on his own, as it was getting late, but at the last second Uncle Gordo grabbed him and they disappeared together. It would have been instinctive for him to do that if he thought he could be of any help...'

'...because he was so nice!' cried the captain, triumphantly.

'...but he never came back.' She looked at Holly, apologetic that the story had so inconclusive an ending. 'Whether the Solver ran out of time and couldn't bring him back, or whether they got separated...'

Hearing a crack in Kia's voice, Lady gently rocked her arm and smiled at her.

'Tomatoes, ham, eggs,' she said, sadly.

'Oh yes,' the captain conceded, 'a great shame. But that doesn't alter the fact that...'

Although the captain's mouth continued to move, Holly was first bewildered to notice that he could no longer hear him, then amused to see the captain's look of bewilderment when he realised that he could no longer hear himself, and finally alarmed as they all simultaneously registered the fact that nothing was audible any more, not their own voices, not the birds, not the wind, not even the leaves rustling in the trees. It was as though all sound had been sucked out of the world.

Unsettling though this was, and it certainly gave Holly a drowning sensation, it only lasted about four seconds, and was followed by a bass drum beat like none of them had ever heard, a bass drum they found themselves inside – not a particularly loud pulse, but one of such unspeakably low frequency that Holly felt every part of himself vibrate. It was as though sound itself had first been inhaled in preparation of a concentrated release, like the tide receding before the arrival of a tidal wave.

As the subsonic thud, and with it the sensation, faded away, the birds, the leaves and the wind faded back in, disconcertingly loud after the silence yet presumably no louder than they had been before, sure enough taking little time to settle down to an ignorable background noise – to such an extent, in fact, that Holly started to doubt whether he had actually heard anything out of the ordinary. He was about to get confirmation that he had, however, and in a way that was at least as chilling as the sound had been.

'What the hell was that? And who are all you people? And why are you covered in ivy?'

The words would have been worrying enough had they come from Kia or the captain, but what turned their concern into genuine horror was that the voice was Lady's.

[1]C	A	[2]T	E	[3]G	O	[4]R	I	[5]S	E	■	[6]H	[7]A	R	[8]M
R	■	R	■	E	■		■		■	[9]	■		■	
[10]A	G	A	I	N	S	T	■	[11]L	A	W	L	O	R	D
F	■	M	■	E	■		■		■		■		■	
[12]T	O	L	E	R	A	N	C	E	■	[13]P	A	N	I	C
■	■	I	■	A	■		■		■		■	■	■	
[14]P	A	N	E	L	■	[15]E	X	T	O	R	T	[16]I	O	N
E	■	E	■	S	■	■	■	■	■		■		■	
[17]D		S		U	■	[18]		[19]	■	[20]				
O	■	■	■	R	■		■		■		■		■	■
[21]M		[22]G		G	■	[23]								[24]
E	■	A	■	E	■		■		■		■		■	
[25]T	A	B	L	O	I	D	■	[26]A	R	T	I	S	A	N
E	■	L	■	N	■		■		■		■		■	
[27]R	E	E	K	■	[28]A	R	I	T	H	M	E	T	I	C

CHAPTER TWENTY-TWO

It took quite a while to calm Lady down. She had found the setting she seemed to have suddenly appeared in alarming enough, reminding Holly of his own initially adverse reaction to the place. But to be approached by a crowd of strangely clad people, however well meaning, all of whose heads somehow became detached as they drew nearer, was enough to induce near hysteria in the poor woman. Only when Kia had shooed off the men did Lady's anxiety show any signs of abating. The baron, the captain and the two uncles went and huddled together a respectful distance away, with Lady keeping a constant suspicious eye on them. She had grabbed Kia's sleeve and wouldn't let go, admitting, albeit reluctantly, that she seemed a nice girl. For her part, Kia made sure that by kneeling she was at the same height as the seated woman, well below the level of the top of the wall, thereby keeping the floating head thing to a minimum.

A short way from the group of men, Holly was still in the same place he had been sitting, but was now standing. Watching Kia cope so impressively with yet another crisis filled Holly with curiosity. How had she acquired this role, and how long ago, and how long was she expected to carry it on? Did she even know the answers herself? It seemed hardly fair to Holly that someone of her age should have to deal with such responsibility, and yet she appeared to take it as read that it was hers to bear. He wondered how much of a childhood she had actually had, and where her parents were.

He felt a hand on his shoulder. It was Great Uncle Sid. The old man had shot out of his seat at the same time as Holly had stood up, but had then remained similarly rooted to the spot. Lady's anguish had spread to them all, but none more so, Holly could see, than Great Uncle Sid. The look he now gave Holly was a mixture of horror and helplessness.

Still grasping Holly's shoulder, he was clearly struggling to formulate what he wanted to say. Holly wondered for the first time what it must be like, only being able to communicate in codes, or anagrams, or synonyms – how what he had until now considered a useful gift could just as easily be seen as a source of frustration.

Eventually the old man sighed and seemed to give up, resorting instead to what, for him, was the most direct approach.

'Hard energy record,' he said in a voice that quavered more than usual, and then again, more plaintively, 'hard energy record.'

Holly knew instinctively, before he had even identified the abbreviations of the three words as H, E and LP respectively, that he was being asked for help. He nodded, he hoped reassuringly, reached up and patted the hand on his shoulder, which was then slowly withdrawn.

Holly gestured to the other men to come over and join him. They in turn looked anxiously over at Lady, keen not to set her off again with any sudden movements, but she was wholly engrossed, concentrating on whatever explanation Kia was trying to give her. They could tell from the look on Lady's face that Kia was having trouble making her story convincing. But at least it was diverting, so they gingerly made their way over, Uncle Jasper having to take special care not to jangle too much, a particular challenge, given his ever-increasing limp.

'What's up with the old – with Lady?' the captain began, wilting under the withering look Great Uncle Sid was giving him. Holly could only shake his head.

'It must have had something to do with that – sound,' suggested the baron, 'that – resonance, that –'

'Boom!' expanded Uncle Jasper, instantly undoing all his careful shuffling by making Lady jump violently. It took all of Kia's efforts to reclaim Lady's attention. Uncle Jasper looked so annoyed at himself that Holly felt sorry for him, especially as he could see that he was the only one who did. Again Holly shook his head.

'It must be connected,' he agreed, 'but what on earth it was I can't imagine.' His eyes searched the skies for anything unusual, but he wasn't surprised when there was nothing out of the ordinary to be seen. The sound could, after all, have come from absolutely anywhere, even from out of the ground, and from any distance.

His thoughts went back to the calm sea and the warm sun, to the sailing ship and the peace of mind he had felt on it. Overall he decided that it was just as well he had solved it, as the temptation to say '1 Down' right now would probably have proved overwhelming. He forced himself to concentrate.

'It was certainly no natural phenomenon,' he concluded.

‘No, it was deliberate,’ murmured the captain, frowning at nothing in particular on the horizon. ‘And it found its intended target.’

He looked at the others defiantly, bracing himself for incredulity and protest, but found neither. Just unease. Emboldened, he carried on.

‘Call me paranoid, and I know you all do behind my back, but this is more conspiracy than theory. The team was the target, and Lady was only affected because she’s a member of the team. Maybe – probably – the most vulnerable member.’

None of the others could elaborate on this, but more tellingly, weren’t contradicting it either. A contemplative silence followed. Kia and Lady had also stopped talking, and even seemed to be listening in.

‘What about,’ the baron started, hesitantly, ‘what was it the General said? Something about a weapon?’

‘That’s right,’ agreed Holly, slowly. ‘A weapon that would bring about the team’s downfall.’

The captain looked smugly pleased – rather grotesquely so, given the prevailing mood.

‘There you go,’ he said. ‘Told you.’

‘Didn’t the General give this weapon a name?’ Holly asked, ignoring him.

‘Yes,’ nodded the baron, ‘or rather a number. Began with a four. Sticks in the memory, that sort of thing.’

‘Yes it does,’ said Holly, glad to be back in the familiar realm of numbers. ‘He called it a 4-18.’

Another pause for thought as they all pondered the possible numerical significance. Uncle Jasper had got a notepad out of one pocket and a propelling pencil out of another and was busily making various calculations. Holly was going through sequences of squares, primes and the Fibonacci series. Great Uncle Sid was substituting letters for numbers. The others were no less deep in thought, but it all seemed to be going nowhere until Kia broke the silence.

'Gentlemen,' she ventured, quietly, 'I don't know if this is being over-simplistic, but I think you should check the grid.' She shook a finger at Holly who had opened his mouth. 'But don't say the word,' she warned.

Lady had long since given up trying to understand Kia's explanations, but was still following the conversation eagerly enough.

'What word?' she wanted to know. 'Is it a four-letter one?'

'Oh yes,' declared Kia, solemnly. 'The worst one there is.'

Lady looked disapprovingly at Holly. Undeterred, he consulted his copy of the paper, where he noticed, with a chill down his spine, that 4 Down continued directly to 18 Down.

'4-18,' he muttered. Thrilled though he was at this discovery, he couldn't help feeling a little disappointed that the product of his application of higher mathematics had boiled down to a simple seven plus seven, that being the number of letters in each word.

He gave Kia an appreciative nod, but she was clearly in no mood to rejoice in her breakthrough, turning back to the matter of soothing Lady's still evident anxiety.

Knowing how important the solving of these clues, and thereby Lady's recovery, must be to Kia, Holly was touched by the faith she was showing in him, effectively handing him the reins and letting him get on with what he was there to do, while she got on with what she was best suited for. She was certainly a leader who knew how to delegate.

'So, 4 and 18, both Down,' he said, carefully so as not to be taken somewhere he was very sure he didn't want to go. He said it for the benefit of anyone who hadn't yet worked out the significance of the numbers. If anyone hadn't, they didn't show it. 'And the first one reads, "Regret having alien in entourage", seven letters.'

As with the last clue, Holly was annoyed and now a little scared that he couldn't see an immediate way in. He wondered whether the pressure was getting to him. He also wondered whether the clue was making a reference to the traitor they had been warned to look out for, and was then wondering how little trouble an alien would have, blending in with this particular entourage, when Great Uncle Sid grabbed him again, this time by the arm – firmly, but not as firmly as Holly would have imagined.

'Alien,' the old man whispered, forcefully. Initially Holly thought this might be some form of confession, before realising that it must refer to a code, unfortunately one that escaped him for the moment. He could see that his lack of comprehension was becoming hugely frustrating to Great Uncle Sid, who was now struggling to find another way of conveying his message.

'School alien,' he came up with at last, by way of an example. Holly still looked puzzled, but Uncle Jasper had cottoned on and was keen to help.

'Class,' he said to Holly in his deliberate way. 'Collection. Group.'

The old man nodded fervently at him, and then they both paused to look expectantly at Holly. Seeing that the penny still hadn't dropped, they tried again.

'Iron alien,' from Great Uncle Sid.

'Bases. Pedestals,' from Uncle Jasper.

Still no reaction from Holly, who was beginning to feel increasingly stupid, an assessment with which Great Uncle Sid was obviously in agreement, as he was about to communicate in some way when Kia intervened.

'We should be getting back,' she said quietly. 'You're going to have to hold the fort here, Great, while we sort this out.'

So saying, she moved the wrought iron table out of the way, pulled his chair over so that it was right next to Lady's and gently guided him into it. Then she knelt in front of Lady and took her hands again.

'We're just going to see if we can fix things,' she said, in as reassuring a voice as she could manage. 'We'll be back soon. In the meantime, this gentleman will stay and look after you.'

Lady, who had become slightly more agitated on hearing that Kia was about to leave, looked nervously at the old man with the sad, tender smile. Holly watched the anxiety slowly fade from her face, and even imagined he saw some hint of recognition in her eyes, followed by a faint smile in return. Quite what she'd make of him when he opened his mouth, Holly didn't dare guess. But for now at least, she was so captivated that Kia had no trouble slipping away and joining the others. She then herded them quietly towards the transparent house until the seated couple had their backs to them. Only then did she whisper to them to hang on to one another and allow Holly to utter his four-letter word.

CHAPTER TWENTY-THREE

Holly was sitting in his usual place on the sofa, pleasantly tired. He had had a tiring day, but was content in the knowledge that the worst of it was over and the remainder would be stress-free, barring the inevitable tussle over what dinner should be – firstly, whether it should be takeaway or cook-at-home, secondly, which country of origin or which style, depending on the answer to the first question, and finally, should it be the latter, which specific ingredients, and most importantly, who should make it.

Anna didn't have a usual place, the very concept being completely foreign to her, and on this occasion was sitting next to him, leaning back on the high armrest with her legs, crossed at the ankles, resting across his. She was reading the paper – *her* paper as he insisted on calling it – with exaggerated nonchalance, having just lost, yet again, the argument over whether they should get a dog. He knew it was an argument she let him win, that even she could see how impractical it would be with them both out at work all day. And yet she would bring the matter up at least once a week, and he was glad she did, because a victory served up on a plate was still a victory, and it made him smile, as it was making him smile right now. And he knew that she knew that he was smiling, even through the newspaper.

Resting in turn on her legs were the test papers he would have to mark by the morning. He had his green felt-tip pen ready in his hand. He had long since stopped using red. He thought green was less scathing and offered more encouragement.

There were two glasses of red wine in front of them on the coffee table, his already considerably more empty than hers. He always drank faster, if not always more, than she did, unless they were having cocktails, in which case hers barely had time to wet the inside of the glass.

From the hi-fi in the far corner came the serene opening horn melody of Haydn's Symphony No. 22, one of her favourites from her favourite composer, with the added bonus that it was nicknamed 'The Philosopher', the mention of which was normally enough to elicit at least a derisory snort from Holly. He didn't know whether it was the lot of every mathematician to have no time whatsoever for philosophy, but it was certainly his. And as Anna had long ago attended an evening class on the subject on a whim, she had no trouble, indeed took great pleasure, in setting him off by commenting dreamily on a particularly metaphysical development section, or declaring it a categorical imperative that she listen to a particular piece. Holly baiting, she called it, the only sport at which she excelled, by her own admission.

As he looked round, he couldn't imagine a more tranquil, idyllic scene. It was perfect. It was, of course, too perfect. And sure enough, when he actually opened his eyes, the reality was completely different.

The person sitting next to him on the sofa wasn't a relaxed Anna but a very agitated Kia.

'What on earth are you smiling about?' she asked incredulously, thus ensuring that he no longer was.

Haydn had also disappeared, to be replaced by the rather less soothing sound of the others bickering in the kitchen, apparently about what sort of frequency had brought about Lady's transformation back in the Chameleon Realm. Uncle Jasper was chanting hypnotically – 'boom, resonance, detonation, report, blast, peal, thunder,' – while Uncle Sid was trying to drown him out by repeating 'bus coins' over and over again, with the captain in turn trying to shut him up by agreeing that he too would have described the sound as subsonic but that they'd all got the idea by now, thank you.

The glasses of wine were similarly absent. Holly realised with some alarm that, far from finding their removal a relief, what he actually felt was disappointment, even feeling inclined to have a brandy, a desire that hadn't occurred to him for longer than he could remember. Fortunately his new-found paternalism surprised him again by raising its reclusive head, and he shuddered at the image of how he used to be, and how useless his old self would be to the team.

He toyed with the idea of discussing dinner with Kia anyway, if only to relieve some tension, but decided it would be inappropriate. In any case, Kia, having given up waiting for a response to her question, had withdrawn into herself, a picture of worry. Her eyes were tightly shut and she was clearly in no mood to discuss anything.

Left to his own devices for a moment, Holly thought he'd use the time wisely and looked at the crossword he was still obediently holding in an unnecessarily firm grip.

He noticed that they now had quite a few letters already of the other long Down solution, including a final M, which narrowed the field down considerably. Looking at the clue, 9 Down, he read 'Limited election for method of overindulgence (3-5,6)'.

Glancing at the letters already entered in the grid, he could see that the three-letter word had a W in the middle, the five-letter word started with a P and had an R in the middle and the six-letter word didn't have an I two from the end, ruling out the two most common endings in M, -ism and -ium. He was always surprised at how few people realised that the letters could provide as much of a clue as the clue itself.

Sure enough, putting all these pieces of information together, he decided that 'method' must be 'system', and that if it was an election then the middle word was likely to be 'party', after which it took him virtually no time at all to go through the fairly short list of three-letter words with a W at the centre and settle on 'two', giving him 'two-party system'.

Considering this possible answer, he found he could confirm it in three ways. Having only two political camps would indeed make it a limited election. Taken as a double celebration, it would certainly describe a method of overindulgence, given that Holly would already have considered a single party the height of hedonism. And of course it would explain why the only politicians who hadn't disappeared were either Labour or Tory.

His brightly coloured pen faltered over the grid. He was acutely aware of the power he was wielding, that it was his decision whether so many politicians deserved to reappear or remain in oblivion. Most of them, he thought, would have spent their entire careers in political oblivion anyway.

When he finally did commit the solution to paper, it wasn't in the name of democracy, but to ensure that the endeavours of the odious Director and his Merry Men had been in vain. He had eradicated them, and now he had eradicated their actions, and in as far as anything in the field of morals could ever be black and white, he briefly surrendered to the warm glow of having done a good thing.

He braced himself for another outraged challenge to this new smile that he quickly disposed of, but none came. Kia still had her eyes closed in a frown, her knees drawn up to her chin and her arms folded round her legs. He studied her for a moment, but she still presented him with more questions than answers. He reached over and touched her elbow – gently, but still making her jump.

'We'll get her back,' he said. He expected a reassuring smile or a nod of agreement, and got neither. But as she didn't say anything, he knew he had correctly guessed what she was thinking, and her lack of confidence only made him more resolute.

'Come on,' he said, hoping his determination was contagious. 'We've got work to do.'

Still she didn't move. Holly could see that this day was really getting to her, and he found the thought strangely comforting. He didn't like the idea that she would have to go through this every day. But the current events seemed to be extremely out of the ordinary, and he felt honoured to be a part of it – flattered, even. He wondered why he had been chosen for this particular day, but soon found this a fruitless line of enquiry, so pursued it no further.

Kia was finally pulling herself together.

'Boys!' she called over her shoulder. The bickering stopped and the four men shuffled in, Uncle Jasper bringing up the rear, limping more than ever. He didn't even make it into the room but remained in the doorway. Even his keys sounded subdued.

'Before we start, we'll check on the news,' she said, using the remote control to turn the television on. 'We may get some more information on that weapon. Other people may have been aff...'

By now an image had appeared on the screen. So many images had appeared to them before – the quirky, the bizarre, even the grotesque – all of which were instantly swept aside by the scene that greeted them now.

1 C	A	2 T	E	3 G	O	4 R	I	5 S	E	■	6 H	7 A	R	8 M
R	■	R	■	E	■		■		■	9 T	■		■	
10 A	G	A	I	N	S	T	■	11 L	A	W	L	O	R	D
F	■	M	■	E	■		■		■	O	■		■	
12 T	O	L	E	R	A	N	C	E	■	13 P	A	N	I	C
■	■	I	■	A	■		■		■	A	■	■	■	
14 P	A	N	E	L	■	15 E	X	T	O	R	T	16 I	O	N
E	■	E	■	S	■	■	■	■	■	T	■		■	
17 D		S		U		18		19	■	20 Y				
O	■	■	■	R	■		■		■	S	■		■	■
21 M		22 G		G	■	23				Y				24
E	■	A	■	E	■		■		■	S	■		■	
25 T	A	B	L	O	I	D	■	26 A	R	T	I	S	A	N
E	■	L	■	N	■		■		■	E	■		■	
27 R	E	E	K	■	28 A	R	I	T	H	M	E	T	I	C

CHAPTER TWENTY-FOUR

The channel that appeared was a twenty-four-hour news channel. Holly knew the uncles must have been the last to watch the TV, as he never bothered with the news channels. It always amazed him how little news they managed to cover. Murnaghan's Law, he called it, after the newsreader he associated it with – the observation that a news item expanded to fill the time available. Three stories, he decided, was their preferred amount, which they then proceeded to scroll round again and again. Today was making life particularly easy for them, as there appeared to be only one.

The image on the screen was shaky and was obviously being filmed from a helicopter. It was looking directly down on to a stretch of open, fairly calm water, in which could be seen a number of pale round objects in a group, each with a dark patch on the same side. Holly imagined at first that they were just floating on the top, but realised they didn't so much bob around on the waves as plough through them regardless. As the helicopter overtook them and zoomed in, the objects finally revealed themselves for what they were.

They were heads, eleven in number, almost spherical, perched on what could now be seen as broad shoulders. Also visible was the occasional flash of an arm as it broke water. The entire ensemble was of the same off-white colour, which seemed, from a close-up of the heads, to be a type of fur. This arrangement was only broken by the dark patches which turned out to be their faces, identical mask-like features totally devoid of expression. The head-swivelling, air-gulping manoeuvres displayed by experienced swimmers were entirely absent – the heads remained constant and the small horizontal mouths remained shut. The texture of their faces reminded Holly of a Brazil nut's shell.

The scene was so exotic, even alien, that Holly would have assumed these creatures to have been spotted messing about in their natural habitat in some remote watering hole, had it not been for their resolute progress in one definite direction, and the caption at the bottom of the screen, just above the 'Breaking News' scrolling headlines, which bore the words 'English Channel'.

As the helicopter maintained its gaze, the camera's unsteady movements seeming to mimic those of the waves it was looking at, the shell-shocked voice of the studio anchorman related, for the benefit of those who may have only just tuned in – rather conveniently, Holly thought – the facts of this story since the creatures had first been sighted.

This had been by some Russian sailors on a cargo ship on the river Volga at 08:45 GMT. They were slightly north of Volgograd, having just left that city on the way to Novgorod, when these things had suddenly appeared on the eastern shore, dived straight in, shimmered vaguely as they swam under the ship, causing it to sway alarmingly although no direct contact was made, only to reappear briefly at the opposite shore, and then vanish again into the distance.

The authorities had duly been notified, but the story had got no further, the official explanation being vodka-induced visions rather than actual sightings.

The next, and first credible, mass sighting had come more than three hours later. Coincidentally, this had also been at a river, this time the Dnieper just south of Kiev. The Ukrainians had taken the reports more seriously than the Russians, and within minutes the news had gone global. From then on sightings were being phoned in with increasing regularity and from all over the region, even as far north as Minsk, although these did indeed turn out to be vodka-induced visions.

By the time the more sober coordinates had been correlated, the path taken by the creatures turned out to be remarkably straight – 'practically geometric', as one American reporter put it. They were heading almost due west, with a slight leaning to the north. This had taken them from the Ukraine into Poland, where they had brushed the southern outskirts of Cracow.

It was from here that the people of the world had been shown their first glimpse of the marauders. Helicopters and planes had been in the air for a good two hours by now, but as the sheer speed of the creatures had been underestimated, they had been looking in the wrong places.

From then on they were tracked ceaselessly, being passed from one country's news agency to the next. So it was that the Poles handed the baton to the Czechs, who watched with relief as the route passed comfortably to the north of Prague.

It was soon after the next border crossing that their speed had changed noticeably. Their progress up until now had been impressive enough, given that they were negotiating forests and farmland, but once inside Germany it didn't take them long to latch on to the motorway system and step up a gear. Accidents were surprisingly few, the creatures proving to be astonishingly sure-footed, weaving through the traffic as expertly as a Parisian round the Arc de Triomphe, even on landing after vaulting the many bridges and overpasses.

The other result of this change of tactic was that at almost exactly 4 p.m., Bonn became the first major urban area to be affected by the visitors' presence. The authorities had hastily tried to erect some sort of roadblock, but this had proved no barrier whatsoever, and the city suffered extensive damage and a considerable number of casualties.

This in turn brought the animal rights groups into the frame, albeit very obviously only in England. The fatalities were collateral damage, they believed, and were in any case brought about unwittingly, even incidentally. The general European line seemed to be unanimously to shoot the creatures with something. The French hunting lobby was getting itchy fingers, and the Dutch were particularly vocal in their preference for the use of drugs, although whether on themselves or the animals wasn't quite clear.

Meanwhile the next scene of destruction was the heart of Brussels. There the powers that be had been given plenty of warning, but by the time disaster struck, the Flemings and the Walloons still hadn't decided on which language to use for arranging the defences, much less arrange the defences themselves.

And so it was that a mere half hour later the creatures crossed their most recent land border and, the odd Frenchman with his shotgun taking random potshots notwithstanding, reached the Channel relatively unopposed and dived in.

And that brought the story to the present time. That was as much as anyone knew. As to the creatures' motive and intended destination, they were still completely in the dark. The team, sitting in stunned silence in Holly's lounge, were all too aware of both.

In England, it appeared, all sorts of forces were being mobilised. The creatures' most likely route had been projected, given their current bearing and their previous deviation history, an uncomplicated reading of zero. This would take them, rather alarmingly, just north of the centre of London. Not having the team's insider knowledge, they saw no reason to suppose the route would end there, so their line had continued merrily on westwards.

The next area of significance, to their way of thinking, would be Ludlow. The people of this Shropshire market town had already polarised into two distinct camps.

The first one was convinced that their home was indeed the final destination, rejoicing in the confirmation that they were, as they had always suspected, living at the centre of the universe. They were busily designing 'Welcome to Ludlow' banners and had already worked out an itinerary taking in all the local sights and amenities.

The second was equally jubilant that their long-dormant castle was finally to be called into service to repulse someone other than the Welsh, and were equally busily investigating whether the cannon still functioned.

Back in Kent, all motorways into London had been evacuated. A huge army presence had been assembled on the north bank of the River Medway to meet the illegal aliens crossing it on the M2. So far, all they had encountered was a correspondingly large group of animal rights and non-violence campaigners. The police were currently trying to deal with fighting that had broken out between members of the League for Peaceful Solutions and a crowd of antiglobalisation activists who were convinced that the creatures were just part of a publicity stunt by some huge corporation.

The protest had been organised by a Liberal Democrat MP, whose very existence cheered Holly greatly.

'Lib Dem!' he declared, pointing at the screen and making everyone jump. The faces now looking at him betrayed no knowledge of what he was talking about.

'He's neither Labour nor Tory,' he elucidated, or thought he had. 'I solved it.' His confidence was suffering from a slow puncture. 'Two-party system.' He feebly waved his paper at them. Fortunately he was spared any more embarrassment, as at that moment the creatures could be seen reaching shore.

This was the first time the team had seen them in their entirety, and the windows of Holly's lounge rattled quietly at the simultaneous intakes of breath.

The thing that struck the team most was the sheer size of the newcomers. Emerging from the water in a town provided far easier comparisons than rocks and trees, and they dwarfed most of the houses on the seafront. The street lamps also made them far more visible, as the daylight was now starting to fade.

The next most noteworthy features were their faces, hard dark ovals in complete contrast in both colour and texture to the surrounding pale fur that, despite being waterlogged and plastered down as they climbed ashore, was already starting to dry. It seemed to Holly that they had bought a job lot of identical masks, giving them the aura of bank robbers or hitmen. He shuddered at the aptness of that image.

The way they moved also turned his stomach, a collective movement, as though they were all obeying the same remote control. Those at the front couldn't be said to be leading the others, they just happened to be ahead of them. And they all seemed to have an equal share in a homing instinct that allowed for no doubt as to which way they should go to reach their goal. To reach him. He briefly imagined that they'd been able to pick up his scent halfway round the world, but despite the events of the day so far, his core belief in rationality wouldn't allow the possibility.

The last thing the viewers noticed before the creatures took off again was their feet, which were quite long, a cross between a kangaroo's feet and a clown's shoes. Holly just had time to connect the design of these feet to the astonishing speed of their owners before that speed was demonstrated again, although Holly was surprised at how slowly they accelerated as they gained momentum. All the same, it only seemed to take them seconds to find the deserted motorway, making it much easier for them to reach maximum velocity and resume the appearance of the unstoppable force that everyone, except the team, had been avidly watching all afternoon.

CHAPTER TWENTY-FIVE

The motorway, however, was the wrong one. The news presenter, still only a voice over the uninterruptible images, was explaining an unexpected deviation from the predicted course of events in a tone that betrayed the general feeling that marauding monsters making their way at breakneck speed across the entire continent of Europe to land on our shores was one thing, but that our boffins making such a schoolboy error in their calculations was quite another.

It turned out that they had omitted, unbelievably, to take account of the effects of the tide or the currents, and that the creatures had been swept off course to reach dry land not at Dover, as predicted, but at Folkestone. Consequently, they were now to be seen streaking up the M20, not the M2. This caused consternation among the military, who found themselves entrenched in the wrong trench, but jubilation among the animal rights campaigners, at least until they realised they wouldn't be getting their close encounter with the recipients of their good intentions.

In Holly's lounge, one good intention was about to be replaced with another. Kia had seen enough.

‘Priorities,’ she said, with as much conviction as she could muster in an effort to persuade herself as well as everyone else. ‘We have to deal with this. Lady will have to wait.’ By now her conviction had wilted, and her voice trailed off.

‘Thaw?’ Uncle Sid was the first to express the outrage that Holly could see was shared by the whole team – even by himself, he realised.

‘People are dying, Uncle Sid,’ Kia said, quietly but firmly. The questioning of her decision had made her focus on it, making her more convinced that it was the right one. ‘That’s the bottom line. And that’s why we’re here.’

She looked round at Uncle Sid, who still looked like he was going to explode with indignation. The captain was taking a few surreptitious steps away from him so as not to be caught in the impending blast.

‘It’s what Lady would have done,’ Kia went on, knowing that was her trump card.

At Uncle Sid’s other side, Uncle Jasper, although clearly sharing his companion’s sentiment, was as always the quicker to accept the reality of the situation. He put a hand on Uncle Sid’s shoulder, but Uncle Sid brusquely turned aside, unfortunately in the direction of the captain, who took a couple more hurried paces backwards, stepping on the baron’s foot in the process.

Kia stood up, followed instinctively by Holly.

‘Quickly,’ she said to him, ‘search the clues. Look for anything – creature-y.’

Holly scanned the remaining clues, glad that he’d followed his usual habit of crossing out the numbers of the clues that had been solved – such a habit, indeed, that he hadn’t been aware that he had done so today, in spite of everything. It meant he could immediately discount the first eight, after which the second one available caught his eye.

' "Unknown site swarming with monsters",' he offered, hopefully. 'Five letters.' Kia nodded.

'Has to be worth a go,' she said. 'Any ideas?'

Holly looked at it for a moment, then shook his head.

'Nothing immediate. You?' he asked the baron.

'Not yet. Trying to think what an unknown site might be.'

'You buying a round?' suggested the captain.

'S-I-T-E,' corrected the baron, showing the captain the spelling on the page. He shrugged. 'Otherwise a sound proposal.'

'Alright, what about the other clue. Maybe that'll help,' Kia persisted. Consulting her own copy, she read out, ' "Tried buds out, getting upset". That's a nine-letter word.'

' "Out" could be an anagram indicator,' Holly mused, 'and "Tried buds" is nine letters. Uncle Sid?'

The target of his query was still glaring at the carpet with his back to everybody, looking for all the world like a naughty boy told to stand in the corner. If he had heard the question, he wasn't showing it.

'Uncle Sid, we don't have time,' Kia implored, watching live coverage of the creatures crossing the M25, the London orbital road. 'Lady doesn't have time. The sooner we deal with this, the sooner we can concentrate on helping her. It doesn't help, being moody.'

'Disturbed,' came the muffled response.

'You can say that again,' muttered the captain.

'Alright, disturbed,' conceded Kia, exasperatedly. 'Let's not quibble.'

Uncle Sid finally turned to face them, and prodded the paper Uncle Jasper was clutching against his chest, almost making Uncle Jasper lose his balance.

'Disturbed,' he breathed menacingly, staring at Kia, who in turn gave Holly a questioning look.

'Anagram of "Tried buds",' he confirmed. ' "Disturbed," meaning "upset". Thank you.'

Uncle Sid graciously acknowledged the acknowledgement as Holly entered the new word into his grid. As soon as he had finished, Kia grabbed his arm.

'OK, let's go,' she said, her eyes shining. Holly automatically tried to pull back, but she wouldn't allow it.

'Are you serious?' he demanded.

'Best way to solve a situation is from the inside. Isn't that right, Uncle Jasper?'

Uncle Jasper's reaction was far from supportive. Kia held her free hand out to the others anyway.

'Who's coming?' she challenged.

'Too right!' blurted out the captain, grabbing her hand, and then in response to the looks of surprise and trepidation around him, 'Oh, come on! Seeing those things? It's a once in a lifetime opportunity.'

'And quite possibly an end of a lifetime opportunity,' protested the baron half-heartedly, grabbing the captain's sleeve anyway.

That just left the uncles. Uncle Jasper shook his head with a look of horror, but Uncle Sid, clearly galvanised into action by the thought of dealing with this problem as fast as possible so as to go on to more pressing matters, managed to latch on to both Kia's hand and the arm of Uncle Jasper, who resisted as little as the baron had done.

'So, Mr Holly,' said Kia, with obvious pride in her team, 'where are we going?'

It was now Holly's turn to concede, which he did

considerably more slowly than the others. Eventually, seeing there was no alternative, he looked down at his paper and located the relevant unsolved clue. Even then, he couldn't bring himself to name it, pausing first to look into the eyes of each person making this disjointed chain that reminded Holly of a diagram of a molecule.

Reassured by seeing, among the different cocktails of emotions, a common ingredient of determination, he whispered, '20 Across.'

Shap. Slight nausea. Drop in temperature. Chilly wind. Outside. Dark, but lots of lights. Soft under foot. Grass. Hum of traffic. Sound of people, lots of people, but quiet, expectant, like an audience in an auditorium as the lights go down for a concert. Strange building rising up twenty feet ahead, rounded, sloping. Holly recognised it, but couldn't place it.

It was Uncle Sid who pinpointed their location.

'One word,' he said, pointing off to Holly's right, 'no loft.'

Holly prided himself on being good at anagrams, and would have loved the chance to rise to the challenge, but Logic the Dictator dictated that, time being of the essence, it would be a lot quicker simply to look in the direction indicated. Sure enough, when he did so, he found he was looking across the river at the Tower of London.

Forgetting momentarily why they were there, Holly felt exhilarated at finding himself in the heart of the capital, in an area he hadn't visited in a very long time. Technically speaking, he hadn't ever been to this particular spot, as this side of the Thames, the southern shore, had been redeveloped fairly recently. He had an idea this part of the Embankment was called the Queen's Walk, and then remembered that the previously unidentifiable building was in fact the London mayor's new office. Like so many of London's new buildings, its shape had generated a nickname, although Holly wasn't sure what it was – the Sliced Lemon, was it, or maybe the Headlamp. To him, it had more the air of an Easter Island statue, looking implacably across at its considerably older neighbour.

Looking to the right of the eleventh-century stronghold on the other side of the river, Holly marvelled at the even more imposing vision that is Tower Bridge, its four towers – the two large inner towers framing the central part of the bridge that opened to let the larger ships through, and the two outer ones, less than half the size, that marked the ends of the suspension sections – displayed in full theatrical lighting.

The high walkway across the two central towers reminded Holly that this was yet another place he had meant to visit, a lifetime ago.

The entire group had by now wandered off the manicured patch of grass on to the wide paved area and over to the stone wall of overlapping blocks that ran along the edge of the river. They all seemed similarly affected by their new location, looking wide-eyed in every direction without saying a word. Even Uncle Jasper, now hopping on his right leg rather than putting any weight on his other foot, did so almost without wincing.

The crowd they could still hear mumbling amongst themselves were all between them and the bridge, and all facing it. That must be why nobody reacted to seeing six people suddenly appear out of thin air, Holly surmised, unless being able to come and go unnoticed was another one of the new rules of this place.

What snapped the members of the team out of tourist mode, making them follow the gaze of the murmuring throng, was a change of sound.

The wall they were now leaning against ran all the way to the first of the bridge's small towers. From there, looking to the right, they could clearly see a long, uninterrupted stretch of the bridge's approach road, as the only houses along it were on the far side. This motley collection of houses, a couple of dozen or so, represented the styles of several centuries – even the twentieth, Holly noted ruefully. It was where this road disappeared from view behind a building Holly took to have been a Victorian school, now probably luxury flats, that the change of sound came.

First came the distant sound of car horns – some sporadic, either in anger or as a warning, others, increasing in number and proximity, continuous tones. Holly found these more disturbing, but didn't have much time to ponder why they weren't stopping.

This was followed by a growing cacophony of general destruction, a melee of smashes, crunches, shatters and screeches. Holly thought it was worse, not being able to see what was causing it. But he was wrong.

Then a new noise joined the crescendo, adding a mechanical drone – two helicopters, circling each other in a slow, stately dance. The media had arrived, the eyes of the world.

The last change was human, and it was screaming, in all conceivable registers. Unsettling as this was, it was only a few seconds before the reasons for this vocalised terror leapt into view.

The street lamps seemed to make the fur glow, the dark oval faces thrown into even more relief. The television pictures hadn't done them justice. From the team's horizontal perspective, even with the river of heads in front of them, the creatures' full stature could be appreciated, the taller ones breaching the skyline of the buildings behind them.

The river of heads suddenly burst its banks, the people having unanimously decided that the very thing they had come to see, they didn't want to see after all. The team clung firmly to the stone wall as the yelling crowd fled past them, desperate not to be swept away in the flood.

Considering their speed, the creatures moved in a very close formation, further testament to their agility and coordination. In just a few seconds all eleven reached the first tower, effortlessly ducking under the arch that was barely half their height as though they were negotiating an assault course.

Immediately, though, there was a change of pace. They continued through the second arch, but Holly felt he was watching a film that was slowing down. By the time the front runner alone had passed through the third arch, they came to a complete standstill. It was as if someone had pushed the pause button, but for the hysterical crowd still firmly in fast forward.

After a brief pause of immobility, eleven heads started turning simultaneously, the rest of their bodies remaining perfectly motionless, and the heads continued turning until they were all facing the transfixed team. Or – to be more pedantic, as Holly now was – at him. If Holly's natural response to stressful situations was to freeze, he was now in cryogenic stasis. He was utterly paralysed and utterly vulnerable, and he knew it. He was in the middle of questioning why his legs wouldn't run, why his vocal cords wouldn't scream, why these demonic things didn't just get it over with, and most of all why he'd come to the location of this clue in the first place, when something wholly unexpected happened.

The front runner, alone on the third section of the bridge, where the suspension cables were so low they almost touched the road, suddenly jolted and crashed over the side on to the shore in front of the Tower, having received a full-size bulldozer full in the face.

1 C	A	2 T	E	3 G	O	4 R	I	5 S	E	■	6 H	7 A	R	8 M
R	■	R	■	E	■		■		■	9 T	■		■	
10 A	G	A	I	N	S	T	■	11 L	A	W	L	O	R	D
F	■	M	■	E	■		■		■	O	■		■	
12 T	O	L	E	R	A	N	C	E	■	13 P	A	N	I	C
■	■	I	■	A	■		■		■	A	■	■	■	
14 P	A	N	E	L	■	15 E	X	T	O	R	T	16 I	O	N
E	■	E	■	S	■	■	■	■	■	T	■		■	
17 D	I	S	T	U	R	18 B	E	19 D	■	20 Y				
O	■	■	■	R	■		■		■	S	■		■	■
21 M		22 G		G	■	23				Y				24
E	■	A	■	E	■		■		■	S	■		■	
25 T	A	B	L	O	I	D	■	26 A	R	T	I	S	A	N
E	■	L	■	N	■		■		■	E	■		■	
27 R	E	E	K	■	28 A	R	I	T	H	M	E	T	I	C

CHAPTER TWENTY-SIX

In Wapping, the mood had started to change almost the minute the media circus had packed up and left. The gigantic little boy hadn't even looked up as they departed, preoccupied as he was with a scaled-up torch, the companion piece to the oversized binoculars. He had delighted in making the dot of light dance on the walls and ceiling, and had shown an inordinate fascination in the on/off switch and his sudden ability to cause light to come and go. He had then shone it in his own eyes, recoiling at first, finally turning it into a game, squealing happily every time and screwing up his eyes. Fearing for his son's eyesight, his father had successfully taught him, by demonstration, how covering up the light with his fingers made them glow red. He had immediately regretted it, questioning the wisdom of asking a three-year-old to close his fist round a 500-watt light bulb, but the youngster seemed genuinely unaffected by the heat, and undeniably enchanted at the effect.

After a while, however, it was noticed that he had lost all interest in this new toy, which was unusual. The lad was not known to have a short attention span, in fact quite the reverse, occasionally bordering on the obsessive. Soon his lack of interest in anything at all became the cause of some concern.

Not that he was showing any signs of boredom. His face and eyes were as alert as ever. He gave the impression of someone intently following an argument or narrative on the radio through headphones, inaudible to anyone but himself. But there were no headphones, the specially made pair he had been presented with earlier in the year having been summarily rejected. He didn't trust them.

Then began what can only be described as a vigil, the boy standing by the windows that ran along the top of the wall at the front of the warehouse, looking south across the Thames. Occasionally he would call his new binoculars into use, reassuring his parents briefly that he had regained some interest in the day's festivities. But eventually they had to concede that he wasn't so much playing with them as utilising them.

The fact that he was refusing food, or more accurately that he was ignoring all entreaties with him to have some, was initially underplayed, at least by his father, put down to the enormous amount of cake he had seen off earlier. But this, too, had to be added to the worry list by the time even a large bowl of his beloved grated strong Cheddar couldn't gain his attention.

As the light started to fail outside, so did his composure inside. Far from needing a rest after standing for so long, he began to pace up and down, every now and then muttering 'pom, pom, pom, pom, pom' to himself, making it sound march-like, yet strikingly not in sync with his own footsteps, all the while with his eyes fixed unwaveringly on the opposite side of the river.

His despairing parents had no idea what to make of all this. They did at least have the presence of mind to dismiss the theory of the child's behavioural therapist, who suggested the boy was suffering from the trauma of the realisation that he had reached the ripe old age of three, and the thoughts of his impending mortality brought on by that realisation. Given that this was the same therapist who had recommended the father accompany his son in the back of the van on the aborted move to the country, a plan that had resulted in the father having to take a month off work as his ribs fused back together, it was a constant mystery to him why this woman was still involved, despite his numerous best efforts to have her replaced, or better still, simply removed. His wife had intervened each time, claiming that their son relied on the woman, that she represented some stability in his otherwise disjointed life, to which he had always responded that the boy saw the same people and the same surroundings every day of his life, how much stability did she think he was lacking. But to no avail. And it was as he was pondering what his next approach to this eviction could be, that the focus of all their lives suddenly turned and spoke to them, the first time he had even acknowledged their existence in a number of hours.

'Doan worry,' he said, imitating his mother, including her tone of addressing a child. From his great height, he was speaking down to them in both senses of the phrase. 'Oi haff go to work now.' Another sentence familiar to him, this time from his father. Confident that he had explained himself enough, he went over to the huge door, opened it and stepped into the courtyard.

A cold wind forced its way inside, and the boy's mother stifled an instinctive appeal to her son to put on a coat. He was at least fully dressed, wearing black Velcro-fastening shoes, brown corduroy trousers – his little old man's outfit, his mother called it – all specially made, and a knitted jumper, one of the day's gifts, which was pale blue with a picture of a mischievous elephant over the word 'Trouble'. This was an in-joke, being his nickname, particularly among the staff, to which he always delighted in taking offence. 'Oi not trouble,' he would protest, beaming proudly. He had taken to the jumper immediately, grinning back at the elephant for ages as though he were looking into a mirror before actually putting the jumper on.

Having left the door open, his entourage could see him standing just outside, scanning the area. There was a lean-to covering an assortment of bicycles, tricycles and scooters, all now too small, and the place was littered with balls of varying size but uniformly gaudy. There was a mini trampoline with a raised bar for holding on to, also severely outgrown, not that he had used it much, having once fallen off, plus a large number of the plastic workman's tools he loved to use, including a bright yellow hard hat. But his restless eyes finally settled on his latest and still gleaming acquisition sitting peacefully yet powerfully in the corner, his very own bulldozer.

He went over to it, causing his intent spectators to move to the windows overlooking his play area in order to maintain their view of him, but calmly and without panic. They knew he couldn't leave the courtyard.

After a brief but worrying pause staring at his new toy, seemingly back in his previous trance, he suddenly picked it up and tucked it under his arm, producing a gasp among his audience. They had expected him only to be able to push it around like a toy car. Despite being all too aware of his ever-increasing strength, this came as a shock.

Bulldozer firmly in place, he walked over to the long wall at the back of the courtyard that separated it from the street behind, casting an almost professional eye over it as though calculating an estimate for work to be done.

Apparently satisfied with his inspection, he lifted his head and shouted, clearly for the benefit of any people who might be on the other side, 'Oi go break wall now!'

This caused a little more concern from the viewers inside the house, but they still felt no need for active intervention, whatever that might entail. It was a high brick wall that certainly gave the impression of being an impenetrable barrier. The general consensus was that his most likely tactic would be to strike the wall with the bulldozer in a vain attempt to damage it.

In the event, the bulldozer was no more than a passenger. The boy simply stuck his free hand straight through the wall, causing a large section of it to come cascading down, for all the world as if its builders had forgotten to use mortar between the bricks. As luck would have it, there hadn't been anybody on the pavement outside to hear his considerate warning, and the demolition had been so gently done that the falling bricks hadn't even reached the cars that were parked alongside, which suffered no more than a coating of dust.

The cause of this destruction stuck his head through the large breach in the wall and surveyed his handiwork with the same professional air as before. Visibly content with the result, he gingerly stepped through, still clutching his now redundant plaything, surprisingly sure-footed on the pile of loose masonry. Without a moment's doubt about which way to go, or a single backwards glance at his now panic-stricken entourage, he disappeared from their view.

Finding it awkward to convey himself and his cargo along the narrow pavement, he crossed into the road at the earliest opportunity. Being a quiet area, he encountered little traffic, and avoiding the pavements meant he posed less of a danger to the numerous pedestrians who were striding about with such purpose at this time of day that amazingly few even noticed him. The cars he did meet received a contrite 'sorry' for causing such obvious distress to the gaping motorists as he hurried past.

The first widespread interest he generated, although he was oblivious to it, was when his route took him to a corner of St Katherine's Dock, a redeveloped area full of moored yachts and restaurants where the preferred gait was a gentle, observant stroll rather than a relentless, head down rush. The low murmur of private conversation became a higher pitched buzz of general excitement, and the flash flurry of cameras and camera phones gave the boy the appearance of running through an electrical storm.

He ran across a short cantilevered bridge over a lock and took a sharp left, which brought him to a wide paved area right on the bank of the river in front of a large hotel building and the sudden dramatic appearance of Tower Bridge. Another thing he was oblivious to was the fact that he arrived at this spot at exactly the same time as Holly and his companions materialised diagonally opposite, being on the other side of both the river and the bridge.

Having reached this spot, the child seemed unsure what to do next. His instinct had brought him this far but now left him to it. He started walking tentatively towards Tower Bridge, passing groups of bewildered tourists, more flashes, his industrial cargo still nestling comfortably under his arm. The constant hubbub around him, created by his appearance, meant that it took him longer to notice the sounds of mayhem that Holly was immediately aware of, but as they became more noticeable the crowd grew uneasy and silent, making it easier for him to identify which direction the sounds were coming from. As he looked towards the other side of the river, he saw a blurred movement through the arch of the bridge's furthest tower and froze.

The blur turned out to be an off-white furry creature that the boy would have found cute and cuddly but for the scary face and the menacing, purposeful stride, stooping to get under the arch, then rising to its full height, eventually dwarfing the entire tower.

By the time this apparition had repeated the manoeuvre twice and had emerged from the third archway, it had been joined on the bridge by a number of others, roughly similar in size and shape, identical in expression, and they had all started slowing down.

The boy by now had reached the bridge, and the first creature passed him before they all came to a complete standstill. Then they simultaneously turned their heads to look at something on the far side of the bridge. The one at the front had to turn its head so much that the lad could clearly see its face. And it was then that he launched the only missile he had to hand.

CHAPTER TWENTY-SEVEN

The creature fell lifeless to the ground in front of a sign giving directions to the Tower via Dead Man's Hole. The bulldozer bounced off the side of the bridge and fell into the water by the wall, where most of it remained visible due to the low tide, twinkling in the bright artificial lighting.

Holly watched it come to rest, and continued to stare at it. The paralysing fear he had been feeling wasn't so much replaced by confusion at this mystifying event as heightened by it, if that were possible. Not until the other creatures slowly reacted, again as a unit, turning their heads back towards this new development and away from him, did he feel he was regaining any control over his limbs, even if it was only to allow them to tremble.

But this control was immediately in danger of being lost, as indeed, he felt, was his sanity, when he saw what looked like, but surely wasn't, a boy of tender years and impossible size clamber determinedly on to the bridge from the far side to the spot where the felled creature had drawn its last breath, give his victim's companions his sternest look and shout 'Go way!' at the top of his considerable voice.

Only when Holly tried to figure out why he was associating the boy with the word 'adorable', not a way he normally described children, certainly not in recent years, did he remember that they had seen him before, on television, and that 'adorable' had been Kia's assessment. Glancing over at her horror-stricken face now, he thought 'abominable' might be nearer the mark, but whether she was looking at the boy or the creatures, he couldn't tell.

Back on the bridge, the situation could only be described as a stand-off, the boy clenching his fists and giving his adversaries his best frown. His expression was a three-year-old's idea of resolute and defiant, in other words, petulant. The recipients, having no variation of expression, were having to rely on poise to convey menace, which it did remarkably effectively. Crouched down so as to be able to see their juvenile obstacle through the arches, their backs also arched, they appeared to be on the point of pouncing.

Relieved no longer to be the focus of the creatures' attention, Holly could feel that he had now fully regained physical control of his legs, but had lost any compulsion to use them. Like his companions, he could sense, he was now riveted by fascination rather than paralysis.

What he was not aware of was that the whole team, himself included, were slowly leaning forward in exactly the same way as the creatures on the bridge, yet when the creatures, or at least the five or six in the middle section of the bridge, finally did launch themselves forward, the team did the opposite, recoiling as though slapped in the face. Kia even let out an involuntary shriek, immediately covering her mouth with her hand, as the young boy disappeared under a mound of fur.

The vacancies left by the assailants in the middle section of the bridge were immediately filled by their remaining companions, giving the impression, by now characteristic, of a well-rehearsed drill. Once in place they froze, their unwavering focus on the commotion ahead.

The sounds of that commotion were all coming from the boy. There was a constant stream of grunts and shrieks, punctuated by the regular admonishing cry of 'No!' and the occasional 'Dop it!'. All that could be seen of him at first was the odd blurred fist, the scene resembling a catfight, the fur literally flying. As he got more of a purchase on the creatures, having more success in pushing them away, the team caught glimpses of pale blue sleeves and even a black shoe. Finally, having apparently raised himself on one knee, he managed in one swiping movement to free himself of all of them, flinging them in every direction. One of them crashed against the huge tower in front of the boy, bouncing off and landing deftly on its feet. Two of them were thrown against the suspension cables where they remained, watching him malevolently like spiders in a web.

There was a pause as all the combatants regained their breath. The boy stumbled to his feet, his hair even more tousled than usual. The members of the team were shocked at the jagged tears in his trousers, and amazed to see that the only casualty of this last skirmish was the elephant on his jumper which had been cruelly dissected, some of it missing altogether as frayed shreds of knitting hung down, resulting in the jumper now bearing the word 'rouble'. Also revealed was why they had only seen one shoe flailing about, as the other was now visible lying on its side a few feet away.

The young lad was panting and glaring at his adversaries, giving them the extruded bottom lip treatment again.

‘Not,’ he forced through his teeth between gasps, ‘happy.’

The creatures he had been fighting could now easily be distinguished from the rearguard on the other side of the tower, as they were missing large patches of fur, revealing a skin that turned out to be a painful shade of pink, giving them a distinctly mangy look. Any last vestiges of cute teddy bear appeal they may have had were now completely lost, and surely only the most delusional and blinkered animal lover could have come up with anything to say in their defence.

Coincidentally, just such a person had made her way on to the bridge and was now walking down the middle of the road between the two central towers, bearing a placard that read ‘HANDS OFF OUR FURRY COUNTERPARTS’. The counterparts themselves gave no sign that they had even registered her presence.

It was precisely her constant ability to come up with slogans that were heaving with a snigger factor to which she was herself completely ignorant that had made her weary companions give her the wrong time to meet the minibus they had hired to take them to the M2 protest site, thus ensuring that they had a fifty-mile head start. Undeterred and without considering for a moment that the mix-up could possibly have been anything other than an honest mistake, she and her placard had felt drawn to the river and found themselves at the front of the crowd that had waited so diligently to catch the briefest glimpse of the visitors before running away screaming. She alone not only stood firm at their arrival but even leapt for joy, shouting ‘Thank you for coming!’ and similarly welcoming phrases, her joy reaching fever pitch as they seemed to hear her, slow to a halt and turn their heads in what she thought was her direction.

Her ecstasy instantly switched to indignation and fury at the appearance of the bulldozer, and the ensuing battle galvanised her into action. From her front row position on the embankment, she raced through the tunnel under the road and ran up the stairs, tiptoeing on each step. Once on the bridge itself, she marched ostentatiously along the dotted white line in the middle of the road, loudly chanting the words she was holding aloft at an angle that would make them easy for the helicopter cameras to make out. The message that these poor creatures should not be oppressed had to get out, and the fact that it wasn't the military attacking them, as had been predicted, but actually they who were assaulting a three-year-old boy wasn't going to dampen her zeal.

Her arrival at the central section of the bridge coincided with the brief cessation of hostilities beyond the next arch, and for a while the only sound that could be heard was her mantra, shouted encouragingly at the oblivious creatures.

It was as she reached the exact midpoint of the bridge that the creatures launched their next onslaught. The boy seemed to have learnt from the earlier attack and was ready for them. This time he stood his ground and managed to stay on his feet, his face screwed up and his eyes almost completely shut under the barrage of blows. And as he fended them off, he was making sure that they ended up in front of him.

Eventually, when the right moment presented itself, he made a sudden move forward, forming a one-man rugby scrum, forcing all of his opponents into the archway, his arms working furiously to force all the flailing furry limbs through the inadequate opening.

The sight of half a dozen of these creatures bursting out of the archway in front of her stopped the protester in mid chant, but what nearly made her drop her placard was the sight of the remaining four, until now utterly motionless, simultaneously rocketing into the air around her. Two of them took up new positions hanging off either end of one of the suspended walkways, while the other two jumped straight through the gap between the two walkways and landed on top, peering intently down, barely visible against the dark sky.

Buoyed by the headway he had made, the youngster drove onwards, apparently intent on forcing the intruders back to the southern shore of the river. The tornado of limbs reached the centre of the bridge, sending the increasingly vocal activist scurrying to the pavement on the western side. Moments later, a well-timed swing of the lad's right arm found the sweet spot of the creature on that side, launching it on to the wall of the bridge where it thrashed crazily, trying to regain its balance. Its arm in turn then caught the hapless protester full on, jettisoning her towards the enthralled team, holding her placard horizontally above her as though in a vain attempt to hang-glide back to dry land.

Before she had a chance to hit the water, the swaying creature lost its battle with gravity and toppled mutely over the edge. It would have entered the river before her, had it not first made contact with the base of the tower that jutted out just above the waterline, striking its head with a sickening crack followed by the exaggerated splash of a belly flop.

Its only movements thereafter were caused by the currents. It loitered, floating face down by the stone pillar, just long enough for the struggling activist, who couldn't swim, to catch up and grab hold. The team watched the bedraggled woman and her lost cause spinning slowly under the bridge and out of sight.

CHAPTER TWENTY-EIGHT

Holly had been utterly spellbound by the events on and under the bridge, but the spell was now broken by a sharp pain in his left arm, a pain that felt so appropriate to the violence he was watching that he thought at first he might be identifying vividly with the beleaguered little boy. Then he very briefly had the idea that it might be the onset of a heart attack, an idea he greeted with surprisingly little concern, before realising that the pain was actually caused by Kia's nails digging in through his shirt sleeve. The look of horror on her face had remained unchanged, and however evenly matched the fight generally appeared, the sight of the young lad taking an undeniable battering was becoming too much for her.

'Do something!' she screamed at him, shaking him by the arm now, causing a considerable rise in pain level. He let himself be shaken, thinking maybe the pain was a deliberate ploy on her part to get him to focus his mind, but one look at her told him that she was beyond doing anything deliberate.

He knew that it was indeed up to him to do something, that it was somehow in his power to make the whole thing go away, to end the suffering of the poor boy, of Kia and particularly of his left arm – even of the creatures, who were after all only obeying some irresistible instinct. But he still couldn't tear himself away from what was happening on the bridge.

Despite the unwavering ferocity of his opponents, the boy was still making slow progress. He had left some way behind him an amorphous, occasionally twitching mound of fur that Holly deduced consisted of two of the creatures from the fact that the two that had been hanging from the walkways had immediately dropped down to take their places.

The boy then managed to repeat his previous manoeuvre, picking just the right moment to drive his relentless foe through the arch under the second main tower and on to the final third of the bridge, once more flanked by suspension cables.

In doing so, the lad sustained a particularly stomach-turning blow to the head, which Holly had to admit caused him mixed feelings, as it made Kia finally release his arm in order to return both her hands to her mouth.

It was also the final straw that made Holly able at last to look away. He studied his companions in an effort to regain some sort of composure.

The captain had the look of a child taken to see his first pantomime. The baron's worried eyes couldn't decide between the bridge and Kia. Uncle Jasper's boiler suit looked luminous in the artificial light, his arms hanging by his sides, making the odd involuntary motion in frustration. Uncle Sid's bony, bare arms were considerably more animated, engrossed as they were in shadow-boxing.

'Jet flab,' he could be heard muttering through his teeth, 'jet flab.'

Unobserved by Holly, it was precisely such a left jab from the infant pugilist that sent another unfortunate creature careering into the lattice of suspension cables, where it got its neck caught. After a brief, valiant but ultimately futile struggle, it came to rest, hanging limply over the far side of the bridge, its feet barely above the water.

This brought into play the final two non-combatants who had been watching from above like a couple of gargoyles. All six of the remaining creatures now formed a swirling shell around the young boy. The battle was at its most evenly matched, and it seemed to be a matter of who would tire first.

But before Holly could clear his mind enough even to begin to think constructively, his attention was indeed drawn back to the bridge, this time by a new sound. Above the erratic drum roll of the fight and the ever-present drone of the helicopters that washed in and out like slow-motion waves breaking on a beach, a woman's voice could be heard. It was a lower voice than that of the protester and carried infinitely more emotion.

Looking round, it didn't take Holly long to spot her. She had run on to the bridge following the same path the boy had taken, and was now pulling up just before the last tower that separated her from the violent skirmish ahead. A man was running some way behind her, visibly struggling to keep up.

Holly and the team had been slowly and unwittingly advancing on the bridge all this time, but the distance to the woman still meant that Holly couldn't make out her face. Recalling images they had seen earlier on the television, however, he was in no doubt that the distinctive red hair belonged to the boy's mother, and he had no trouble remembering that face, with its equally distinctive blend of pride and sadness.

'Goggy, don't!' she was shouting. 'Please! Goggy! Stop it! *Stop* it!'

Pausing just long enough to see that her words were having no effect on her son, Holly turned to Kia, whose face still consisted only of her eyes and her hands. As soon as she caught his look, though, she knew he was on to something and finally took her hands away – unfortunately for Holly, just so that she could grab his arm again.

'You know something,' she said, almost accusingly. 'What is it? Can you stop this?'

He put his hand over hers and it had the effect he'd hoped it would, reassuring her enough to loosen her grip. Then he looked back at the little boy, or at least at the odd glimpse he could get of him amid the furry maelstrom, and squinted.

'It couldn't be,' he muttered in a tone that said he knew it could. 'Surely.'

The wall they had all been inching along was studded periodically by short, fat stone pillars, each with a slightly taller lamp post crowned with a spherical opaque shade that gave a ghostly white light. Holly gently disengaged himself from Kia's grip and went and sat on the pavement with his back to one of these pillars, facing away from the bridge, with his legs straight out in front of him, just as he had on the ship. The resemblance was not lost on him, and once again he felt a pang of regret at having disposed of a potential source of comfort.

He did find some comfort, however, in the fact that not only could he no longer see the demented goings-on on the bridge, but also that they could no longer see him. He was also relieved to find that the light from the white globe was perfectly adequate for him to be able to read the clues on the paper he now held in front of him. The others joined him in a circle, squatting or sitting cross-legged, except for Uncle Sid who remained standing, his arms mirroring, as though remote-controlled, the all-in wrestling moves he was powerless to stop watching.

Holly decided it would be quicker to look at the grid first, and soon found what he was looking for.

'There it is,' he said triumphantly. 'I thought so.'

He beckoned to the others to come closer. He thought it highly unlikely that the subjects of the clues would be able to hear him above the considerable background noise, but he wasn't taking any chances. He tapped the relevant clue.

'Here,' he explained, redundantly. 'It's not actually the clue that brought us here, it's the next one, and it's on the next line, but I remembered the unusual letters already in the grid. Five-letter word, and the clue reads "Giant cat collects silver".'

There was a pause as minds went to work, and as always Kia's was the first to reach a conclusion, one that made her look round in alarm.

'Oh no,' she cried in panic. 'Don't tell me there's a giant cat on the way as well?'

'A giant cat burglar,' suggested the captain, as usual picking up a stray ball and running with it. 'After the silver.'

Before Holly could kick the ball firmly into touch where it belonged, the baron suddenly stood up and gave the youngster the same intent look Holly had given him moments before.

'It could be,' he said, as though in a trance. 'It does make some sort of sense.'

'What does?' Kia was getting impatient. 'Are you saying

that adorable little boy is actually a cat? Or are those hideous – things – some sort of mutated felines?'

Holly shook his head patiently.

'No,' he said, 'the cat in the clue is...'

'Mog!' Uncle Jasper sat bolt upright as though he had just been plugged into the mains, his whiskers needing time to catch up with the rest of him. The confidence of his smile was not misplaced.

'Exactly,' agreed Holly. 'And "silver" is usually its chemical symbol "Ag". Which means that our little boy...' He couldn't help getting up and following the baron's gaze. '...is Magog.'

Uncle Jasper followed suit, also looking at the lad with renewed respect. Kia stayed where she was, not hugely enlightened, her ignorance in the matter second only to that of the captain.

'Who was – a giant of some sort?' Kia ventured.

Holly felt his attention being sucked back to the bridge where the battle continued unabated, the only change being that the little giant had managed to shift the proceedings further towards the final, small tower. This tower was in a direct line with the wall Holly had been hiding behind, and he could see that, should the boy succeed in his apparent aim of forcing the intruders back through the final archway, the team would once again be in full view.

With some effort, he tore himself free and sat down again, glad of the relief his concealment brought, but all too aware of how short-lived it could be.

'Giant, yes. Two, actually.' He struggled to piece together whatever facts he had stored away. 'Gog and Magog. Several mentions in the Bible, particularly in the Book of Revelation, if I remember rightly. Associated with Armageddon.'

Seeing the look on Kia's face, he instantly regretted dredging up that specific detail.

'But they're much better known,' he hurried on, 'as the last survivors of a race of giants that inhabited prehistoric Britain. As I recall, the story has it that some Trojan soldier...'

'Brutus,' chanted the baron, still in his awestruck trance.

'...Brutus, yes, thank you, over here fleeing the Trojan War, conquered these two giants and had them chained to his stronghold in London to act as a couple of bouncers.' He was rushing, almost tripping over himself, ever mindful that time for explanations might be limited. 'And since then they've been the traditional guardians of the City of London.' Come on, what else did he know? 'There are statues of them in the Guildhall.' Anything else? 'Figures of them have been part of the Lord Mayor's annual procession since the reign of...'

'Henry V,' intoned the baron.

'...Really? That far back? Well, well.'

Despite everything that was going on, Kia was having the greatest difficulty hiding the fact that she was finding Holly's mild hysteria highly amusing.

'Anyway, that's why he's here,' he went on, almost unaware of the entertainment he was providing. 'That's why he's put himself in harm's way at this particular spot.'

'He's defending the City of London,' breathed the baron.

'That's right,' nodded Holly. 'He's driving back the marauding hordes.'

'So,' Kia prompted with as straight a face as she could manage, 'I can see that we only have one of these two giants because that's all the grid's given us, but why is he just a kid?'

'Kid? Kid. Well, that's because... be-cause... oh, because of the other clue...' he consulted the paper with a mixture of triumph and desperation, '...which reads "Development stage fashioned dearly, say". Fashioned. Anagram indicator, perhaps? Uncle Sid? "Dearly, say"?'

The oblivious anagram expert was jabbing as often as before, but was now wincing and pulling pained expressions a lot more. This didn't bode well, and Holly was glad he couldn't see the fight.

The captain, who was still sitting next to where Uncle Sid was standing, tugged on the older man's trouser leg.

'Uncle Sid!' he shouted. 'Anagram of "dearly, say"! Today would be good!'

Without missing a beat, Uncle Sid calmly replied, 'Early days!'

'No, we really are in a bit of a hurry!' persisted the captain, ready to pursue the matter further, but for a calming gesture from Holly.

'It's alright, Captain,' he said. 'That's the answer. "Development stage" is "early days".'

The captain, never one to pretend to be anything other than what he was, grinned broadly.

'Oh yes,' he said, happily. 'Hah! So it is.'

Holly turned back to Kia, ignoring the fact that she was now openly giggling.

'So there you have it. "Magog" and "Early days" combine to make a giant toddler fighting off monsters on Tower Bridge. Simple.'

Overjoyed to feel he was finally making some headway, and overexuberant in his eagerness to make that headway permanent, Holly brought out his garish biro. But before he could reunite it with the newspaper, his arm felt the return of the fingernails. Kia was already on her feet, albeit still squatting on them, and her face had switched instantly back to schoolmistress.

'Are you sure?' she stared down at him. 'Our little Magog is all that's currently standing between those monsters,' she leant in closer to him, 'and you.'

Before Holly had a chance to concede to this logic, much less put his pen safely away, a sudden increase in volume heralded the arrival of the relentlessly swirling melee through the last archway and into their direct line of vision.

CHAPTER TWENTY-NINE

Holly instinctively held up whatever he had in his hand in an effort to hide. Had he been left-handed, his newspaper might have afforded him some protection. As it was, his pen was more likely to attract attention than deflect it. Realising this, and feeling not a little foolish anyway, he lowered it immediately, and as he did so, the worst happened.

Little Magog still appeared as intent as ever, despite his mother's constant entreaties, to drive the invaders off and beyond the bridge. Whether by coincidence or subconscious design on the creatures' part, the snarling fur ball lurched off the bridge towards the team, dropping the twenty odd feet on to the open paved area below, the boy skilfully making sure there were two of his enemies underneath him to break his fall.

As the scrum loosened slightly on impact, one of the creatures broke free altogether, landing in a dazed heap some yards closer. It had by now lost so many random patches of fur it looked like a prize poodle whose owner had gone berserk with the clippers. But the break in contact with the boy seemed to make it more aware of its surroundings, and

Holly watched in increasing horror as, once again, it very slowly turned its head towards him.

Holly had never even come close to winning a staring contest, but was now doing better than he had ever done, albeit only because he couldn't have torn himself away if his life depended on it. When the creature started to get up without breaking eye contact, suddenly seeming none the worse for his recent exertions, Holly's only thought was that his life did depend on it. Even so, it took a shout from Uncle Jasper to get him to move.

'Manage! Fleece!'

Kia responded to the blank look on Holly's face.

'Run! Hide!' she elaborated, dragging him away from the ever-growing threat in front of him, then giving him a shove in the same direction as she went back to help Uncle Jasper who had all but collapsed the first time he had tried to put his weight on his ailing left foot.

Holly ran after the others, but soon started to question the logic of what he was doing.

'What's the point?' he found himself muttering out loud. 'There's no way on earth we can outrun this thing, and even if we manage to evade this one, it's only a matter of time before the whole place is swarming with monsters.'

He stopped running. The captain, the baron and Uncle Sid, a few paces in front, saw him stop and followed suit. They were back where they had started, right in front of the new mayor's building. But it wasn't a sense of futility that had stopped him in his tracks. Nor was it a concern for the straggling Kia and Uncle Jasper. He knew they'd be safe as long as he was around, because he was the primary target.

It was an echo that had brought him to a standstill, an echo of words he had just heard himself using, words that he had heard before. And then he recognised them as being from the clue that had transported them to this location in the first place.

' "Unknown site swarming with monsters",' he remembered. Five letters, was it?

Against his better judgment, he turned round. Surprisingly, his first feeling was relief at seeing that Kia and Uncle Jasper had abandoned trying to catch up with the others and were instead crouching against one of the lantern pillars. Relief was followed, even more surprisingly, by amusement as he saw that Kia had been attempting to shield Uncle Jasper who, as usual becoming pain-free as soon as he stopped moving, was having none of it.

Eventually – actually still only a split second later – he arrived at the chill down the spine he'd been expecting. The monster from the clue had just started closing the 100-yard gap between them, now totally oblivious to the fight still raging behind it, a fight that had so recently commanded its full attention.

Holly's mind, luckily, was accelerating faster. It raced through as many approaches to the clue as it could, but to no avail. It was only when he started panicking at his lack of progress, considering how few variables there were in the clue, that his Eureka moment arrived.

Variables, that was it! Unknowns! He had been caught in a rut, looking for a word for 'unknown site' when in fact 'unknown' wasn't an adjective at all, but a noun – *an* unknown, used by crossword compilers to mean an X or a Y. Which left four letters unaccounted for. Possibly 'site'? With 'swarming' as an anagram indicator?

'I've got it!' he shouted triumphantly, waving his pen in the air, only then realising that the creature was now a mere twenty yards away and closing fast. There wouldn't be time to find the relevant place in the grid, much less write anything in it. He could hear Kia screaming at him to get out of the way. He knew he would have to break the habit of a lifetime and not do his usual impression of a rabbit caught in the headlights.

But before he had a chance to pass or fail the test, the little giant came to his rescue again. The youngster had been steadily driving his attackers on, also in Holly's direction. By now he had lost both his shoes, half of one sock, his trousers had become shorts, which seemed to emphasise his young age, and a light blue collar over a newly revealed torn white vest was the only reminder of the jumper he was wearing for the first time.

One of the creatures hadn't got up after serving as the young giant's landing cushion. The lad had one of the others by the ankle and was swinging it round, keeping the remaining three at bay. And it was at this point that he let go.

The hapless creature flew off at great speed. Having been launched from around ground level, it was still travelling upwards as it caught its companion who had been making a beeline for Holly. The two of them then sailed over Holly's head, the surprised front runner barely having time to take a swipe as he careered past, managing only to knock the hand that Holly was still holding aloft.

The pen in this case proved considerably less mighty than the sword, flying out of Holly's grasp and out of sight.

Submerged into the pavement just beyond the mayor's building was a shallow oval amphitheatre in minimalist granite with seating in a staggered spiral growing from one to nine rows. Holly could just make out the words 'The Scoop' high on its far side. It was used for open-air performances, though fortunately not on this particular evening, for it was precisely here that the two creatures landed.

The one that had been thrown landed on the stone seating at the back. It was immediately apparent from the grotesque way it was piled up on its own neck with one leg pointing implacably skywards that it was never going to get up again. The other hadn't travelled quite as far and was consequently out of sight behind the amphitheatre's shallow wall. Holly fervently hoped his stalker had befallen a similar fate, and was barely halfway through a sigh of relief when its huge head suddenly loomed into view.

It was clearly alive but hardly unscathed. Its oval mask-like face had acquired a slightly diagonal crack across its entire width with its mouth at the centre, a crack roughly an inch wide with a pink froth audibly bubbling out of it. The creature appeared dazed and sluggish.

Before Holly could react, Kia had reached him and had spun him round by his arm.

'Get away! Get away now! You have to get away!' she was ranting, breathlessly. 'Just say "grid" and sort it out from home! Just go!'

Holly shook his head in horror.

'I can't do that,' he protested. 'I can't leave you all here. There isn't time to get you all together.'

'We don't matter!' Kia shouted. 'It's not about us. It's about you! And we'll be fine.'

'No!' Holly was equally adamant. 'You won't! With me out of reach, they'll turn on you! You're only safe as long as I'm here!'

'I don't want to be safe!' The last of Kia's self-control finally crumbled, and she burst into tears. 'I want you to be,' she cried, shaking his arm. 'I can't watch that thing kill you! I can't lose you! Not today!'

She pulled herself closer so her face was right in front of his.

'Please,' she hissed. 'Go!'

Unfortunately for her, the more she asked him to go, the more determined he was to stay. Skulking back home, leaving them to an unknown fate – he'd be in no shape to solve anything.

Resisting her imploring look, he could only shake his head. She welled up again, groaned and let her head fall against his shoulder. Regaining his field of vision, he noticed that the creature was on the move.

It crawled its way laboriously out of the pit, as ever towards Holly who now at least had the presence of mind to back off, shooing a disconsolate Kia towards the river wall and hopefully out of immediate harm's way. It became apparent that the creature only had one arm and one leg functional enough to drag itself along.

Impaired as it was, it still moved faster than Holly, who knew that time was now running out. This was a new situation for him – he had the grid, he had the solution, but he didn't have anything to write with. He found the appropriate space on the grid with a quick glance, leaving his thumb there as a marker.

'A pen!' he shouted at no-one in particular, still firmly in reverse gear, not taking his eyes off his would-be assassin. 'Any pen!'

'He suits!' came Uncle Sid's unmistakable voice. He had passed Kia and now joined Holly in his retreat, holding out a black biro. Holly reached for it and, in the grand tradition of the British relay team passing the baton, dropped it, losing his balance as he did so and falling heavily on his back several paces away from the vital implement.

He stared back at it in disbelief. His assailant was too close. He'd never get to it in time.

'No time,' he echoed, uselessly.

This received a snort from Uncle Sid. With a look of grim determination and pausing only to turn to Uncle Jasper, giving him the briefest of salutes and shouting 'Kippers!', he took three running steps, managing in one of them to kick the isolated pen back towards Holly, and then launched himself towards the moth-eaten demon with a heartfelt cry of 'Notch me one!'.

The change from attacking to being attacked stopped the creature in its tracks, but only for a split second before it registered the futility of the assault. It casually raised its good arm and flicked Uncle Sid aside as if he'd been a mosquito.

The have-a-go hero flew at least thirty feet through the air, already limp, before wrapping himself sickeningly round one of the lamp posts and finally crashing in a heap at its base.

Time stopped, at least for the members of the team who stared numbly at their fallen comrade. There were no tears, no words, no breathing. Just shock and open mouths, each one of them looking like they were screaming, but without making a sound.

The agent of Uncle Sid's demise, however, was unaffected and resumed its previous course, bringing Holly out of his trance sufficiently to reach for the fateful pen.

The creature was on him instantly. It raised its arm, and Holly saw, albeit blurrily through the tears that were now stinging his eyes, the pink pads of its huge hand as it towered high above him. He held up his newspaper, as much to create an ineffectual shield as to be able to write on it.

Pen made contact with paper, Holly hoping that his thumb had remained in the right place after his fall, that he would get the spacing of the letters right without being able to see, that he'd even got the correct solution and that this pen would work upside down.

CHAPTER THIRTY

Time was back on hold. Holly noticed he wasn't breathing, but felt no pressing need to do so. He could hear the reassuring sounds of the river and distant traffic, but he could also hear the helicopters hovering nearby. Why would they still be there, if not to film the creatures? But then why hadn't he been reduced to a two-dimensional stain on the pavement? Obviously the thing to do would be to lower his newspaper, but that was simply out of the question.

The matter was taken out of his hands, almost literally, as the paper, instead of being forced towards him at a stupefying rate as he expected, was knocked sideways to reveal, rather than an arm the size and appearance of a woolly girder, the slightly less alarming sight of a beaming Uncle Sid.

'Neon ice!' he chuckled, whistling in admiration before snatching back the pen Holly still held in his other hand. 'A toy hunk!'

Holly gasped and stared at the ridiculously jolly man in wonder.

'No, thank *you*,' he managed at last, finding himself grinning back. Uncle Sid drew closer, shaking his head.

‘A toy hunk,’ he whispered more earnestly. Then the big smile reappeared and he gave Holly a couple of good-natured slaps on the face before standing up, whereupon he was nearly knocked over by Kia.

‘You mad son of a –,’ she was ranting. ‘What the hell do you think you were –. Don’t you ever –.’ Then she threw her arms round his neck and held on as though she would never let go. That idea also seemed to have occurred to Uncle Sid who, still laughing, gently loosened her grip and pushed her away.

He then went over to where the captain and the baron had been rooted to the spot all this time, starting off a round of backslapping, congratulations and insults flying around in equal measure. Finally he wandered a little further to where Uncle Jasper was still sitting in stunned silence. Uncle Sid sat next to him and gave him a playful punch on the shoulder, getting a faint smile in return.

‘And thank you from me,’ Holly heard Kia say. He hadn’t noticed that she was kneeling over him.

‘You’re welcome,’ he grunted as he lifted himself on to one elbow.

‘Are you OK?’ she demanded. He was reminded with some embarrassment of his less than impressive arrival on the sailing ship. He waved his hand.

‘Yes, I’m fine, I’m just – fine. Look – I can breathe and everything.’

Reassured, she leaned back, still kneeling. Holly looked over at Uncle Sid, happy to see he was now having more success cheering his companion.

‘I suppose you’re going to tell me he does that every day?’

Kia followed his gaze.

'No. Heavens, no. That was another first. Hopefully never again.' She looked at Holly, a little suspiciously, he thought. 'He must have some faith in you.'

Holly looked back at the unassuming man with increased awe, and a certain amount of nausea as he considered how many things could have gone wrong in the solving of that last, literally vital clue, how fragile the chain of events had been. He shuddered, prompting Kia to change the subject.

'So,' she continued, trying to sound nonchalant. 'What were those things?'

'Those,' Holly answered, looking around nervously to make sure they really had disappeared, 'were yetis.'

Kia blinked at him.

'Yetis,' she echoed, clearly in need of convincing.

'So it would appear,' he said, frowning, his voice betraying the fact that he was a little incredulous himself. The captain and the baron had now joined them and were already revelling in stunned disbelief.

' "Disturbed yetis", to be precise,' he continued. 'Which would I suppose account for their rather frenzied demeanour.'

Kia shook her head, still unsure.

'And how did we arrive at that?'

'Well,' Holly began reluctantly, for the first time not particularly keen to revisit one of his triumphs, 'the clue was "Unknown site swarming with monsters". So Y is an unknown, always an X or a Y, followed by "site" – "swarming", i.e. an anagram. So – yetis.'

Keen as he was to get this over with, the faces staring at him seemed to demand some sort of corroboration.

'It fits with the timeline,' he suggested, after a moment trying to remember what they had heard on the news. 'Yetis are traditionally Himalayan. If they'd set off from there as soon as this grid called them into being, which I assume would have been midnight...'

Kia nodded.

'...then, given their rather scary speed, that would tie in with them reaching the eastern edge of Europe early in the morning and then here by the evening – some 3,000 miles later.' He shuddered at the sense of purpose they must have had to accomplish such a feat.

The others seemed to find the argument convincing, contemplative nods all round. Holly started the arduous task of getting upright.

'Excuse me, but I believe this is yours.'

Holly stopped mid manoeuvre, kneeling on one knee with both hands on the ground as though he were waiting for the starter's gun. He looked up to find someone holding out his pen. If the red hair hadn't given the game away immediately, the face, or rather its expression, would have been enough to tell Holly it was the boy's mother.

In her hand, the gaudy pen looked so jarringly tasteless that under different circumstances Holly might have denied that it was his. As he took it, he wished he was wearing a jacket with a pocket to bury it in.

'Thank you,' he said, trying to make the last bit of getting up look as effortless as possible.

He had just been starting to wonder why a man lying on his back in the middle of a wide pavement had attracted so little attention, even given that this was the centre of London and it wasn't that uncommon a sight. Now he noticed that the numerous people walking past, all towards the bridge, were far too preoccupied with what lay in front of them. Seeing that his benefactor was also looking in that direction, with that same mixture of pride and sadness he had seen before, he wasn't surprised, when he too looked that way, to see her son. What did surprise him, was the lad's appearance.

Magog was sitting on the pavement, still towering over the crowd that had assembled round him. His clothes were just as they were when he had first appeared on the bridge – neat black shoes, smart brown corduroy trousers and to crown it all off, his brand-new pale blue jumper. Even the elephant had been resurrected. And at that very moment, at a cue from his father prompted by that jumper, he was uttering his new favourite phrase for the umpteenth time that day, 'Oi not trouble!' to which the crowd roared with laughter, to his obvious delight.

There followed a question and response routine, the man shouting out animals' names and his son giving the appropriate noise. The biggest crowd-pleasers were the 'Oo, oo, ah, ah, ah!' of a monkey and the way he rolled his eyes when he went 'Moo!' both of which recurred several times. The father seemed very at home with this double act, although Holly did notice that whenever his son made any movement towards him, he would cross his arms in front of his chest and give the boy an even wider berth than the audience did.

After a while the little giant lost interest in this game, turning back to play with his best birthday present – a gleaming new bulldozer that he'd been allowed to take with him on this birthday outing. The bulldozer was still resolutely called a tractor, and with its proud owner providing the sound effects as he pushed it back and forth, it sounded exactly like a train.

Why, Holly thought, had he been so surprised at the lad's tidy appearance? The yetis had after all been solved, so it was as if they had never existed. There were no mangled creatures littering the streets, no animal rights activists floating unhappily down the river, no motorway blockades had been set up, even Bonn's city centre was unscathed. And unknown to Holly, a six-year-old Chinese boy wouldn't have a lifelong fear of the moon.

He turned to Kia, who was once again utterly enchanted.

'What do we do?' he asked, having had to shake her gently to break the trance.

'Do?' she asked, dreamily. Holly was reluctant to pursue the issue, but felt he must.

'He shouldn't be here any more than those creatures,' he said as quietly as he could over the noise of the crowd. Her face didn't change.

'He's so-ooo cute,' she cooed. Holly was giving up hope of getting any sense out of her on the matter when she suddenly snapped out of it, although clearly without a change of heart.

'He'll always be there to guard London,' she suggested eagerly, 'to guard us, against – whatever appears in the future.'

She looked up at him like a little girl asking for sweets. Given what had been after him in the very recent past, Holly couldn't help finding the argument compelling.

'And who knows,' she continued, 'he may be very happy. He may lead a normal life.'

'Normal? He will never lead a normal life.'

Holly hadn't had time to come up with such a common-sense observation, wouldn't have said it with such conviction and certainly couldn't have imbued it with such emotion. The words had come from the boy's mother. Holly had forgotten she had been standing on the opposite side of him to Kia.

‘This is how it is,’ she went on emptily, without once taking her eyes off her husband, her child and the show they were putting on, ‘and this is how it will always be.’

Kia and Holly exchanged sombre glances, Kia’s euphoric mood having instantly evaporated.

‘This circus act,’ the woman continued, her voice cracking slightly. ‘No matter what he does, people will always look at him like this – like a freak show.’

Kia started to say something. Holly couldn’t imagine what it was going to be, and he never found out.

‘And I can’t even hold him!’ The woman finally turned to them, almost accusingly. ‘I can’t comfort him, I can barely touch him. They don’t let me near him because he’s too – dangerous. And even if I could cuddle him, what would be the point? I can’t even get my arms round his leg.’ She laughed briefly, before the tears took over.

Kia brushed past Holly and took the hand the woman was trying to cover her face with, in an effort to hide the now copious tears.

‘I just want to be his mother,’ she managed to get out between sobs, ‘and I can’t.’

At this her head went down and she shook uncontrollably.

Without letting go of the woman’s hand, Kia looked round at Holly with an undecided look. Holly’s response was non-committal. Kia knew this world and the possible ramifications of solutions and non-solutions better than he did. It would have to be her decision.

She looked into the distance for a moment, a trait Holly was pleased to notice they shared, and then seemed to make up her mind. She turned back to the sobbing woman.

‘Would you like your son to be a normal boy? To have

a normal life?' she asked.

The woman's head shot up and she stared Kia full in the face.

'I'd give anything for that,' she said hoarsely, before hopelessness set in again. 'Anything.' Her head went back down.

Kia absently patted the hand she was still holding, and then let it go. The woman let it fall limply to her side. Kia slowly moved back to Holly and gestured with her head at the paper in his hand. Getting no response, she did it again with a little more emphasis, before wrapping her arms round the top of Holly's writing arm, still allowing him to use his pen, and then resting her forehead on his shoulder. Sensing there was still no response, she squeezed his arm, but without looking up.

Finally, Holly lifted both pen and paper together. He knew he was doing the right thing – maybe not for himself, or the City of London, and certainly not for Kia, but for this distraught woman, for the little giant himself, and not least, he had to admit, for logic. He was following the rules.

He gritted his teeth and entered the words 'Magog', 'early' and 'days'. Then he closed his eyes. For a while both of them stood there, neither wanting to see that there was no longer anything to be seen.

The sounds told Holly everything he needed to know. There was normal conversation between people moving around them in all directions. There were normal traffic noises coming from the bridge. And there were no helicopters. He sighed.

But then there was another sound, a small, high-pitched voice next to them.

'Doan croy,' it said.

They both opened their eyes and looked down to see a young boy with a huge smile staring up at them. He had tousled blond hair, his pale blue jumper bore an elephant that was no longer life-size and in his hand was a tiny, gleaming yellow bulldozer.

'It's moy birfday!' he announced.

Kia's mouth was wide open, but there seemed little chance of any words coming out, so Holly shocked himself by being the first to say anything.

'Is it?' he said in mock surprise. 'How old are you?'

'Oim free!' came the delighted reply.

The way he screwed up his face and eyes on the word 'free' provoked an involuntary laugh from Kia, which cheered Holly at least as much as the reappearance of the young lad.

'And are you having a nice day?' he continued, wishing he didn't sound so formal. That didn't matter to the boy, of course, who seemed to appreciate the question.

'Olly happy!' he declared.

'Oliver! Oliver, there you are!'

The boy's mother came up and brusquely took his hand.

'Come on, Oliver. Back to Pimlico. That's quite enough excitement for one day,' she said, pulling him away. 'And what have I told you about talking to strangers?'

Giving Holly a pointedly distrustful look, she dragged the tottering lad over to where his father was standing with a pained expression.

'There wasn't any need for that,' he protested.

'There are some very odd characters around,' she countered. 'You can't be too careful.'

'Maybe if you'd kept more of an eye on him...'

And with that, the three of them disappeared into the crowd.

It took another squeeze of Holly's arm for him to realise that she had been watching him with concern for some time – all the time, it turned out, that he'd been watching the space the boy and his parents had vacated.

'She didn't know,' she said, sadly. 'That's the way it happens. I'm sorry.' She wanted to be reassuring, but couldn't. 'You don't get used to that.'

Once again, he was humbled at the thought that, however he may be feeling right now, this girl had to go through this, if not quite on a daily basis, then considerably more frequently than he could bear to contemplate.

He nodded and lifted his head in a vain attempt to look more unaffected than he was. The two of them walked slowly over to the others who had congregated around the now practically static Uncle Jasper.

As they joined them the captain patted Holly jovially on the shoulder and said something characteristically light-hearted, or so at least Holly assumed, as he couldn't hear him. Then he realised that he couldn't hear anything – no cars, no buses, no water, no people, no wind.

And the silence lasted four seconds.

1C	A	2T	E	3G	O	4R	I	5S	E	■	6H	7A	R	8M
R	■	R	■	E	■		■		■	9T	■		■	
10A	G	A	I	N	S	T	■	11L	A	W	L	O	R	D
F	■	M	■	E	■		■		■	O	■		■	
12T	O	L	E	R	A	N	C	E	■	13P	A	N	I	C
■	■	I	■	A	■		■		■	A	■	■	■	
14P	A	N	E	L	■	15E	X	T	O	R	T	16I	O	N
E	■	E	■	S	■	■	■	■	■	T	■		■	
17D	I	S	T	U	R	18B	E	19D	■	20Y	E	T	I	S
O	■	■	■	R	■		■		■	S	■		■	■
21M	A	22G	O	G	■	23E	A	R	L	Y	D	A	Y	24S
E	■	A	■	E	■		■		■	S	■		■	
25T	A	B	L	O	I	D	■	26A	R	T	I	S	A	N
E	■	L	■	N	■		■		■	E	■		■	
27R	E	E	K	■	28A	R	I	T	H	M	E	T	I	C

CHAPTER THIRTY-ONE

Four seconds was long enough for the captain's face to register his incredulity that once again this was happening while he was talking, but that didn't stop him ducking involuntarily with everyone else when the boom came.

Everyone else in the team, that is. The pedestrians out for an evening stroll showed no sign of hearing anything, although one or two of them did cast a suspicious eye on the strange group huddled together performing synchronised convulsions, no doubt taking them for a mime troupe.

As the resonant thud faded, all the sounds flooded back simultaneously. Holly felt like a deaf person who had suddenly acquired hearing – all the background sounds he had taken for granted were actually deafening, at least compared to silence.

By the time they had all started to acclimatise and had straightened again, there began a latticework of nervous glances in a mute attempt to discover if they had lost any more members of the team. The captain was the first to give a verbal confirmation.

‘No,’ he said, emphatically. ‘Not me. Nothing wrong with me.’

‘That wasn’t wrong already,’ completed the baron.

‘You’re OK too, then,’ ventured Kia. ‘You OK?’ she asked Holly. He shrugged.

‘As far as I can tell,’ he said without much conviction.

They turned towards the two uncles. Uncle Sid was peering distractedly at the pavement with his hands in his pockets.

‘Bus coins,’ he muttered. The others nodded in recognition and attention turned to Uncle Jasper, who was looking increasingly anxious. He stared at each one of them in turn.

‘Subsonic,’ he said at last, as though giving a password. ‘Low frequency. Deep resonance.’ He only smiled when the others did, out of relief that this time none of them seemed to have been affected.

‘No, no, I mean I had some coins here for the bus. Now how am I going to get home? I can’t even think where home is at the moment. That noise really did me head in. What in the world was it? It made me bones rattle.’

The resonant bass note had made Holly feel nauseous enough, but this little speech from Uncle Sid got much closer to actually making him throw up. What brought him back from the brink was having to take Kia’s entire weight on his left arm as her legs gave way.

‘No,’ she wailed, struggling to hang on to Holly’s arm. The baron appeared at her side to provide support.

‘It did, straight up it did,’ Uncle Sid continued. ‘I’ve come over all unnecessary. I could certainly use a drink, that usually does the trick. Anyone care to join me?’

‘No,’ Kia moaned again, swaying between her two human pillars.

'No?' Uncle Sid looked at her. 'Perhaps not. You look as though you've had a skinful already. Oh well. Anyone else?' He looked round at the other horror-stricken faces. 'Blimey,' he chuckled. 'What are you all? Sally Army?'

The baron beckoned the captain over.

'Get Uncle Sid a few beers and then get him home,' he said under his breath, 'while we try and sort things out.'

'Ducking out of buying a round again, eh?' joked the captain, holding up his hands to deflect the look the baron was giving him. 'No problem. Leave it to me. Just the man for the job.' He took Uncle Sid by the elbow and led him off. 'Come along, old fellow. A dose of the Bentley's will see you right. If memory serves, we should only have to turn that corner.'

Uncle Jasper, who had vigorously shaken his head when the captain had given him a questioning jerk of his head to see if he wanted to come along, was the last to turn away from the retreating duo. He stared at some point on the ground ahead of him, shell-shocked.

'No,' Kia was moaning again. 'First Lady, then Uncle Sid. What's Great Uncle Sid going to say? This is all my fault.'

'No, it isn't,' chorused the baron and Holly.

'And we're not just making excuses for you,' the baron continued, 'so don't go hyperventilating on us again. We all know whose fault this is. Time is running out and we need to stop him.'

'Stop!'

Uncle Jasper pounced on the word as it floated past, and when he looked up there was a glint in his eye.

'Stop,' he repeated, making his way laboriously towards the other three. 'Hinder – obstruct –,' using his left foot so little he was almost hopping on his right one with every word, '– check –,' the effort audible in his voice, '– break –,' he was now standing in front of Kia, '– unravel –,' he turned to face Holly full on, '– solve.'

He gave Holly one of those inescapable, challenging looks, eyebrows raised, eyes wide and unblinking, a look that gives the recipient no option but to squirm and wish it would go away. When it finally did, much to Holly's relief, it was merely transferred to Kia, where it stayed for an uncomfortable length of time.

But it worked.

'OK, OK,' conceded Kia, bringing a hand up to shield her face. 'Not The Look. Anything but The Look.' She pulled herself free of her supporters, drew herself shakily to her full height and took a deep breath. 'See? Pulling myself together. Put it away.'

After a moment's hesitation to make sure she didn't have a relapse, Uncle Jasper gave a couple of nods and resumed his normal expression. Kia peeked from behind the hand she was still holding up, just to make certain. Reassured, she used the hand to tidy a few strands of stray hair that had freed themselves from her ponytail before relaxing her arm.

'Right then,' she said, matter-of-factly. 'As you said, Baron, we know who the Culprit is. Let's go.'

'Hang on,' protested the baron. 'Yes – we do know it's – him, but you're seriously suggesting we just go and drop in? Social visit? Cosy little chat? Would he mind awfully not picking us off one by one? Why can't we just sit here, calmly, and solve all the remaining clues? I'm sure between us we could manage it.'

Quick though the baron had been to object, Holly fancied these thoughts had occurred to him first, but his incurable habit of rehearsing in his mind everything he said before he said it had saved him the potential embarrassment of being the one who looked scared. This habit was usually a source of frustration to him, but every now and then he was glad of it.

Kia was adamant, and her voice had a cold edge.

'That's no longer good enough,' she intoned. 'Whatever this weapon is – this 4-18 – just getting rid of it today doesn't mean he won't come up with it again tomorrow, now he's had the idea. So we have to make sure, if we can, that he doesn't. And that means going to him.'

Despite the deliberately frosty tone, her voice still wavered a little at the end.

'But we don't know where he is.' Holly felt the baron needed some backing. 'I mean, we know how to get to him, but we have no idea where we'll end up if we name the clue.'

Kia shook her head absently. Uncle Jasper turned to Holly and reactivated The Look.

'Rowers – feathers,' he said, slowly and deliberately.

After a moment's pause, the baron nodded.

'Oh, very good. Four Down. "Down" is another word for "feathers", and "rowers" is used in crosswords to mean "four", as in a rowing four, a team of four rowers.' He stopped and frowned. 'Hang on, though, there's a rowing eight as well, so you could just as easily be saying "8 D..." '

The Look had switched targets. The baron wisely let it pass.

'Rowers – feathers,' Uncle Jasper repeated.

Holly exchanged glances with the baron, who was just glad to be able to break eye contact with the man in the boiler suit. Then he sought confirmation from Kia, but she seemed preoccupied with coming to terms with what they were about to do.

'All right,' he declared, quietly. 'Let's do it.'

Uncle Jasper took hold of Holly's sleeve with one hand, and put the other on the baron's shoulder. Holly gingerly held Kia's arm, and she finally lifted her head and looked him in the eye, with an expression that was clearly determined to appear determined, and almost succeeded. They were ready.

Holly had one last look round at the bridge. No longer festooned with vanquished monsters, life there had returned to normal and traffic was flowing freely. He noticed for the first time how cold it had become, and he shivered. He had no idea how much colder it was about to get.

'Rowers and feathers.' He smiled at Uncle Jasper. 'Four Down.'

As their surroundings dissolved, Holly heard his last words as a report on a number of troops that had fallen on active duty, and hoped it wouldn't turn out to be an accurate prediction for his reduced team. In a conscious effort to minimise casualties, he had the word 'grid' ready at the tip of his tongue, just in case enemy territory turned out to be overwhelmingly hostile. But as their new environment faded into view, its only qualities that were overwhelming were dismal and cold, so Holly stood his tongue down. It was so gloomy and murky that Holly waited several seconds for his vision to clear before realising that it wasn't going to.

At first, all Holly could make out of the space they found themselves in was that it was roughly square, a room with only one light source, a dull, sickly yellow glow coming through a frosted Perspex panel in one end of the suspended ceiling. As his eyes grew more accustomed to the light, or lack of it, he saw that it wasn't so much a room as a convergence of several corridors, and that what he had mistaken for a couple of the walls were in fact just dark, empty openings. Peer into these as he might, the darkness seemed to get ever more impenetrable, so he gave that up and turned his attention to the other two.

Directly in front of him and below the feeble light was a closed set of double swinging doors, each with a large square window in the top half. Beyond them he could see a passage stretching away, initially brightly lit but then succumbing yet again to the all-pervasive gloom, so that it was impossible to tell how long it was.

To the right of these doors was another pair at right angles to the first, forming the beginning of the last wall. The left one of this pair was open into another corridor, and through this door another light, equally thin but whiter, seemed to be floating in before dissipating. From where Holly was standing, he couldn't see where this light was coming from.

So far, none of them had moved. Nor had anyone said anything, preferring to let their teeth do the chattering. None of them had really been sufficiently dressed to cope with central London in December, even a mild one – they were woefully ill-equipped for these conditions. The only one who didn't look physically traumatised by the cold, indeed seemed oblivious to it, was Uncle Jasper. Holly wondered how many other layers were concealed beneath the boiler suit.

Uncle Jasper's relative composure was also evident from his breathing, which was far slower and calmer than that of his companions, an easy comparison to make now that their breath was so visible in the freezing air. Looking back at the patches of light wafting through the open door, Holly imagined it was the corridor itself breathing on them.

Either that, or something in the corridor. He suppressed the thought and looked away uneasily.

Chattering of teeth aside, the only sounds to be heard were a drone of white noise – wind, Holly imagined, but muffled – and two high-pitched whines of air being continuously forced through small openings, whines that fluctuated and danced round each other like a pair of butterflies.

Holly listened to this musical dance for a while, mesmerised. Then, pulling himself together, he was about to broach the subject of a possible plan of action, when another sound froze his vocal cords altogether – a distant sound, but not nearly distant enough for Holly.

It started off as an angry male growl, rising steadily in volume and to an impossibly high pitch before suddenly being wrenched out of existence, not even leaving an echo.

CHAPTER THIRTY-TWO

The silence, background noise apart, had been broken, and with it an intuitive obligation not to talk. The baron was the first to take advantage of this freedom, but still did so in a whisper.

'What – the – *hell* – was that?' he wanted to know.

'You don't want to know,' replied Kia.

'Well, no, possibly not,' the baron conceded, 'but...' He stopped, realising that her tone had been more knowledgeable than he had expected. 'Hang on – that was meant to be rhetorical...' He peered at her more intently. 'What – you mean you actually know what that was?'

She nodded. The others waited, but nothing was forthcoming.

'Well?' the baron tried again.

Kia took a deep breath.

'I've been here before,' she started, hesitantly. Holly could tell from Uncle Jasper's surprised expression that Kia must only have had another Solver for company on that particular excursion.

'I don't recognise this,' she went on, looking round. 'It must have been a different bit. But I recognise that –

that noise. That's what we were here to solve. But we ran out of time.'

She hung her head for a moment. Her companions could sense her feeling of responsibility, that it was her fault they were facing this thing again, but they were reluctant on this occasion to wade in with words of consolation, given what had greeted them before. When she lifted her head again to survey her surroundings, it was with a more positive air.

'Well at least this isn't the bell tower,' she said in her best silver-lining tone.

This time Holly was the first to break under curiosity.

'Why?'

Before Kia could answer, the subject of their conversation joined in with another swooping utterance, although not as expansively, confining itself to the middle register.

There was a pause before everyone resumed breathing.

'Because that,' Kia nodded in the general direction of the outlandish cry, 'is the Bell Tower Demon.'

This seemed the perfect opportunity for the creature to respond to its name, but its decision to remain silent only served to heighten the tension. The men were relieved when Kia resumed her story.

'We didn't solve it on the day, but we've heard it mentioned since.'

Uncle Jasper nodded thoughtfully. Holly could see him marrying a name he'd heard to a sound he probably wished he hadn't.

'Fortunately,' Kia went on, 'only in connection with the bell tower itself. Its name seems to restrict its field of activity. And as this doesn't look like the bell tower,' she looked round with mock optimism, 'we should at least not have that to worry about.'

The others looked less than convinced, particularly as it reminded them of what they did have to worry about.

'Whether the Culprit was also here at the time,' Kia said, following the same train of thought, 'I have no idea. I certainly wouldn't have come here if I'd thought he was. Ironic,' she added, ruefully, 'as that's why we're here now.'

'And where is here, exactly?' asked the baron with a mixture of genuine curiosity and a desire to lead the conversation in a different direction. 'Or don't I want to know that either?'

Kia smiled.

'This is Chateau Remorse,' she said, her smile fading over the course of those four words. 'Not as chateau-like as I remember. This must be a more recent extension. It feels like an office block.' She pointed into one of the dark corners, where a person-sized metal trolley could just be seen emerging from the darkness. 'Or maybe a hospital wing.'

The idea that this place could in any way be linked to anything medical moved through them like a shock wave, followed by a pressing desire to be elsewhere.

'Well, not that this isn't awfully jolly,' said the baron in as upbeat a tone as he could manage, 'but this doesn't seem to be getting us very far, and we don't want to run out of time.' Recalling Kia's reason for not having dealt with the Bell Tower Demon, he instantly regretted making that remark. 'So,' he continued hastily, 'where do we have to go, and what do we have to do to get there?'

The pause of indecision that followed was punctuated only by another shriek from the demon, this time back to showing off its entire vocal range.

'There?' echoed Uncle Jasper, pointing tentatively at the door that was breathing light at them. 'Yonder?'

It was as good a way as any, and considerably less dark than some of the others, and a collective shrug of the shoulders saw them all move in that direction.

Holly led the way, and was relieved to find, on reaching the door, that there was nothing breathing smoke lying in wait for them, but that it was merely fog floating in, a fog that seemed to be lit from the inside.

In contrast to the corridor that had been directly in front of them, this one was lit throughout, so that even the closed doors at the other end could be seen. The light, however, wasn't coming from anything on the ceiling, but appeared to be emanating solely from the fog which was pouring in through the numerous broken windows that lined the left side of the passageway, after which it seemed reluctant to touch any solid surface, preferring instead to float along the centre. To Holly's mind, the entire corridor resembled a huge fluorescent lamp.

The windows themselves may as well have been opaque, but the constant stream of fog through the shattered glass panes indicated that this was responsible for the non-existent view. The source of its light was impossible to tell – it could have been the moon, or maybe a light somewhere else in the building – as was the nature of the space beyond the windows, whether it was exterior or merely an inner courtyard.

Holly stepped gingerly through the door, followed by Kia. The baron and Uncle Jasper clashed midway in an effort not to be last, before chivalry took over, after which neither wanted to be first. An admonishing 'Psst!' from Kia brought them both squeezing through simultaneously.

The group moved slowly along the corridor, Holly's eyes darting in all directions, Kia mainly concerned that the doors ahead stayed shut, the other two exclusively looking behind them to make sure they weren't being followed. It was Holly who saw something first. He held out an arm to block the others, then raised it to quell the numerous protestations as the reversing baron and Uncle Jasper collided with Kia.

They were about a third of the way along the passage, and it took a couple of seconds for them to locate what Holly was looking at, but when they did, they froze.

A little way ahead, on the other side of the broken window panes, stood the shadowy form of a man. It was barely discernable against the fog that could now be seen to be swirling round it. The figure, by contrast, was motionless.

Time passed, during which the only thing that moved was the dense, freezing mist. Even Kia's teeth had stopped chattering.

Eventually Holly took a couple of steps forward, hunched, ready to run. Kia swung an arm out to try and pull him back but missed and gave up. Taking even the two steps needed to catch him up and try again was out of the question. The three of them watched him intently. Although still within spitting distance, Holly had already acquired a ghostly soft focus.

After peering through the window for a while, he suddenly straightened up. He walked a few more paces until he reached the halfway point of the corridor, all the while staring into the glowing void, flinching a couple of times as a stream of fog caught him full in the face. There he stopped and beckoned the others to join him. Reluctantly, after an exchange of nervous glances, they set off, keeping a watchful eye on the silhouette through the glass.

As they approached, the vague form acquired a more detailed outline, an outline of precise curves and straight lines – an outline, as it turned out, of a machine. A humanoid machine, to be sure, but an automaton nonetheless. As the details became clearer, other figures started to loom out of the gloom, and by the time the three incredulous stragglers reached Holly they were looking at a group of seven of these contraptions.

They were all roughly man-sized and roughly man-shaped. The design was crude and mechanical, and the colour was of iron that had long since succumbed to rust. They all stood fairly upright and held their arms out in front of them. Grasped in the clumsy clamps that served as their hands were metal rods with small, hard rubber balls on the ends, and suspended below these, riveted to their hips, each one had a differently sized section of a metal drum.

Kia's face had softened from fear to compassion.

'That's the Robot Steel Band,' she said with obvious fondness, putting a hand up against one of the few unbroken panes. 'Oh, but they look so sad. What happened to them?'

Having a weakness for mechanical and clockwork objects, Holly was delighted at this unexpected chance to find out more about these magnificent, if corroded, constructions.

'You know them?' he asked eagerly.

'Oh yes,' she replied without taking her eyes off them. 'They appeared one morning on the South Bank. Nobody seemed to know where they came from, so we knew straight away that they were part of that day's puzzle. Playing away. Non-stop. The Solver was so taken with them she refused to solve them.' Kia giggled. 'Point blank. Wouldn't do it. We tried to explain to her that, cute as they were, we had no way of knowing the consequences of leaving them unsolved, but she wouldn't hear of it.'

Holly tried to imagine what they must have looked like, new and gleaming, and what they must have sounded like. He himself wasn't the greatest fan of steel band music, but given his admiration for their design, he knew he would at least have faltered at their solution, if not demurred altogether.

'So we left them there,' Kia continued, wistfully. 'Everyone loved them. Big tourist attraction.' Her eyebrows dropped into a frown. 'And then one day, they just weren't there any more. Nobody had any more idea where they went as where they had come from.' Her face went full circle back to compassion. 'They must have been here ever since. This fog certainly hasn't done them any favours.'

The distant shriek that followed seemed to echo Kia's indignation, but the demon was already starting to lose its shock value, and the four travellers barely heard it.

That shock value was transferred to the next sound, even though it was the quieter of the two, as beyond the doors they were heading for, someone coughed.

CHAPTER THIRTY-THREE

It wasn't the polite cough of someone trying to attract another's attention before starting a conversation, rather the self-indulgent hacking fit of someone confident that there is nobody else within earshot. Hoping that their presence was indeed unknown, and overcome by curiosity, the quartet crept stealthily along until they reached the windows in the doors and looked through.

The room was almost identical to the one they had just been only too glad to leave, right down to the unfathomable darkness at one end. The one lit ceiling panel may have been a little more central, but other than that it might have been a mirror image. The one thing that set it apart was its occupant.

Almost directly underneath the single source of light was a dilapidated metal hospital trolley with a thin, blue, plastic-coated mattress on which a man was lying. He was tall – or rather long, being horizontal – and unnaturally thin, with straight fair hair that hung in strands over his gaunt face. The lighting from above made his nose look exaggeratedly long and pointed.

He was lying on his back, propped up on his elbows, and breathing hard in an effort to recover from his recent hack attack. The pale sheet and blanket, in themselves ludicrously inadequate in the face of the arctic conditions, even failed to reach his feet and his equally bare shoulders.

Harmless as the man appeared, Holly was still stunned to see Kia push open not just one of the doors but both – apparently expecting her companions to follow her – and walk in.

'What are *you* doing here?' she asked – a little sharply, Holly thought. He would also have expected, given the unnerving nature of the setting, that the poor man would have jumped a mile on having several people burst into his room without warning. But either the man had been waiting for them or was simply disinclined to show, or perhaps even feel, surprise. His response implied that both were true.

'Ah, there you are,' he panted. 'Sneaking around as usual, eh?'

The baron felt there was a matter even more important at this point than formal introductions.

'Are you warm enough with those?' he wanted to know, indicating the man's bed linen that was looking more threadbare the closer they got.

'Oh, don't worry about me,' said the man, groaning as he lay his head laboriously back on the wafer-thin pillow. 'I'm as comfortable as I'm ever going to be.'

The distinct lack of compassion in Kia's face was not lost on Holly, and she in turn noticed his puzzled look.

'This,' she said by way of explanation, 'is the Inoperable Hero.'

The man made a great show of barely lifting a hand in recognition of his full title. Holly and the baron nodded in greeting. Holly noticed that Uncle Jasper shared Kia's look of distrustful disdain.

'It's true,' the unlikely Hero wheezed. 'They can't do a thing for me. It's only a matter of time.'

Kia looked at Holly and raised her eyes to the ceiling.

'But it's more about what I can do for you,' the ailing man said with considerably more composure, 'and your time might be running out before mine.'

Before Kia could question this theory, the demon expressed its displeasure at being ignored with a particularly desperate shriek.

'That's one, isn't it?' the man said in a voice now free of effort. He practically leapt up, again belying his supposed afflictions, this time on to just one elbow so that he could face them. 'You didn't solve that, did you? And you won't ever be able to solve any more. That's the Culprit's aim.'

At this point he seemed to realise that he was slipping out of character, so relapsed into a particularly self-conscious fit of coughing, during which Kia leant over to Holly and whispered, 'We never did find out his real name, but with acting like that, I don't suppose it's Oscar.'

She waited patiently, shaking her head from time to time, until the self-indulgence subsided.

'What do you mean?' she finally got to ask.

The man's elbow had by now pitifully slid away, and he was lying on his shoulder, still facing them, valiantly trying to keep his head horizontal. After a lengthy bout of panting for dramatic effect, he continued.

'He's – come up with – a machine,' he struggled to say. 'A device – that specifically targets – anyone who knows about – the grid. It somehow neutralises – that part of you – that makes you different.'

Kia stared at him, for the first time without contempt. 'But that would make us...'

He nodded and fell heavily on to his back.

'The same as everyone else,' he murmured.

Kia looked away, her eyes darting restlessly about.

'We'd be powerless to stop him,' she muttered to herself. 'He could do whatever he liked.' Her eyes suddenly came to rest. 'And so would everything else. Anything that appeared on any given day. Free rein. Chaos.' She looked imploringly at Holly. 'The end.'

Holly tried to imagine what that would be like, but couldn't. He'd only been here a day, and the idea of the demonic furry creatures on the bridge running around unchecked was bad enough, but he had no way of knowing what untold horrors Kia and her team had dispatched in the past. And had they not, all these things would now be coexisting in this world, vying for supremacy. He wondered where humanity would be in that pecking order, if anywhere.

The word Solver loomed in front of him, with the sickening realisation that the title was his.

'Where is he?' he asked the stricken man quietly.

'Ah, there you are,' came the reply. The patient didn't open his eyes. His voice was still weak but had acquired a menacing tone. 'The man of the moment. And unless you're very good, maybe the last of a dying breed.'

At this point he too seemed to be reminded of his allocated role. He opened his eyes and looked pitifully at Holly and raised a trembling arm.

'He's on the top floor,' he groaned, almost extending a finger. 'His machine must be more effective from up there. Go.' He hauled himself painfully back on to his elbow. 'Go. You must stop him. I've done all I can. You're the only hope we have left.'

With that, the Inoperable Hero's last strength appeared to desert him and he crumpled on to his side with a loud sigh. The others looked at one another, uncertain as to how to proceed.

'Except to say,' the man suddenly announced, shooting up again and making them all jump, 'that when you reach a point where you're not sure which door to take, always send a scout on ahead. It's not safe for you all to go through together.'

Now thoroughly spent, he fell on to his back, an alarming rattle coming from his throat. Holly attempted to get more information out of him on his last pronouncement, but was feebly waved away with a series of gurgling noises, one of which may or may not have been the word 'Hurry'.

Realising that there was now nothing for it but to make their way higher in the building, Holly looked around and noticed a sign that said STAIRS, accompanied by an arrow. The arrow indicated the passageway that would take them along another side of the space that housed the Robot Steel Band, implying that the impenetrable, glowing space was, after all, a courtyard.

The other three followed the direction of Holly's nod at the sign and dubiously nodded in reply. They had only taken one step, however, when Uncle Jasper let out a yell and fell on one knee, after which he clutched at his foot. Kia was the first to reach him.

'What is it?' she asked with concern. The man shook his head, making his whiskers twitch. He was panting heavily. 'The same thing again?' she wanted to know. He nodded, sweat starting to form on his brow.

'OK, well, listen,' Kia said, in a tone that told Holly she was used to coming up with plans to deal with any situation – her own type of solution. 'You rest here awhile. We'll have to get going, but we'll take the most direct route we can, so you should be able to follow us when you feel up to it. Alright?'

Uncle Jasper nodded in pain and frustration. He didn't watch the other three reluctantly leave him, choosing instead to glower at the man on the trolley, who, not to be outdone, had started panting even more noisily.

The baron pushed aside one of the double doors that led into the new passageway and held it open for his two companions, Kia bringing up the rear, giving one last sorrowful look at the crouching man in the boiler suit.

As the door closed behind them, the ever-present sound of swirling wind became suddenly muffled. Holly deduced that this was because the windows in this passageway were all inexplicably intact. Although it had no functioning light source of its own, not even the luminous fog of the other corridor, the glow through the glass was more than enough to enable them to see where they were going, at least as far as yet another set of doors.

Through these doors was a room not dissimilar to the first two. Thinking geometrically as ever, Holly knew that they were now on the diagonally opposite corner of the courtyard from where they had arrived. As it turned out, this would be the last time he could be sure of his bearings.

This room had the distinction of being the darkest of the three. The only light, indeed, came from a broken sign above a door some way in to the room, on which the word STAIRS was just still legible. The door itself had a long, vertical pane of frosted glass, through which could be seen a light of a ghostly green hue, flickering slowly on and off in a pattern that was random and, to Holly's mind, deranged.

Kia went straight over to this door and pulled the handle, but to no avail. The two men combined their strengths and, after a couple of attempts and rather to their disappointment, it finally creaked into action. They stepped through, reluctant to allow it to close behind them, should the next one prove even harder to move.

The stairwell looked as though it may once have been painted white. The stairs led in both directions, the only strip light suspended over the ascending flight, the other leading into total darkness, so things could conceivably have been worse, Holly thought grimly. With the door now firmly closed behind them, the light didn't seem so green any more.

They took a deep breath and started to climb, expecting a long haul, and were surprised when the steps ran out after ascending just two floors. They were confronted by an identical door to the one through which they had entered the stairwell, and Kia's efforts yielded identical results, as did the men's, but in a different way. The hinges on this door had rusted to such a degree that, instead of the door swinging open, it simply fell in with an almighty crash, taking the baron with it, Holly having caught hold of the door frame just in time.

The noise echoed around them for what seemed an age, easily long enough for the demon to respond with a spectacular three-part shriek, each part finishing higher than the last like a racing car changing gear, before the rumble faded and blended seamlessly with the white noise of the storm outside.

Only when she was sure that nothing could be heard coming towards them did Kia and Holly step over the baron, who gestured that he was alright but seemed in no hurry to get up, and enter the room.

Holly's immediate feeling was disorientation. He was sure this door faced the same way as the previous one, in which case the windows on to the glowing courtyard should have been to their right. In their place was an open set of doors leading into another dark corridor with blank walls on either side that was littered with wheelchairs in various states of disrepair.

There were windows at the opposite end of the room, but the atmosphere outside them was so much less murky that an empty courtyard was clearly visible. More unsettling for Holly was that, on closer inspection, the gravel-covered ground of this courtyard could clearly be seen to be on the same floor they were now on, despite them having just ascended from two floors below. The far sides of this square space could just be made out, as could dark windows on higher floors, before the view petered out.

Higher still, an intense light was blazing. The three of them stood staring at it for a moment, sharing the tacit understanding that this beacon was showing them their destination.

CHAPTER THIRTY-FOUR

Two doors, each with its own STAIRS sign, each leading along a different side of the courtyard, both equally dark, both with unbroken windows along one side, one empty, one with another hospital trolley diagonally across it about halfway along. The three remaining members of the team again shared the same thought – that this was one of the forks the Inoperable Hero had warned them about.

Kia took charge. She faced the two men squarely, although it didn't escape Holly that she couldn't actually look them in the eye.

'Right,' she said. 'This is how it's going to happen. If I'm not back within two minutes to give you the all-clear...'

'Whoa, whoa, hang on,' the baron interrupted. 'That's not how it's going to happen at all.'

'Baron, please don't argue,' Kia implored, her voice shaking. 'I'm the team leader...'

'Exactly, Kia,' the baron persisted. 'You're the team leader, and leading in this instance doesn't mean going in front, it means coordinating and giving orders. And if you're out there on your own, you won't have a team to lead. At least if the two of you are here together, you'll have him to boss around.'

Holly smiled and nodded almost eagerly. But Kia didn't seem able to concede.

'No, no,' she wailed, on the verge of tears, 'I have to do the right thing...'

'...which in this case is to delegate,' said the baron, calmly but firmly. 'Sending lieutenants out into the field. Being authoritative and decisive. Even if, in this case,' he paused until she finally made eye contact, 'I have to make the decision for you.'

She continued staring at him, and said nothing.

'Kia,' he went on, quietly, 'this is the only sensible deployment of the forces that remain available to you. You're the leader and Holly's the Solver. Without you two, none of this is going to get fixed. I'm the most expendable. And besides, if it wasn't for your – I would love to say generosity, but I suppose I mean your inability to solve me on the day – I wouldn't even be here. So maybe me being here now is the reason you were so rubbish back then.'

He smiled hopefully. Kia wrestled inwardly for a moment, then nodded sadly.

'Go on, then,' she said with nearly all her usual composure, adding, 'but if you don't come back, I'll never speak to you again.'

'Very likely,' agreed the baron. He made a few cheerful eeny, meeny motions between his two options, eventually choosing the right-hand door which led into the passageway with the trolley, for no better reason than it seemed an appropriate omen, the man on the trolley having been the cause of this solo mission.

He was reaching for the handle when Kia caught his arm, indicating that she wanted to whisper something to him.

When he bent down to receive his final instructions, she kissed him lightly on the cheek. He nearly lost his balance in surprise.

'Oh dear,' he said to the door as he straightened up. 'Oh dear, oh dear. Now I really am scared.'

Without looking back, he pushed the door open and set off with a purposeful stride.

Kia and Holly watched him through the window in the door as his dark clothing faded into its surroundings. By the time he reached the far end, all that could be seen of him was his silver hair, which somehow managed to open the door and float through the gap.

When the sound of footsteps had died away, Holly noticed that the fluctuating accompaniment of the wind, now at its most muted since they had arrived, was being offset by a constant drone, a hum that could be felt as much as heard, like that of a giant transformer.

Another layer of sound was provided by the reactivation of Kia's teeth, which chattered merrily along like a pair of overactive castanets until she caught Holly looking at her, at which point she clamped them firmly together.

'Don't you feel the cold?' she asked with some annoyance, hunched over her folded arms.

'Well, yes and no,' replied Holly after a moment's thought. 'The truth is, I'm always cold, I just choose not to feel it. Or maybe I'm just used to it.'

He moved over to the window and surveyed the hazy enclosed space beyond. Even though this window was unbroken, he saw for the first time that the gravel, already shiny from the moist fog, was also littered with shattered glass, presumably from the floors above.

'Anna was always trying to get me to put on more layers,' he continued, absently, 'but I kept telling her there was no point. It made no difference, other than to make me feel like an over-inflated tyre.'

Kia slowly went and stood next to him, joining him in staring at the play of light on the medley of glass and stone.

'Holly,' she began, hesitantly. 'If – we don't – get through this,' she paused to give her bottom lip a few playful bites, 'there's something you really ought to know...'

'No.' Holly's tone was adamant. 'There isn't.' He turned and spoke down to her, suddenly back at school. 'And that's not because I have the faintest idea what you're going to say. Because I haven't. But I do know that there's more than enough going on here already, and that's our priority.' He remembered one of the first things he had heard her say. 'And we have to prioritise, as I recall.'

Whether she realised she was having her words thrown back at her, he couldn't tell. Eventually she nodded, but without any real conviction. The full stop to the conversation was provided by the demon with a particularly loud swooping shriek.

'It's too quiet,' Kia said, a little incongruously to Holly's mind, but he knew instantly what she meant. The baron hadn't checked in.

Kia went back to the door and peered through the window.

'Something's not right,' she murmured. 'And I can't see that we're any safer waiting here than going on.' She gestured with her head for Holly to join her. 'Let's get after him.'

They pushed the door open together and entered the passageway, both glad to be moving again. Just waiting helplessly was bad enough, but in this temperature it was immeasurably worse.

As they crept along, instead of their eyes getting used to the lack of light, the reverse seemed to be true – the darkness grew in intensity, as did their apprehension at what they would find at the other end. It also made the corridor feel a great deal longer than they had first thought.

When they did finally reach the other end, they slid gingerly through the smallest gap they could make between the doors. They needn't have worried about keeping quiet, because the volume level of the wind instantly raised a few notches.

In the far right corner of an otherwise completely dark room, one of the double doors was open, revealing another howling fluorescent lamp of a corridor just like the one that had led them past the Robot Steel Band, complete with swirling fog and shattered windows. Indeed, Holly would have sworn it was the same courtyard, albeit a couple of floors higher, but given the route they had taken, he didn't see how it could be.

They made their way, Kia in front, towards these doors, both because this was the only exit they could see, and because they bore the next STAIRS sign above them. Holly was feeling particularly uneasy at the fact that, in such a run-down, neglected place, their path was being so well signposted. His unease trebled when Kia stopped and screamed.

Looking past her, he could now see that the reason the door was open was that there was a body lying in it. The fog was having trouble picking out any features from its dark mass, but closest to them they could just make out a pair of shoes. What really gave it away was the tangled mass of silver hair at the other end.

Holly instinctively tried to hold an arm out in front of Kia so that he could go and investigate first, but she brushed him aside and ran forward.

'Baron!' she shouted, bending down next to the prone figure. By the time Holly had caught her up, she had already swept the baron's hair back from his face, except for one strand. They both watched with fascination and enormous relief as this single lock of hair wafted rhythmically back and forth.

'He's breathing,' said Kia, finally allowing herself to do the same. She stared sadly at her stricken colleague.

'Maybe the captain was right,' she murmured. 'Maybe being nice really doesn't get you anywhere.' Her voice was starting to crack. 'No good deed goes unpunished,' she said, desolately.

'Well, he hasn't been knocked down,' Holly deduced, having found no obvious sign of injury. 'From the way he's curled up, it's as if he carefully laid himself down on the floor.'

They gently slid the baron's inert form a short way further into the fog-laden corridor, just far enough for his knees to clear the spring-loaded door which wasted no time in falling shut.

After a few vain attempts at revival, Holly and Kia had just sat back, wondering how to proceed, when they both heard something. Bending forward, they realised to their amazement that not only was the baron breathing, he was snoring.

'He's – asleep,' she proclaimed, audibly aware of how stupid that sounded. 'A very deep sleep. Maybe some sort of trance?'

For some reason, Holly had always found the sound of snoring deeply unsettling. On the rare occasions his wife had snored – more accurately the rare occasions he was awake and she wasn't – he had either got up or gently nudged her until she changed position. Hearing it now, in this setting, made his hair stand on end. He would have been glad of a distraction, but when it came it was even more unsettling.

It was a voice, and it wasn't the baron's. It was Uncle Jasper's, riding the fog through the cracks in the windows.

'Large drink sign. Twice as angry,' it said in that unmistakably deliberate tone. It wasn't quite a shout, but it didn't need to be – it was declaimed in a way designed to be heard over a great distance, and it was meant as a warning.

Kia stared out into the featureless glow, clearly shaken at hearing her beloved adviser's voice through the raging wind.

'He's used that before,' she moaned. 'But what does it mean?' Her face grew pained. 'Why can't I get these things? Why don't I listen?'

Holly watched her as she grew more and more agitated, her hands becoming increasingly animated. Then they stopped and her eyes widened.

'Large drink – sign. Double – cross. That's it! Twice as – angry. Double – cross. Yes! He's warning us about a double-cross!' Her brief tone of triumph disintegrated. 'Oh no.'

Her breathing was getting shorter again, and faster. The pained expression had returned, her eyes were darting around wildly and one hand had gone up to her neck.

'No, oh no. It can't be.'

The onset of panic was so similar to the ones she had had earlier, Holly wondered whether he had inadvertently been tolerant about something.

'He's warning me,' she wheezed. 'It's me – that clue was for me – I'm the one facing the Law Lord.' She was shaking her head in anguish. 'The General told us. The one we had to look out for. The last thing he said. "He's always c..." He must have meant – "cold".' Her expression was now one of abject despair. 'You just said it. You're always cold.'

She turned to Holly, hopelessness streaming out of her eyes.

'It's all you. You're the traitor!'

CHAPTER THIRTY-FIVE

Holly could only stare back at Kia. His voice had frozen, and his expression had frozen. And this just helped to confirm Kia's suspicions.

Her face contorted in anguish and anger, and uttering a loud sound the demon would have been proud of, which started as a grunt and ended as a squeal, she shoved Holly backwards. He would have caught himself easily enough, had he not tried to avoid the baron's legs. After some awkward manoeuvring he ended up on his back, and by the time he lifted his head, all he could see in the distance was one of the doors flapping shut.

'Kia!' he shouted, relieved to have regained command of his voice. 'Kia, come back!'

He struggled to his feet, and with one last jealous look at the peacefully curled up baron, he stumbled after her.

There seemed little point any more in stealth. The team had disintegrated, and their progress throughout had clearly been well orchestrated. The only priority now was finding Kia.

He burst through the doors and without hesitating made straight for the next doors with a STAIRS sign over them, thinking that Kia would have done the same, even in her state. These doors received the same brusque treatment.

He had found the next stairwell. The lighting arrangement was the same – use of the descending flight was obviously being discouraged. Happily following the path of least resistance, Holly bounded up the steps two at a time. Again, he was only allowed to get two floors closer to his goal. This time he stuck his head round the exit door on the intermediate floor to see if there was any sign of Kia before continuing upwards.

He emerged into a room that was so dark he had no idea of its size or layout. The only faint light came from a set of doors to his right, one of which was open, this time without the aid of a body, he was glad to notice. He didn't know that he was about to discover another one anyway, and yet something did make him slow down and enter the room cautiously.

It looked like it had once been some sort of waiting room. It housed an odd collection of chairs, a few of which seemed to have been thrown in. Towards the far end of the room was a coffee table, behind which the only other set of doors seemed to be whistling to themselves. Closer to Holly, against the right-hand wall was an old filing cabinet, its empty bottom drawer jutting out like a protruding chin. And huddled against it in the corner, her head resting on her knees and her arms hanging limply at her sides, was Kia.

'There you are,' Holly puffed, rather embarrassed to be still severely out of breath after such brief exertions. Then rather sharply, 'Have you come to your senses yet?'

As he approached her, he could see that he was wasting what precious little breath he had. Kia was as comatose as the baron had been and, like the baron, appeared to have settled gently into a sleeping position. Her breathing was deep and slow, but she showed no other signs of life. And with that realisation, any last resolve Holly may have had sank to the floor, taking him with it.

He sat on his knees on the floor facing her, reminded of the last time they had sat like this, on the ship. Then – had that really only been earlier today? – she had comforted him. Now he was powerless to comfort her. He wanted to put his arms around her as she had done to him, and tell her everything was going to be alright. But he couldn't bring himself to, consoling himself with the thought that she wouldn't be able to hear him. But the bottom line was that he didn't believe everything would be alright.

He shifted laboriously round and sat next to her. In this position he felt able at least to put one arm across her shoulders. This meant that, for the first time since they had all arrived in Chateau Remorse, or perhaps even earlier, the newspaper he was still diligently carrying had to change hands. Her head moved a little, falling lightly against his chest.

They sat like this for a while, silent and motionless, as he stared blankly through the door into the room he had just left.

'I'm sorry,' he said at last. He wasn't even aware he was speaking out loud. 'You really seemed to think I'd be good at this. You really wanted me to be good at this. And I should be. Lord knows I've wasted enough time on these puzzles. When it didn't matter. And now that it does matter, I've let you down. I've let you all down.' He frowned at the floor. 'I've allowed an entire world – to end.'

He waited for the full enormity of that sentence to sink in, but it didn't. It was too abstract. It was too impersonal.

‘And it has to be personal,’ he said tentatively to himself, as though coming to the end of a particularly complex mathematical equation and not quite daring to believe the result, ‘because the only person I really care about letting down,’ he looked at Kia in a moment of quiet revelation, ‘is you.’

His eyes rediscovered their favourite non-existent point of focus, his thinking spot, and for a moment he was transfixed, his mind racing. It had been so long since he had cared, really cared, for somebody that the memories of that feeling that were now surfacing and passing in front of him like a conveyor belt were dragging him back a full two decades.

In all that time he had been wallowing in what he considered a healthy contempt for mankind in general, with himself at the top of the list. And this reawakened feeling – a yearning, a desperation to be with someone, to protect them from any harm – a feeling that had blown his world apart on the day of the crash – had been suppressed. This was out of fear, he now saw, because this feeling makes you vulnerable. But he also saw that it can give you purpose, possibly the only purpose you will ever need.

The last memory that was paraded in front of him was of the two policemen who came knocking on his door with the bad news. That was the day this feeling was replaced by one of anger and remorse. He should have been there, he couldn't help thinking, despite knowing what little difference that would have made. No, surely things would have been alright if only he had been there.

But this time I am here, he thought. And while I'm still here, maybe there's a chance that things will turn out to be alright, however slight that chance might be. And while there was any hope at all, he would have to try.

His resolve had returned so fast and with such intensity that he felt dizzy. Nonetheless, he knew that if he was to make any use of it, he had no time to delay.

He removed his arm from Kia's shoulders, feeling the pins and needles in it for the first time. He then gently let her fall sideways to the ground, putting his newspaper under her head. Thinking better of that, he took off his jumper, folded it and swapped it for the paper.

Her ponytail had fallen over her face, and he pushed it back, just as Kia had done for the baron. As he gazed at her, he resolved that her lasting memory of him, should she have one, would not be of a traitor. He had no idea whether she had correctly interpreted Uncle Jasper's warning of a double-cross – it made sense in a cryptic sort of way, although he had no idea what it referred to – but he couldn't help smiling at how she had got the General's clue so characteristically, and spectacularly, wrong.

He stood up quickly, which made him feel even more light-headed, and made his way to the whistling doors. Their music stopped as he opened them, as though they were holding their breath, and then resumed once he was safely through.

It was unfortunate at this point that he didn't have a giant ball of string to unravel behind him, marking out the meandering route he was taking through this labyrinth, because that was the only way he was ever going to find his way out again. The truth was, he now had purpose and resolve by the bucketload, but no plan whatsoever. He was running entirely on instinct, an instinct that simply told him to keep following the STAIRS signs. Apart from these directions, he was completely oblivious to his surroundings.

After a countless succession of rooms and corridors and at least six flights of stairs, he blundered into by far the largest room he had been in, more accurately a hall, and stopped. It was as wide as any previous room, but higher and several times longer, with barely discernable single doors dotted along either side and a big wall-to-wall, floor-to-ceiling window at either end.

The window closest to him, the one to his left, revealed nothing more than a featureless glow that was brighter at the top. He could feel that the source of this light was where he had to be.

He could also feel the glass of this window vibrate, as though it was somehow containing something raging on the other side, but he couldn't hear anything, at least not from this window. He did fancy, though, that he could hear the faintest sound coming from the other one, and was compelled to investigate.

Although this window also had an opaque look, Holly thought he could make out a vague shape through it, a large smudge. As he made his way slowly towards it, the faint noise condensed into a slow ticking, and the shape gradually sharpened into that of a huge tree.

While the turbulent space beyond the first window gave the impression of unfathomable depth, entirely in keeping with the number of steps Holly had climbed to get here, he was startled to find, behind this second window, another gravel-strewn courtyard, the ground again on the same level as his floor. Its four walls were visible through the haze, and revealed to Holly that there was only one floor above his. Beyond that he could see dark, starless sky.

Dramatically lit against this sky, thrusting straight out of the gravel, was the tree, which filled the courtyard and extended at least one floor above the building. It was entirely bare but for one leaf on one of its lower branches, a paddle-shaped leaf that swung constantly back and forth. And it was from this leaf that the sound was coming.

Holly recognised it immediately from his time on the ship. Metronome leaves, Kia had called them. As then, he was completely mesmerised. He thought it entirely logical that it would be a slow one that was the last to fall. He imagined the faster ones dropping early, the tree gradually grinding to a halt as only the slower ones remained.

As Holly watched, this last leaf finally gave up its lonely vigil, fluttered gracefully to the ground, and the tree fell silent. Holly felt a surge in the vibration from the other side of the hall, and glancing over his shoulder, noticed that the glow had become a little more intense.

Turning back, he was enchanted to see that, parodying the leaf's last movements, a few snowflakes had suddenly appeared. By the time the first wave had landed on the ground, their numbers had greatly increased, and by the time Holly managed to tear himself away, the courtyard reminded him of a snow globe that had just been shaken.

All that swirling reflected the state of his mind. He needed to focus. This running around was all very well, but only his mind had any chance of solving anything. He remembered the baron outside the pub using the phrase 'knowledge is power'. He needed more knowledge. And the idea of solutions told him what he had to do.

Walking back along the hall, he noticed a light coming from under one of the doors on the right. Opening the door revealed a storage room with a single bright bulb hanging from the middle of the ceiling. Against both the side walls were a number of tall metal cupboards, green with double doors, one of which had a door open, showing Holly an empty, shelfless interior.

Holly purposefully entered the room, climbed into the cupboard and closed the door behind him.

CHAPTER THIRTY-SIX

This time when Holly closed his eyes, there was no sofa. There was no Anna, no domestic bliss, no glass of Cabernet Anaesthetic. Even Haydn had gone AWOL. Try as he might Holly couldn't dredge up a single comforting thought. And he was glad, because he needed to think.

He needed to spend what he had heard people call quality time with his newspaper, although he knew that the quality in this case was going to be nerve-wracking. He had no idea how much of this day he had left – he felt maybe a couple of hours, but as he had long since got out of the habit of wearing a watch, there was no way of telling.

The doors of the cupboard were mercifully so warped that there was a sizeable gap between them, letting in a shaft of light more than bright enough to read by. As he looked down at the fateful puzzle, he marvelled at the difference between the respect he was showing it now and the flippant way he had chucked it on the kitchen table after he had brought it back from the newsagent's that morning. He was even reluctant to hold it out in front of him, so obsessively had he been clutching it to his chest.

Looking at it, he registered for the first time, with some satisfaction, the fact that all the horizontal words had been completed. That should make solving the vertical ones that much easier. The only gaps now were four pairs of Down clues, including the dreaded 4-18.

He looked at the clue to 4 Down again, but still couldn't make any headway. Despite Great Uncle Sid's 'alien' promptings and having every other letter, all he could come up with were the words 'retence' and 'ratinge', both of which he knew didn't exist, other than in his mind. Inventing plausible words had always been a diverting by-product of solving puzzles, and he and Eric had often proposed the idea of producing an alternative dictionary to house them and all their possible definitions.

He gave up and cut straight to 18 Down instead. He was experienced enough to know not to get stuck on one clue when you're up against a mental block.

'Note to loan shark gets kitchen appliance', he read, but no longer aloud. Seven letters. The solution took him no time at all. 'Note' was usually any letter from A to G, a musical note, and a loan shark was a lender. Tempting as 'flender' and 'glender' were, they would have to wait for that dictionary. He settled on 'blender', which had the added attraction of being a kitchen appliance, and wrote it into thc grid.

Infuriatingly, his block was still firmly in place, and the phrase 'something blender' yielded no results. No time to waste, onwards.

The next pair began with the clue 'Ale isn't terribly striking', another seven-letter word. Holly was pleased that, despite having been part of this team for so short a time, he was already expecting to hear the captain tell some groanworthy, beer-related joke, or at least a tall tale involving their beloved Bentleys. In consolation, he thought, at least it was quicker to solve the clue without the wisecracks. And so it was.

He recognised 'terribly' as one of the most common anagram indicators, obviously referring to 'ale isn't' as these words conveniently amounted to seven letters, and given the letters already provided in the grid and the definition 'striking', he was led directly to the solution 'salient', which he also entered.

Completing the pair was the clue 'Trod warily around fellow who's sleeping', seven letters yet again, and yet again posing little difficulty. 'Warily' fulfilled the same role as 'terribly' had in the previous clue, and 'around' meant that the letters T, R, O and D were somehow arranged around something, in this case another word for 'fellow'. Settling on 'man', and double-checking with the letters he already had, Holly arrived at 'dormant', a synonym for 'sleeping'.

Solving one of the all-important pairs of words and not understanding its meaning was even more frustrating than not having solved it at all. Try as he might, he just couldn't make 'salient dormant' mean anything, let alone something that might be relevant to today's events.

He wrote the letters into their appropriate squares, and held his breath. Other than a slight dizziness returning, nothing happened. Disappointed but undaunted, he cracked on.

Breaking the pattern, the third couple began with a five-letter word, the clue being 'Article on bad jokes bears fruit'. 'Article' usually denoted the words 'a', 'an', or 'the'. This word began with an A, which probably excluded the latter. It didn't take Holly long to guess at 'corn' for 'bad jokes', which resulted in 'acorn', being the fruit of an oak tree. His guessing fell a long way short of revealing where this might be leading, so he swiftly moved on to the next clue.

Two words this time, two and seven letters respectively, 'Moving tin trains about'. He was pretty sure it would be an anagram, 'tin trains' being the required nine letters, and both 'moving' and 'about' being possible indicators.

Speed being of the essence, he decided to use the empty space provided below the grid. He wrote the letters out in his usual way – in reverse order in two rows, vowels at the top, consonants at the bottom. That way, he found, the letters were least likely to suggest their original arrangement. He was reassured by the speed with which he arrived at the words 'in transit'.

What didn't reassure him was that, once again, this made no sense to him, and its inclusion in the grid had no discernible effect either. 'Acorn in transit', he pondered, picturing the tiny object on a self-propelled journey around the world. Well at least it's making more progress than I am, he thought glumly, before turning his attention to the final pair. Surely this combination would make sense of it all.

First impressions of the clue 'Snide mice involved in drugs', nine letters, weren't promising, other than providing an intriguing premise for a cartoon series. It was also not much of a challenge – the letters of 'snide mice' were 'involved' to make 'medicines', or drugs.

The last five-letter word proved no different. Indeed, Holly had solved it before he had even seen the clue, 'Coins shaped using sound'. The S-blank-N-blank-C arrangement allowed for no word he could think of but 'sonic' – as it turned out, an anagram of 'coins' meaning 'using sound'.

Writing over, he stared in disbelief at these two words, 'medicines sonic'. They had been his last hope at some level of understanding, the key to seeing the bigger picture, but he felt no closer to that now than he had been when he entered the cupboard. Solving these last clues, resolving all outstanding issues and emerging triumphant – that had been the plan and it had seemed so simple.

But the whole exercise had been a waste of time. Holly felt stupid and embarrassed, and certainly questioned the wisdom of hiding, like a Russian doll, inside a dead-end cupboard inside a dead-end room. The words 'sitting duck' loomed large over him, and he had a sudden attack of claustrophobia.

He vacated the cupboard and the room, emerging back into the dark hall. In the distance to his left, the picturesque scene he remembered had been transformed. The stately tree, although itself still the image of serenity, was now barely visible inside a violent blizzard, a hurricane of snow.

In the malevolent glow at the other end, snow could also be seen following random, restless currents, but in this light the larger flakes appeared dark instead of white. Holly also noticed that the glow was now pulsating slowly, as was the humming noise, and that the glow and the hum were disconcertingly out of phase.

He went slowly over to this window and looked up at where the glow was most intense. The beauty of the plan of solving the last clues was that it would now all be over. He wouldn't have to go up the final flight of stairs and confront whatever was there. He had absolutely no curiosity as to what that might be. The idea that he could go home without ever finding out caused him no problem whatsoever, indeed he would be happy to live with that ignorance, as long as it meant that he would live at all – not for himself, but because for him to survive meant that the others would also survive.

He saw with resignation that the last door on the right bore the now familiar STAIRS sign. He wearily pushed it open, walked with leaden feet along the last corridor before reaching the last stairwell. The steps here didn't even allow him an option, but only went up.

He slowly obeyed them, making heavy use of the banister he was sure hadn't been provided on any of the other stairs.

Having reached the top, he stopped. He could tell from the gaps round the door that there was so much light on the other side that he was reluctant to open it – a reluctance that only increased when a voice that seemed to be made of gas wafted through those same gaps.

'Well come in, come in,' it wheezed. 'Come in and say goodbye.'

[1]C	A	[2]T	E	[3]G	O	[4]R	I	[5]S	E	■	[6]H	[7]A	R	[8]M
R	■	R	■	E	■		■	A	■	[9]T	■	C	■	E
[10]A	G	A	I	N	S	T	■	[11]L	A	W	L	O	R	D
F	■	M	■	E	■		■	I	■	O	■	R	■	I
[12]T	O	L	E	R	A	N	C	E	■	[13]P	A	N	I	C
■	■	I	■	A	■		■	N	■	A	■	■	■	I
[14]P	A	N	E	L	■	[15]E	X	T	O	R	T	[16]I	O	N
E	■	E	■	S	■	■	■	■	■	T	■	N	■	E
[17]D	I	S	T	U	R	[18]B	E	[19]D	■	[20]Y	E	T	I	S
O	■	■	■	R	■	L	■	O	■	S	■	R	■	■
[21]M	A	[22]G	O	G	■	[23]E	A	R	L	Y	D	A	Y	[24]S
E	■	A	■	E	■	N	■	M	■	S	■	N	■	O
[25]T	A	B	L	O	I	D	■	[26]A	R	T	I	S	A	N
E	■	L	■	N	■	E	■	N	■	E	■	I	■	I
[27]R	E	E	K	■	[28]A	R	I	T	H	M	E	T	I	C

CHAPTER THIRTY-SEVEN

Holly froze, but only for a second. In the absence of any cars or lamp posts to hide behind, there seemed little point in delaying the inevitable. Pretending to tie his shoelaces now would clearly prove even less effective than it would have been in his own street that morning. He sighed and slowly pushed open the door. The brightness was indeed blinding, but soon began to fade.

As it did so, the room slowly came into focus. It was a fairly large room, although nothing like the hall downstairs. It did have a common feature with the hall, however, in that there were wall-to-wall windows at either end, even if these ones didn't reach the floor. They both showed the same furious blizzard, the window to Holly's left being the more accommodating as the cracks and gaping, jagged holes offered shelter from the storm to some snowflakes and clouds of the ever-present fog, thus ensuring that Holly's focus remained slightly hazy.

At either end of both walls was a set of swinging doors, the handles of which, Holly noticed with more puzzlement than unease, were chained together.

In the centre of the room was the source of the maddening, pulsating hum, which was now loud enough almost to drown out the considerable noise of the wind whistling through the shards of glass. Perched across a motley collection of tables was an even more motley collection of machines, devices and apparatuses, sporting a bewildering array of meters, dials, sliders, switches, screens, valves and LEDs, all wired together in the most precarious-looking manner imaginable.

But for the computer at its heart, it reminded Holly of a Hollywood B-movie depiction of Frankenstein's laboratory. He half expected to see a heavy cable running from it out through the window and up to the roof and the lightning rod. He was therefore only half surprised to find a thick black cable doing precisely that, although he presumed it was carrying some sort of signal out to a transmitter rather than conducting electricity the other way – that would have been rather redundant, given the large number of mains leads he could see snaking into a hefty generator under the tables.

As he stared at this monstrous contraption, he thought he caught a shadow moving to his right out of the corner of his eye. He turned his head to find that he had been right. It was a man-sized shadow. Only there was no man there to cast it. And out of it came that voice.

'Mr Holly, I presume?' it breezed, its vindictive quality making it easily audible against the layers of background noise, despite its gaseous nature.

Holly peered intently at this apparition, trying to make out more detail. What detail he did manage to find was not cheering.

The figure did indeed seem to be made of smoke. He was of roughly the same height and shape as Holly, as far as Holly could tell – the outline of his form was blurred, and it was hard to make out where the smoke finished and the air took over. The only part of him which displayed any definition was his face, of which only the cold, yellow eyes were static, the rest shifting like sand as he spoke.

'I can see from your relative composure that you already know of me,' the voice wafted on, 'but then, from what I know of you, keeping a composed exterior has never posed you any difficulty.'

Holly noticed that as the shadow was talking, his mouth actually blew the frayed edges of his lips outwards.

'You're the Culprit,' was all Holly could find in reply. Although he had spoken softly, his voice was so much more substantial that he felt he was shouting.

The Culprit laughed, making a sound like air escaping from a balloon. As he did so, a dark hole briefly appeared in his face.

'In so many ways,' he said at last. 'And in this particular instance, Culprit by name and culprit by nature. But you'll know me in any number of other forms.'

He started to circle Holly, walking in front of his invention. The side he led with was smooth, Holly noticed, while his following edge trailed behind him like shreds of lace.

'I'm every shadowy figure you've ever come across,' he continued. 'I'm the foggiest notion you always swear you haven't got. I may even be the shadow Peter Pan came looking for – the one that got away.' Another laugh, this time more shrill. As he said this he seemed momentarily to get more transparent before fading back in again.

He stopped and put his hands on his hips – whether in a deliberate parody of Peter Pan or simply out of frustration at getting no response, Holly couldn't tell.

‘Oh dear. Kia had such high hopes for you. And yet here you are. All alone.’

Hearing this abomination even speak Kia’s name roused Holly’s anger, as of course had been the intention. He was going to have to hold his own in this battle of wills. He was going to have to be devastatingly witty.

‘So are you,’ he said, sadly aware that he sounded like a petulant nine-year-old, disappointing himself once again. The Culprit must also have been expecting something better, as he drooped visibly and let his arms hang down.

‘Yes, well,’ he said, sounding bored. ‘In the first place, I didn’t start the day with a crack team at my disposal that I then succeeded in frittering away, one by one.’

Holly hoped that, back in his teaching days, when he had addressed his pupils, they hadn’t felt as small as he felt right now, but rather imagined that they did.

‘And in the second place,’ his lecturer continued, now with a little more relish, ‘who said I was alone?’

Taking its cue, a trolley slowly slid from behind the dense machinery and the forest of wires, gradually revealing its occupant, feet first, to be the Inoperable Hero.

He was using the various tables to propel himself along with his emaciated arms, grimacing as he did so. Having made his strenuous way to the front, he flopped melodramatically on to his back while still allowing himself to give Holly a smug grin and a feeble wave of acknowledgement.

‘There he is,’ simpered the Culprit, as though talking about a pet. ‘The Hero of the moment.’

Holly remembered the man on the trolley addressing him in a similar way, and wondered if the Culprit was being equally sarcastic.

'But I'm afraid the old family retainer was right, bless his whiskers.' Holly was amazed at how jovial this steam-powered voice could sound. 'There was a double-cross. And a traitor. Although how anyone could be stupid enough to associate either of those with good old Holly is entirely beyond me.'

Holly felt his hackles rise again, this time also getting annoyed that he was so easily being made to feel annoyed. The Inoperable Hero added to his irritation by having another of his affected bouts of coughing, at which the dark hole reappeared in the Culprit's face, which Holly took to be a silent laugh.

'There's the General's generous clue!' the Culprit breathed, triumphantly, having indulgently waited for the attack to subside. 'He's always – coughing!' Another laugh. 'Not cold! Oh yes,' he added in a more conspiratorial tone, 'I've been keeping an ear on your progress, or lack of it.' The joviality returned. 'But coming out with "I'm always cold" when you did – what are the chances of that? I couldn't have scripted that one better myself!'

Holly didn't react, but for once he was deliberately not reacting. He had calculated that a complete lack of response on his part was the only thing likely to unsettle this vain wisp of smoke who clearly loved nothing more than the sound of his own breath. But at the same time he was casting his eyes about for an object that was portable yet heavy enough to lay into the machinery with. He didn't think Mr Wispy would be able to offer much in the way of opposition, but what happened next severely disillusioned him on that score.

'But what about that double-cross?' the Culprit was still gloating. 'Have you got that far yet?'

Without any warning, and despite being several paces away, the Culprit suddenly shot out an arm, which not only reached Holly but managed to snatch the newspaper out of his hand. The Culprit's fingers had condensed, apparently concentrating their matter to such an extent that, as they brushed past Holly's hand, they felt like rough steel rods.

Holly took a step back, profoundly shocked. If this character could manipulate himself to this degree, there was no telling what he could do. The Culprit meanwhile pretended not to notice the effect he had produced, busying himself instead with inspecting the almost completed grid.

At length he whistled – in admiration, although the impression was more of letting off steam.

'You have done well,' he patronised. 'So nearly there. All but a single word.' He looked up. 'And you have solved the double-cross. But I bet you don't even know which one it is.'

He left an expectant pause for thought, which Holly also ruefully recognised as a habit of his own, and then tapped the relevant spot on the paper.

'Salient dormant,' he offered, as though it was the most obvious thing in the world. 'But you thought "salient" only meant "prominent", didn't you? No, *a* salient can be used to mean a projection of the front line into enemy territory. How appropriate is that? In this case, a scout or forerunner. What a judicious choice of words.'

Holly began to get an idea of how his own eulogising must have made Uncle Sid feel.

'So I just had to make sure Mr Incurable here convinced you to keep sending people ahead on their own, after which they'd be out for the count, and out of the running.'

The man on the trolley let his head fall to one side.

'Oh it was nothing,' he whimpered. 'Nothing at all.'

'Ah, modest to the end,' the Culprit purred. 'A hero through and through.'

He slapped Holly's newspaper down on the chest of the ailing man, who coughed once and automatically covered the paper with his hand.

'But as you can see, Mr Solver,' resumed the voice, back to its malevolent best, 'in the event, he was my Hero, not yours.'

He floated round to the end of the trolley nearest Holly.

'And heroes need rewarding. And what better reward for an Inoperable Hero than the ultimate cure?'

Something in the tone of voice made the supposedly hopeless case snap his head up sharply, just in time to see the figure of smoke suddenly reduce its entire body to the solid rods Holly had felt just moments before. With one swift movement, this grotesque stick figure launched the trolley and its cargo at the broken window.

The trolley came to a catastrophic stop against the wall, but the few remaining shards of glass in the window offered no resistance to its occupant, and with a deafening howl that belied his innumerable illnesses, the Inoperable Hero, still clutching Holly's newspaper, disappeared into the swirling void.

CHAPTER THIRTY-EIGHT

'He took his bedclothes with him. Such a modest man. He will be sorely missed.'

Holly could only stare at the speaker, horrified that anyone, or anything, could be so calm under these circumstances, horrified that he had just witnessed a fellow human being, however loathsome, being dispatched with such indifference, and horrified that his copy of the paper, the only hope he had of stopping this infernal device and thwarting the Culprit's plan, had just vanished. It had been up to him to come up with all the solutions. He was the Solver, and he had lost.

'Well.' The Culprit turned back from admiring his handiwork, having resumed his smoky consistency. 'That just leaves you and me, now that we have both lost our entourage. Which reminds me! The missing word. The only word, fortunately for me, that eluded you. And your – entourage.'

The repeated word was obviously meant to drive the clue home, but Holly's mind wasn't at home. He tried again to wield a poker face as his ultimate weapon, but was sure the poker his face looked like was less the game than the red-hot variety.

'Retinue.' The Culprit rolled the R outrageously.

Holly thought he had already reached the lowest level of inadequacy, but now he discovered there was a sub-sub-basement.

How had he not got that? It certainly seemed blindingly simple now. He could even remember the clue – 'Regret having alien in entourage'. 'Regret' was 'rue' going round the outside, and the alien...

His mind raced back to Great Uncle Sid's valiant but vain attempts to give Holly a head start to this clue. 'School alien', he had said, to which Uncle Jasper had responded with 'class – collection'. Holly saw now that this was S-ET. The old man's second hint had been 'iron alien', Uncle Jasper's response, 'bases – pedestals', the answer, Fe-ET. 'Alien' was of course ET, short for 'extraterrestrial'. No wonder Great Uncle Sid had given Holly a look of such disdain.

'Retinue blender,' the hazy figure announced, throwing out an arm in the direction of the expansive apparatus with such force that its wispy trails threatened to become completely detached. 'A device that only affects your retinue – The Team,' the last two words given the full treatment of sarcasm, 'and homogenises them, making them no more of a danger to me than all the other brainless drones that walk the streets.'

He cocked his head, awaiting the moral outcry, the voice of reason, even just irresistible curiosity. But Holly wasn't going to give him the satisfaction of any of those.

'How does it work, I hear you ask?' offered the Culprit, not to be denied his moment. 'Well, we have the late lamented Hero to thank for that.' Rather more gently than before, he used his other arm to refer his audience to the wreckage of the trolley that was sprawled under the window. 'I'm sure you will not be too surprised to hear that the unfortunate fellow spent a great deal of time in and out of the hospital, where they would test for this and that, hoping to get to the root cause of the poor man's unfathomable, hence inoperable, condition.'

As the shady character's eager speech got into its stride, so did his legs. He started pacing around as though he really was a professor lecturing students, stopping occasionally to emphasise a particular point.

'The tests, of course, never produced anything remotely conclusive, and they were about to throw in the towel when a research student came up to him and asked him if he'd like to take part in a project she was organising. Naturally, he leapt at the chance – or at least limped at it with enthusiasm.'

Holly's eyes were following the raconteur's movements around the room, while occasionally darting furtively over at the machinery, trying to decide which bit looked important enough to be worth attempting to destroy irreparably before he was impaled by those steely fingers.

'It turned out to be about resonance,' the wheezy voice droned on. 'Apparently we all vibrate at different frequencies, and one of the tests had shown that our Hero's frequency was unusual, but what made it really noteworthy was that it was a frequency that he shared exactly with some others, and the woman got very excited and said that never happened, not exactly. So our Hero makes some enquiries, does a bit of delving and discovers that the people with this common frequency are all...' he nodded, assuming – correctly, as it turned out – that Holly could fill in the blank himself, '...grid related.'

Holly might even have been tempted to fill in the blank out loud, but a movement behind the Culprit had caught his eye.

Each of the doors to the room was furnished with a small window, not even a foot square, around head height, and as the Culprit strutted self-importantly in front of the set of doors to the left of the shattered trolley, it was through one of these windows that Holly did indeed see a head. Waiting for an opportune moment when he hoped the professor would be too engrossed to notice, he peered more intently and saw to his astonishment that the head was Uncle Jasper's, instantly recognisable despite the window frame not having the capacity to contain both face and whiskers.

Initially he had been waving – the movement that had attracted Holly's attention – but once that had been achieved, he started pointing vehemently downwards, giving Holly a mild version of The Look he had used by the bridge, before disappearing out of sight again.

'A nifty bit of research, wouldn't you agree?' the voice went on, not bothering to wait for the reply it knew it wouldn't get. 'One our long-suffering Hero was stupid enough to bring to me. And by turning their procedure on its head, we end up with the perfect method for weeding out specifically those elements that our world would be so much better without. Target that frequency, alter that frequency, eliminate the problem.'

The figure wafted right up to Holly, his eyes the only constant in that maelstrom of a face.

'You know that this is real,' it murmured. 'You've seen its effect. Haven't you?'

If this was one last attempt to elicit a response from Holly, it came within a hair's breadth of working. The memories of the changes brought about in Lady and Uncle Sid were painful, and the idea of that happening to Kia was unbearable.

The Culprit snorted in contempt and drifted over to the centre of the array.

'And now we shall unleash the fruits of their wonderful hard labour,' he proclaimed.

So saying, he threw a large switch on a panel next to the computer screen. The ever-present drone of the transformers was joined by a hum that started fairly low in pitch and volume, before slowly increasing in both. The demon, who must have been listening intently to its colleague all this time, seemed to sense a rival and let out a particularly unnerving swooping shriek just to show how it was really done.

Holly looked around in panic. The Culprit turned to him.

'Takes a while to warm up,' he said, almost apologetically. 'But it will be worth it! Just think – tomorrow morning you'll wake up as if nothing has happened, blissfully unaware of all the people here you've let down.'

That was finally too much for Holly. He picked up a stray leg from the Inoperable Hero's trolley that had spun his way after the impact. Choosing an especially busy display panel on the left of the array, he launched himself at it, arm raised to strike.

He didn't even get halfway. The Culprit intercepted him and Holly bounced off the supposed shadow as if he'd hit a brick wall, before finding both his wrists firmly clamped into place, his right arm still aloft. He was surprised to notice that, despite the solidity of the wall-like body and the vice-like hands, the impression of the surfaces was one of felt. Maybe baize, Holly thought.

The machinery was getting louder, a buzzer had started to go off and some of the apparatus was beginning to rattle.

'Was that it?' the voice hissed into Holly's ear. 'The ultimate intellectual solution? The crowning achievement of the great Solver? A piece of Luddite thuggery, a desperate, futile gesture in the face of an inevitable future?'

Holly found himself being thrown effortlessly through the air, landing unceremoniously on his front in a corner. He lay there, stunned.

'I'm grateful you took so long getting here,' the Culprit roared over the spiralling volume of his device. 'Even half an hour ago, I couldn't quite have done that. You work it out.'

Still facing away from his tormentor, Holly had managed to prop himself up on his elbows, but didn't seem to be in any shape to work anything out.

'No? Well then, you just lie back and enjoy the show. Only a few more seconds and all your troubles will be over.'

The machinery produced a final crescendo in preparation of belching forth its decisive broadcast, the last great boom that would bust once and for all the shackles imposed by Kia and her solitary band of experts on anyone and anything that intended chaos and destruction to this world.

Just as the fateful signal left the device, sending a jolt through the thick black cable that snaked its way out of the shattered window and up into the unknown, the sound of heavy industry suddenly vanished, leaving only that of the wind. The assembly of tables, previously groaning under the restless weight of contrived metal and glass, lay bare.

The proud inventor of the absent invention could only stare at the space it had so recently occupied. Eventually, in a great blur, he whirled round at the only other person in the room, and his eloquence failed him.

'What?' was all he could manage, but it was all that was needed.

Holly had been thrown – indeed had made sure he was thrown, having judiciously chosen a convenient part of the machine for an attack he knew would be fruitless – into the corner of the room in front of the doors through which he had seen Uncle Jasper's gestures. Having correctly interpreted those gestures, he now rolled over to one side, pen still in hand, to reveal his dog-eared copy of the newspaper, puzzle to the fore, grid finally completed.

'What!' the Culprit roared again, louder and more drawn out, making the windows at the far end of the room rattle.

Holly slowly and painfully stood up and faced his adversary.

'Retinue,' he said, gesturing with his thumb at Uncle Jasper's beaming face in the window of the door, as the old family retainer waved merrily at the Culprit. 'Thanks for the help.'

The Culprit let out a long, loud snarl and started to expand. Holly moved towards the centre of the room to divert whatever may happen away from Uncle Jasper. The Culprit continued to grow and billow.

Eventually he became a swirling black mass topped with a gargoyle-like grimace of hostility and rage.

'I'm fuming now!' bellowed the cloud of seething smoke, at which point the entire window behind him splintered and showered the room in glass shards, allowing the snow-laden currents free rein, which they gleefully accepted, by racing each other to the already ruined panes on the other side.

Once the glass rain had settled, the Culprit suddenly regained his malicious composure and pounced on Holly, instantly shrinking to his previous humanoid form and pinning Holly to the top of one of the tables.

'Oh well, guess I'll have to make do with the consolation prize,' he panted. 'Another notch for my belt.'

He held up his right hand in front of Holly's face, and slowly reduced the fingers to the lethally dense form Holly had felt before. Not a hint of baize there, Holly thought.

'I could just rip your head off with these,' the restless face snarled, 'but where's the subtlety? You and I both like a little more mystery, don't we? We prefer things a little more – cryptic?'

Holly watched in helpless horror as the hand reverted first to its usual smoky state and then carried on dissipating until it was barely visible. The Culprit then calmly pushed it through Holly's shirt as if it wasn't there, and into his chest.

'Even the foggiest notion can be fatal,' he whispered, as Holly felt the hand close round his heart and start to squeeze, 'as your poor friend, Eric, found out.'

Holly couldn't move, and started to feel he was having trouble breathing, but whether this was due to the pressure on his heart or mere panic, he wasn't sure.

Compounding his distress was a growing feeling of injustice. He had done everything asked of him. He and the team had faced imminent destruction, several clear and present dangers, and each time he had come up with the appropriate solution – granted, not always unaided. He had even gone on to complete the entire grid. The team should have been safe. Everything should have been fine.

So why was he now losing his fight for breath, for his life, and for the chance to get the other members of the team safely home? Was that just the way it went, or had he missed something?

Thrashing his head around, the only thing he could move, he caught sight of Uncle Jasper peering through the window of the door, apparently shouting something, but Holly couldn't hear what above the sound of the hurricane that was now howling across the room.

What he could hear was when Uncle Jasper started pounding on the other side of the door with his open hand out of frustration – a constant beat, as deliberate as his speech.

This was then joined by a more erratic sound, a haphazard pounding – duller, like the padded side of a fist against a door. Looking round, Holly saw that the door in question was one of the set diagonally opposite the pair that excluded Uncle Jasper, and that the invisible fist belonged to Baron Nonentity, whose visible face was also shouting something incomprehensible. Seeing him, Holly was forced to agree with the captain's assessment at their introduction – the baron's name couldn't have been more inappropriate.

And then yet another noise was added to the ensemble, the ghostly sound of chains rattling. Fearfully – as if things could get any worse – Holly located the sound as coming from a third set of doors, the one at the other end of the wall from Uncle Jasper's, and opposite the baron. But the sight that met Holly's eyes would actually have lifted his heart, had it not currently been constricted in a vice-like grip, because, pushing the doors back and forth from the other side against the chain that bound their handles, was Kia.

Holly couldn't imagine how the doors were holding out, Kia was giving them such a workout. She was grimacing with the effort, and she too was shouting – mostly incoherently, but Holly could at least make out his own name.

But comforting as the appearance of his new friends was, he was resigning himself to the fact that it just meant that he wasn't going to die alone, when he noticed a change in the Culprit's demeanour – a marked restlessness, punctuated by the occasional angry glance in the direction of Uncle Jasper.

At first he assumed the Culprit to have superior hearing, reacting to something insulting Uncle Jasper had said that was otherwise inaudible. But it soon occurred to him that it wasn't the words that elicited this reaction, but the incessant pounding on the door. And that's when everything finally made sense.

The Culprit, Holly realised, was a creature of chaos, shunning anything that displayed order or regularity. And the one orderly thing that affronted his senses most was rhythm – any sort of regular rhythm, even footsteps. That was why the Inoperable Hero had to wheel himself around instead of walking. That was why the Robot Steel Band had had to be silenced. And that was why the Culprit had so recently attained his full potential – when the last of the metronome leaves fell. That tree, Holly guessed, must have been put there deliberately to keep the Culprit's powers at bay for as long as possible.

It also explained the last pair of solutions Holly had reached unaided – 'medicines sonic' – solutions that turned out in turn to be another clue, a hint that the final remedies were to be found in sound.

Feeling his strength beginning to fail, Holly knew his opportunity for putting this knowledge to use was running out. Finding his left arm free, he began slapping his open hand against the table in time with Uncle Jasper, feeling, appropriately, like a wrestler beating his submission against the canvas. The Culprit thrashed around in noticeably more agitation, but didn't release his deadly grip.

Holly was then gratified to see, or perhaps imagine in what was now approaching delirium, that both Kia and the baron had cottoned on, amplifying the beat. He also saw, but hoped he only imagined, that his name was now the only word coming from Kia, and that despite her unrelenting fury at the door, her face was already showing bereavement, tears of hopelessness streaming down her cheeks.

Holly felt himself fading as this beat, now provided by two open hands, a fist and a set of chains, became confused with the weakening pulse of his own heart. As the audible beat grew stronger and more persistent, he watched with ever more detachment as the Culprit writhed in what appeared to be agony, then with only the mildest curiosity as the shadowy figure started to appear striated, reminding Holly of a set of blinds, and finally with near indifference as the horizontal lines of smoke narrowed to nothing, and all that remained of the Culprit was the echo of a scream.

At this point Holly's world turned into the most comfortable, inviting bed imaginable, and he dived gratefully in as the lights went out.

CHAPTER THIRTY-NINE

'...and after a two-hour monologue on the merits of model aircraft, he suddenly sits back, waves his eighth pint at me knowingly and says "Regal". That's when I knew things were back to normal.'

Holly listened to the captain's voice, and during the laughter that followed he opened his eyes, just in time to see Uncle Sid sitting in an armchair, still nursing a pint of lager, echoing the word 'Regal' with a contented and decidedly intoxicated smile, which generated another wave of laughter.

Holly was home, and sitting in his usual spot on the sofa. Rather than relief, he initially felt a slight panic, afraid this might be yet another daydream after which he really would open his eyes to find himself in yet another nightmare. But time passed, the laughter continued and the panic subsided.

The captain was perched on the right arm of Uncle Sid's chair, also with a near empty glass in his hand, and seemed to be swaying slightly. They must have started off on their way here immediately after Uncle Sid's recovery, Holly thought, as neither of them now looked capable of walking in a straight line.

He was more relieved to see that Uncle Jasper and the baron had also made it safely back from the chilling Chateau Remorse and were standing either side of the chair, Uncle Jasper with his hands in the pockets of his boiler suit, the baron with his arms folded, both looking calmly contented to be taking their usual back seat to their more talkative companions.

The other thing that convinced Holly he was as awake as he was going to get was a feeling in his left arm. Swivelling his eyes as far in that direction as they would go, he saw that Kia was hanging on it, oblivious as yet, as they all were, that he was conscious. She was sitting with her legs folded to one side, and was beaming proudly at her team.

'I'll drink to that!' announced the captain, clashing glasses with Uncle Sid. 'Of course,' he continued, having drained his glass, 'there aren't many things I wouldn't drink to.' He pondered for a moment. 'That machine,' he settled on at last, 'that blender – that thing that made people really boring – that's not very toastworthy. Never confuse a blender with a toaster.' He paused and frowned, having successfully confused himself. 'But I'll drink to its solution!'

He raised his glass in salute, and then lowered it again in disappointment at finding it inexplicably empty.

'How did he solve that, anyway?' he asked the baron, who winced.

'Well, I have no first-hand knowledge of that,' he said with obvious regret, 'as I had unforgivably fallen asleep on the job at that point.' He nodded at Holly. 'But you can ask him yourself.'

They all turned to Holly, Kia letting out a high-pitched 'Oh!', releasing his arm and clapping her hands together.

The others instinctively took this as a cue and started giving Holly a cheering round of applause.

He painfully pulled himself more upright in his seat.

'How did we get back here?' he asked, as much out of curiosity as in an effort to silence this embarrassing accolade.

'Mate, one side of your face is going to be one big bruise,' the baron told him, laughing. 'Kia didn't stop slapping it, shouting "Say 6 Across, say 6 Across!" as we hung on to her. You were mumbling some pretty weird stuff, but you must have come up with the right word eventually. And you were lucky. That's nothing to what she did to that door. The Skipper and I had to go the long way round to find the door you went through, but the warrior princess here just wrenched the handles straight off hers!'

Holly noticed for the first time that the left side of his face was indeed tingling a little. He looked quizzically at Kia, whose expression was about as unapologetic as it was possible to get.

'Six?' he queried. 'Not grid?'

'I had to check on Lady,' Kia said, perhaps just a little sheepishly, 'and she's fine! Very grateful to you, of course, which accounts for the lipstick on the other side of your face.'

She produced a tissue out of a pocket, licked it and dabbed at his right cheek a couple of times.

'*Then* I had to get you to say grid,' she went on, holding the tissue against the other cheek in mock sympathy.

'You did it, though!' she suddenly shouted, grabbing his hand again. 'You got them all! You completed the grid! You did it!' She suddenly frowned at him. 'How did you do it?' she asked, with some suspicion. 'How on earth did you solve all those last clues?'

It was Holly's turn to look sheepish.

'Oh, I found most of the answers,' he faltered, 'in a cupboard.'

He was anxious to break the surprised silence that followed.

'But none of that would have counted for anything,' he hurried on, 'if Uncle Jasper hadn't somehow returned my paper to me. And beating on that door the way he did was nothing short of inspirational.'

'Majestic!' agreed the captain, raising his glass again, dismayed to find it still hadn't filled itself since the last time he had drained it.

'Regal!' chimed in Uncle Sid, brandishing his similarly empty glass to another outburst of laughter and cheering. Uncle Jasper looked visibly moved and uncomfortable in equal measure.

'Kippers! Regal!' shouted Uncle Sid again, waving his glass more frantically. Uncle Jasper smiled, relieved that his companion hadn't after all been so uncharacteristically complimentary but was merely ordering a refill.

'Coming,' he muttered as he shuffled off to the kitchen, happy to be leaving the limelight. 'Being delivered – arriving – turning up –'

Holly noticed that the man was moving without any trace of his previous limp.

'He's walking OK,' he commented. 'What was that all about?'

'You should know,' ventured the baron, eyebrows raised. 'You solved it.'

Short of raising his eyebrows as well, Holly gave no response.

'It was "Acorn in transit",' the baron was forced to elaborate. 'A corn in transit. A painful affliction of the foot suffered while mobile.'

Holly still looked puzzled.

'Which is why he only felt it when he was moving,' Kia elaborated, 'and totally forgot about it when he wasn't.'

Now fully enlightened, Holly just looked bewildered.

'He hadn't been able to leave the room we left him in until you solved that,' Kia went on. 'And he was still there, trying to figure out what to do, when the Inoperable Hero hit the ground outside the window.' She pulled a face. 'He wouldn't tell us any more about that, he didn't want to talk about it. Other than to say that he noticed your newspaper was there as well, so he knew he had to get it back to you, and he knew that you were directly overhead.'

She paused as the subject of her conversation came back into the room with a bottle of beer, pulled a penknife from one of his innumerable pockets, prised out the bottle opener attachment, used it and passed the bottle to his less than gracious colleague.

'It must have been around then that you solved "salient dormant" as well, and the baron and I woke up and made our way to where the noise was coming from.'

'And did you just fall asleep?' Holly asked the baron.

'That was weird,' the baron said, frowning. 'It was like an immense wave of fatigue. It took, I suppose, about five seconds?' He looked to Kia for confirmation, and got it. 'And I knew what was going to happen, so plenty of time to get down on the floor first. The funny thing is, I usually shut down anyway in particularly stressful situations, some sort of defence mechanism. I start yawning uncontrollably. So that's what I thought was happening, and all the way down I was telling myself not to be such a wimp.'

Kia nodded sympathetically – whether out of a shared experience or in agreement with his self-analysis, he couldn't be sure.

'Salient,' Holly said, shaking his head. 'An advance party sent into enemy territory. Who'd have thought it meant that?' He took on his faraway look. 'You've got to admit, this whole thing is some – construction!'

His admiration was clearly not shared around the room. Uncle Sid leaned forward and pointed at Holly with the end of his bottle.

'A recluse,' he slurred, squinting, 'has our honey.'

Laughter all round again, this time with a few 'ooh's thrown in. Holly found his pen and eagerly started scribbling on any available margin on his paper, pleased to see that the solving bug was far from crushed by the day's events.

Those events seemed to be going round Kia's head as well.

'Magog was such a cute little thing,' she said, absently. 'For a giant.'

'He certainly was a Wapping lad,' offered the captain. 'For a Pimlico boy.'

Holly snorted. Looking up self-consciously he was amused to see that the captain had taken his outburst as appreciation of his own cunning play on words, the actual cause having been Uncle Sid's cunning play on letters. He returned to his task and laid out some letters of his own.

'And what of the Culprit?' the baron wanted to know. 'Has he really gone?'

'Well, yes,' said Kia, hardly daring to believe it herself. 'We saw him disappear. And even if he comes back, we now know how to deal with him. The Indomitable Hero here saw to that.'

Holly snorted again, this time out of embarrassment.

'No, he's gone,' Kia went on, as much to convince herself as anyone else. 'He's beaten.'

‘Beaten,’ agreed Uncle Jasper, nodding his head. ‘Beaten – defeated – crushed – overwhelmed – conquered,’ he grinned mischievously, ‘stuffed.’

The baron meanwhile was still finding the concept of no Culprit hard to accept.

‘I wonder,’ he mused. ‘Can we be really sure?’

‘Really sure,’ said Holly vehemently, making them all turn in surprise, and then, pointing his pen at Uncle Sid, ‘of shoe’, which surprised them again, none more so than Uncle Sid, who sat bolt upright with his mouth open. The baron burst out laughing.

‘Neon ice!’ Uncle Sid gasped at last, breaking into a huge smile. ‘Neon ice! My dog alight!’ He joined the baron with his own hoarse cackle, and held out his hand to Holly, who gladly stood up and accepted it. ‘O, Holly bled!’

‘Fortunately not,’ said Kia, still not quite sure what they were laughing about. ‘That’s about the only thing he hasn’t done today.’

‘And on that happy note,’ announced the captain, the only other person not to have joined in the hilarity, ‘I think it’s time I was on my way.’ He stood up and looked at his watch. ‘It’s still just about today, and the door of the Steed may yet be ajar for those wanting a jar. Time for another, Baron?’

‘Why not, Captain,’ said the baron, wiping tears from his eyes. ‘As it’s Friday.’

This prompted another wave of laughter which this time engulfed them all.

The captain saluted Holly, at which Uncle Sid clumsily attempted to do the same before slumping heavily back into his seat. Holly nodded.

‘Captain,’ he said.

'*Nein, nein, mein Kapitän*,' insisted the captain, saluting and bowing at the same time.

'Mr Holly,' said the baron, offering his hand. 'It's been an honour. Until the next time.'

'No, no, the honour's all mine,' Holly assured him, shaking his hand. 'Next time?'

'Oh, you're too good,' the baron warned him. 'I very much doubt the grid's finished with you.'

A few more waves, bows and salutes, and the two men left the room to let themselves out. Uncle Jasper then went into the kitchen. Uncle Sid was nodding off quietly in the armchair. Holly sat back down on the sofa beside Kia.

'Next time?' he asked again. She shrugged.

'If it was up to you – which I can assure you it isn't – would you come back?'

'Like a shot,' he said, like a shot. 'If I can be of any help,' he added, not wanting to seem too keen.

She considered him for a moment.

'Thank you,' she said, to his surprise.

'What for?'

'Well, for getting us all through this.' She nodded at the grid on the newspaper he was still holding in his left hand, before adding quietly, 'And for being all I ever hoped you'd be.'

Holly got that same feeling of statements generating more questions than answers, but was too tired to pursue the matter.

'I take it I'm no longer to be tried as a traitor, then?'

Kia blushed deeply and looked distressed.

'I don't know how I got there,' she mumbled, unable to look at him. 'It seemed to make perfect sense at the time. But then that Law Lord warning could really only have been meant for you, so that's still unresolved.' She shook her head, sadly. 'Ironic, really, that I should finally get a clue right, and then make such a mess of interpreting it.'

She looked so downcast that Holly couldn't help taking her hand. She smiled faintly, still looking at the carpet.

'Thanks for not telling the others about that.'

'Well,' he chuckled, 'we wouldn't want them to see that their great leader was a mere mortal, would we?'

She finally looked up and for a while they stared at one another, unblinking, as he tried to fathom what it was about this girl that was so familiar to him.

At a sudden loud snort from the sleeping Uncle Sid, he let go of her hand and relaxed against the back of the sofa.

'You know,' he sighed, 'this is the first time I haven't wished I was back on that sailing ship.'

'This *is* the place to be,' agreed Kia, taking his paper from him. She smiled. 'And don't you forget us,' she added, quietly, tapping him playfully on the forehead with it, making him blink.

In the brief moment his eyes were closed, it struck him how odd it was that she had said 'us' and not 'it', as he had expected. But he saw why when he opened his eyes and found he was alone in the room.

[1] C	A	[2] T	E	[3] G	O	[4] R	I	[5] S	E	■	[6] H	[7] A	R	[8] M
R	■	R	■	E	■	E	■	A	■	[9] T	■	C	■	E
[10] A	G	A	I	N	S	T	■	[11] L	A	W	L	O	R	D
F	■	M	■	E	■	I	■	I	■	O	■	R	■	I
[12] T	O	L	E	R	A	N	C	E	■	[13] P	A	N	I	C
■	■	I	■	A	■	U	■	N	■	A	■	■	■	I
[14] P	A	N	E	L	■	[15] E	X	T	O	R	T	[16] I	O	N
E	■	E	■	S	■	■	■	■	■	T	■	N	■	E
[17] D	I	S	T	U	R	[18] B	E	[19] D	■	[20] Y	E	T	I	S
O	■	■	■	R	■	L	■	O	■	S	■	R	■	■
[21] M	A	[22] G	O	G	■	[23] E	A	R	L	Y	D	A	Y	[24] S
E	■	A	■	E	■	N	■	M	■	S	■	N	■	O
[25] T	A	B	L	O	I	D	■	[26] A	R	T	I	S	A	N
E	■	L	■	N	■	E	■	N	■	E	■	I	■	I
[27] R	E	E	K	■	[28] A	R	I	T	H	M	E	T	I	C

CHAPTER FORTY

It had just turned midnight. The house was silent and peaceful. The space on the sofa next to Holly was empty, save for his dog-eared newspaper.

There were no reporters, no generals, no student protesters. There was no corporate threat, no imminent invasion from the east, no moving shadows, and the furniture hadn't taken on the appearance of the wallpaper. He wasn't being squeezed, prodded, or slapped. He wasn't being bombarded with synonyms, anagrams, or dodgy puns.

And he had never felt so lonely in his entire life.

'Get a grip, Holly Oak,' he heard Anna's voice say, reminding him, if nothing else, that there had been at least one other time when he had felt this lonely. 'That was a hell of a day. Would you really rather have just sat there, staring at the walls? That was a great day. And besides.' Holly was sure the voice acquired a twinkle. 'You did good.'

He had to concede, albeit with a sigh, that she was right. He couldn't remember the last time he had experienced such a feeling of achievement, or if he ever had. And it had been a great day.

It did occur to him for a very brief moment that it had never happened, that he really had been sitting on his sofa all day, the events he remembered so vividly being the products of his warped imagination. But he dismissed the idea as irrational, chuckling as he did so at the battering his ideas on rationality had taken since that morning. In any case, all he had to do was look at his right hand which was still holding the multicoloured pen Kia had given him.

His home, until now primarily a sanctuary from the outside world, was suddenly making him feel claustrophobic. He made his way through the house and out towards the road, leaving his front door open. It was almost as quiet outside and there was nobody to be seen in the street, but there was some activity to be heard from the square, and at least he could feel a breeze. It was a mild night despite the clear sky, and Holly felt no need of his absent jumper, although he did shiver when he remembered where he had left it.

When he reached his gate he turned round and looked at the house. I did a good job fixing that, he thought to himself, not a visible sign of repair work anywhere. He was trying to picture which crack had gone where and which part of the chimney had fallen down first, when a voice behind him made him jump.

'Would I be correct in assuming this to be the residence of a Mr Holly?'

Holly froze, but only for a second before whirling round. To his relief, leaning nonchalantly against the lamp post was the ever-immaculate figure of his neighbour, Gus.

'Checking the pointing?' the old gentleman enquired. 'Or considering a moonlight flit? Who's the lucky lady?'

Holly smiled at him, watching him make his way to his own gate which, in contrast to Holly's, was never shut.

'Pleasant evening, Gus?' he asked. 'Visiting your – niece, is it?'

'That's close enough, yes,' Gus nodded. 'I think you missed out a few "great"s, but bless you for that.'

He got out his keys and put one of them in the lock.

'I don't suppose,' Holly faltered, 'you could do with that cocoa now?'

Gus stopped in mid operation and looked round in some surprise.

'Thank you,' he said, resuming unlocking his door. 'Thank you, that would be nice. But not tonight, thanks all the same.'

He turned in his now open doorway to brandish a red folder at Holly.

'Lucy's given me some homework to do, and I'm rather anxious to get started right away. Another time!'

Holly nodded, watched him go inside and then followed the procession of lights going on and off around the house until just one upstairs light remained on.

Holly continued staring through this light for some time, trying to come to terms with what he had seen that day. In the period after the accident, his colleagues, before they stopped coming round altogether, would try to prise him out of the house, telling him there was a whole world out there. How little they knew, he thought, but how right they were.

In just a few hours, Kia and her dedicated team would start trying to unravel the next grid. Things would already have appeared or been set in motion. Who would the Solver be? Would it ever again be Holly? Would he be able to cope if it was?

He tried to imagine what daybreak would bring, how he would treat the new grid, whether he would even buy it. Yes of course he would, he thought – if there was the slightest chance of being called up, he wanted to be ready, even have a head start, if possible.

Two things were certain to him – that he wouldn't go all fanatical about it, as Eric had done – and that he was going to give the newsagent the loudest 'good morning' he had ever received in an effort to make him look up at last.

Breaking free from his neighbour's mesmerising lamp, he himself looked further up to where a full moon was serenely suspended. He had always seen a face in it, and a benign one, but there was something about it now that he found unsettling. Lowering his gaze, his house was looking particularly inviting. It was reverting, at least to some degree, to a sanctuary.

'Get in there,' he muttered, strode through the door and closed it behind him.

EPILOGUE

Holly will be put through the wringer again in

CLOUDED JUDGMENT

BOOK TWO OF THE CRYPTIC CHRONICLES

and he can't wait.

ACKNOWLEDGEMENTS

Aside from the principal dedicatees at the beginning of the book, many people deserve my thanks for their contributions, some for helping with this project directly, others for providing inspiration or well-being generally.

Several family members must be mentioned, chief among them Jill Norman, for lavishing considerable experience, time, effort and no doubt patience on my literary efforts. Also my siblings – Remco and Elinor, for being among the very first to read the thing and for their positive encouragement, and Sasha, for being kind and brave enough to proofread it as well.

Regarding career, I would particularly like to thank Mike Hutchinson, for thinking me worthy of my break into crosswords and helping me through my first faltering cryptic steps, and Peter Stirling, for managing to keep me in work in an increasingly harsh climate.

Never far away, in any sense, are my fellow members of the greatest pub rock band, the Wild Uncles. Dan, Julian and PT have generously contributed names, characters and even a beer, however unwittingly. I salute you.

There are also people you come across occasionally who restore your faith, should it need restoring, in mankind, and for me, the two that stand out have both gone above and beyond in keeping my succession of cars on the road for the past couple of decades. So a big thanks to Joe and Andy.

Any glaring omissions in this list should stop glaring and await the next book.

BIOGRAPHY

To my surprise, I was advised that readers may want to know something about the author, so here goes.

Born in London, to Dutch parents.

Character-wise: Leo Kottke, London Pride, St Ives (Cornwall), Led Zeppelin, cheese, Stravinsky, my Les Paul, storms, Quo (not still, but again), Boulez, brandy, Stevie Ray Vaughan, pesto, Machaut. Did I mention Quo?

Professionally, the last twenty-five years have been spent compiling crosswords for every tabloid in the land, particularly the *Mirror* two speeds (for the full twenty-five years) and the *Express* Crusaders (just the last fifteen), as well as the *Telegraph*, plus periodicals, trade magazines and advertising campaigns. I can reveal that the notorious last *News of the World* crossword, supposedly full of vitriolic references to Rebekah Brooks, contained nothing of the sort, having been submitted, by me, a full week before the shock announcement of the paper's termination. Sad but true.

The previous decade saw me as a musician. It started with me being drafted into a pop band signed to EMI with a couple of singles in the charts, touring with the likes of Elton John and Shakin' Stevens. There followed a number of rock and jazz ventures of my own, none of which I was happy with, and the decade ended with me as Donovan's lead guitarist on the first of his comebacks – not a massively enjoyable experience but at least I can say I've played Wembley Arena.

At this point, in order to keep music enjoyable, it seemed sensible to restrict it to a hobby. It is still both. I still gig occasionally, currently as a Son of Sue and a Wild Uncle. I have also just completed a concerto for two guitars and chamber orchestra.

Plus I have had fun devising, over the years, a number of crossword-related puzzles, mostly 3-D (serialised, manipulated 2-D and true 3-D), including a 3-D crossword in the style of 3-D noughts and crosses.

Social networking sites bring me out in a rash, I'm afraid, but one of these days I will be setting up a marcbreman.london, so will be available at marc@marcbreman.london, an address that completely exhausts my talents for self-publicity.

www.ingramcontent.com/pod-product-compliance
Lightning Source LLC
Chambersburg PA
CBHW060900210726
48293CB00006B/1898

* 9 7 8 1 9 9 9 7 3 3 7 0 4 *